PENGUIN BOOKS AND BLUE SALT

QUANTUM SIEGE

Brijesh Singh is an IPS officer, currently serving in Mumbai. An engineer, he also holds master's degrees in psychology and public administration. Deeply interested in Indology and philosophy, and extremely passionate about computers, he holds technology patents too. He indulges in photography, classical music and poetry. He has two wonderful daughters, Pritha and Arya; his wife, Anjali, has been his greatest strength.

Blue Salt is an imprint dedicated to noir and crime, established by the bestselling writer S. Hussain Zaidi and co-published by Penguin.

QUANTUM SIEGE

BRIJESH SINGH

BLUE
SALT

PENGUIN BOOKS

An imprint of Penguin Random House

PENGUIN BOOKS

USA | Canada | UK | Ireland | Australia
New Zealand | India | South Africa | China | Singapore

Penguin Books is part of the Penguin Random House group of companies
whose addresses can be found at global.penguinrandomhouse.com

Published by Penguin Random House India Pvt. Ltd
4th Floor, Capital Tower 1, MG Road,
Gurugram 122 002, Haryana, India

Penguin
Random House
India

First published by Penguin Books India and Blue Salt 2014

10 9 8 7 6 5 4 3 2

ISBN 9780143422877

Typeset in Sabon by R. Ajith Kumar, New Delhi

Printed at Repro India Limited

www.penguin.co.in

MIX
Paper from
responsible sources
FSC® C047271

This is a legitimate digitally printed version of the book and therefore might not
have certain extra finishing on the cover.

CONTENTS

1

SOMETHING IN THE AIR

It all began with the defection of Iranian General Kemal Shahbazi. On a cold night in January 2007, dressed as the assistant to a truck driver, he slipped into Turkey at the Gurbulak crossing from Bazargan in Iran. For a man of his station, it was a class act. He felt uncomfortable in the dirty clothes he was wearing and the cheap cigarettes he kept smoking as part of his disguise. It further increased his distaste for the state of things. He was convincing enough and the border guards didn't find anything amiss.

The CIA had planned his defection for months. Ten members of his family had already left Tehran, ostensibly for a vacation. Bahram Farrahi, a 'human rights activist', had played a substantial role in the operation. From Germany, he coordinated the defection, arranging for separate entry of the general and his wife into Turkey. He executed the plan flawlessly. The CIA was pleased with their asset.

A liberal, Shahbazi fell out with the more fundamentalist elements in the new government at Tehran elected in 2005. He had risen to become a deputy minister in the earlier regime. Here, his future looked bleak. The West had seen him squirming, and opportunity came knocking, at the right time. He was bitter and hurt and his pride mangled.

Once he had crossed the border into Turkey, he continued travelling through the towns of Karakose, Erzurum and Erzincan by the E88 highway till he reached the province of Sivas. It was almost dinner time and he had been travelling continuously for 750 kilometres. He was hungry, yet not exhausted, when he finally reached the Pasabey Hotel near the railway station.

Once safely in Turkey, he was quickly moved to a new destination and given a new identity. For Iran, he had disappeared into thin air. Turkey was in a tizzy over the episode. They were upset that whosoever had executed this operation was probably an ally, and yet had failed to take them into confidence. Iran retaliated by seizing fifteen British soldiers whom they wanted to trade for the defector. It was too late.

Shahbazi proved to be a goldmine of information, even beyond the expectations of his handlers. His varied experience as head of Revolutionary Guards in Lebanon in his early thirties; as head of Iranian Military Intelligence in the 1990s and his close ties with the Hezbollah, proved to be a treasure trove that the West hadn't even dreamt of.

He was debriefed extensively by various agencies; he made them all happy with first-hand accounts of top-secret missions, prospective plans, stages of development and deployment of various weapons, and location of strategic assets. The Russians and Chinese had got wind of the treachery of this Iranian general; they were on his lookout too. The Americans moved him out of Turkey and then from one US city to another, from Texas to California, and Denver to Detroit.

Today, he and his family lead a luxurious life reaping the fruits of his apostasy.

FEBRUARY 2007, LONDON

A top Syrian official has arrived at a hotel in London, booking it under an alias. Mossad has detected the online booking and has decoded the alias. It has sent hard-core men from the Kidon (assassination) and Negev (break-in) divisions. A separate team has been deputed to track him from Heathrow Airport.

He is identified immediately on arrival and trailed by the Kidon. Meanwhile, the Negev men enter his room when he goes shopping and find his laptop on. They install a monitoring software on it which relays information to obscure servers maintained by Mossad. The contents of his hard disk get uploaded and every email, message and VoIP (Voice Over Internet Protocol) communication is copied and stored. A team of analysts and cyber-forensic experts are constantly decoding the stream of information pouring in.

The material from the laptop includes several photographs, blueprints and names. There are a lot of Iranian and North Korean references in them along with photographs of an eminent Pyongyang arms expert.

WEDNESDAY, 7 MARCH 2007, TEL AVIV

The prime minister of Israel, Baden Menahem, has just returned from Palmachim Air Force station. He was there to witness the trials of the Eltan-Heron super-drone. After reading an Intelligence report, he has cut short his programme. He has hurriedly summoned the chiefs of Army, Air Force and Mossad at his residence.

The look on his face tells it all. He informs them that Iran, Syria and North Korea have formed an evil nexus. Something very sinister has been cooking. It is an existential crisis for the country—they have to act decisively and fast.

The prime minister swears them to secrecy; no one ever comes to know what transpires among them.

JULY 2007

There is a suspicious explosion at a Syrian arms depot, killing seventeen Syrians and eight Iranians. *Jane's Defence Weekly* reports that the explosion happened when Syrian Army personnel were trying to fit a Scud missile with a chemical weapon warhead. There is an indication of a link to Pyongyang, North Korea. The Mossad chief is again summoned by Prime Minister Menahem. It's time for action.

FRIDAY, 17 AUGUST 2007

It is a pitch-dark night. Five Israeli helicopters are flying low over the Euphrates River, deep into Syrian territory. The normally azure waters are looking like black tar, but for the ripples caused by the rotor blades. The choppers ascend a little while crossing the suspension bridge across the river. Within fifteen minutes, they are in the desert, now flying very low. They hover over the sand at a few hundred metres from the Syrian Al-Kibar military installation. Men slither down ropes hurriedly. They are followed by equipment, which is dropped with extreme care. They swiftly move towards the large concrete building situated in the midst of nowhere.

As they are taking samples of the sand, a convoy of Syrian military patrol is seen approaching, firing warning shots. The operation is quickly aborted; the big birds quickly haul the personnel and equipment to fly away at great speed.

WEDNESDAY, 5 SEPTEMBER 2007 [ISRAELI DATE, ELUL 22]

Shortly before 11 p.m., all ten of the F-15 pilots in the squadron at the Ramat David Air Base in Israel are preparing for an emergency exercise. The orders seem routine, they fly north-westwards over Yagur, Nesher and the port city of Haifa, heading for the Mediterranean Sea towards Cyprus. Midway, three of the 'Raam' (thunder) F-15s get orders to turn back. Seven of them suddenly change direction and head east–north-eastwards into the Syrian borders. An ELINT aircraft has joined them. They fly very low to avoid detection, manoeuvring in a right echelon formation. Flying for more than twenty minutes, they have avoided detection by Syrian radars using a combination of terrain-masking and Advanced Airborne Network Attack Systems.

The Syrians have Tor-M1 (SA-15) and Pechora-2A (S-125/SA-3) surface-to-air missiles, but not one is fired. The Israelis precision bomb the Syrian radar site at Tall al-Abuad, completely destroying it. In no time, they are at the Al-Kibar military complex in the Deir ez-Zor desert.

AGM-65 Maverick missiles and 500-pound bombs are used in a surgical way to completely obliterate the structure. In all, seventeen tonnes of explosives are used, with the prime minister himself supervising the operations live from the IDF headquarters (nicknamed The Pit) in Tel Aviv. At 12.53 a.m., the pilots radio back 'Arizona', signalling that the target has been completely destroyed.

THURSDAY, 6 SEPTEMBER 2007, DAMASCUS

Brigadier General Abdel Badi has been summoned to the Presidential Palace on Mount Mezzeh. President Hashem Qabbani-II is furious; when the general comes out of the meeting, he has a dead look on his face; later, a press release is issued.

'Israel bombed an empty military complex under construction in the Deir ez-Zor desert. We condemn the transgression of our borders.'

CNN reports the incident, stating that there are nine North Koreans amongst the deceased.

Initially, there is no reaction from Israel. Two days later, the prime minister issues a statement: 'We applaud the unusual courage shown by the Israeli Defence Forces, but we cannot reveal anything further.'

The din dies, time flies.

TUESDAY, 15 MARCH 2011, SYRIA

Arab Spring hits Syria; demonstrators take to the streets demanding the ouster of President Qabbani-II. It begins after children are arrested in the Izra district for drawing graffiti on walls. A wave of violence sweeps across the country. The Army is split into two, right down the middle. A group of soldiers establish their headquarters in Turkey and provide an umbrella organization for all anti-government forces. General Abdel Badi, an astute strategist, renounces his uniform and escapes to Iran. The game is not over for him just yet.

MONDAY, 2 MAY 2011, PAKISTAN

Osama bin Laden is killed at his secret hideout by the United States' Navy SEAL Team Six in Abbottabad, Pakistan. The sun sets over the Al-Qaeda. There is a temporary vacuum.

The Lashkar-e-Tayyaba has until now concentrated on Kashmir. It had taken the world by storm when it orchestrated spectacular attacks in Mumbai in the winter of 2008. Pakistan's spy agency Inter Services Intelligence has been happy with its protégé which has never barked at the master. The 'war of a thousand cuts' has just gotten better. Major Abdul Muneer of the ISI has been maintaining very close contacts with the Lashkar, overseeing operations, training and funding.

The Lashkar has dreams of establishing an Islamic caliphate throughout the world. Beginning with the plan to 'liberate' the Himalayan province of Kashmir, it has the Balkan caliphate next in sight. The time is ripe for it to take the place of Al-Qaeda and attain centre stage, claiming leadership over all Islamic religious struggles across the world.

The Lashkar has certain advantages which the Al-Qaeda didn't have. A steady stream of volunteers ready to lay down their lives in the cause of religion; very well-developed training facilities and a steady revenue stream. Another advantage is its association with charity and social work, which gives it the opportunity to recruit volunteers, legitimize its cause and present a human face to the world.

After 2008, there has hardly been any major terror attack anywhere in the world that did not have the shadow of the

Lashkar. Emboldened and revitalized, it has now decided to teach India a decisive lesson.

Hakim Mohammed Sheikh, its founder, has spoken in the past about the 'annihilation of India' as his dream. His charm and popularity has many converts to his cause of Jihad; his call is heard across countries and continents. Ansar Suleri, a London-based dot-com billionaire, is one of them. Driven by the stories of Guantanamo Bay, he has come out of his early retirement, relinquished worldly pleasures and taken to a life of piety. His spiritual quest has coalesced with the anger inside, to bring him to Pakistan, the land of his forefathers.

2

CALL FROM BLACK HOLE

The caller is insisting that he talk to the prime minister himself. The prime minister is packing up for the day. The Delhi Police security branch has been alerted by the prime minister's security group (PSG) that the convoy would move at any moment from the Raisina Hill South Block office. It has been a day like any other; the prime minister has had a Cabinet meeting, followed by lunch, post which was a press briefing. The workaholic that he is, he stays late to finish the day's work. He is very tired.

The operator tries to reason, but the cold voice on the other end cuts him off. 'In one hour, the prime minister will call me himself. Watch the television for breaking news from Mumbai. My number is 9918299823. Thank you.'

The operator tries to transfer the call to the prime minister's secretary, but the caller has already hung up.

The operator briefs the secretary and asks him to inform

the police. The PSG officer on duty is informed about the call and he passes the information on to the relevant Intelligence agencies.

It is usual in this country to get a lot of calls like this. There are people who are frustrated, plain adventurous, stupid or overzealous; these are the ones who typically insist on talking directly to the senior functionaries. There have been instances when such callers have turned out to be mentally unstable. Still, any call that has an element of threat is taken seriously and passed on to the agencies and departments concerned as a matter of abundant precaution. The Mumbai police commissioner is asked to be vigilant; 'alert' messages are sent to other important cities too.

Mumbai Police is currently reeling under the allegations of a fake encounter by its Anti-Terror Cell. The Central Bureau of Investigation (CBI) has arrested a senior officer, Rudra Pratap Singh, five days ago. He has been accused of playing a role in the killing of a terrorist. It was a botched-up encounter where two of the suspects escaped with bullet wounds. They then came on national television to discredit the Anti-Terror Cell.

Owing to the public outcry (and political pressure), the CBI has taken up the case and Rudra has been arrested. The force is reeling under this shock; the pride of Mumbai Police has been hurt. Media vans have been stationed at all significant locations—outside Rudra's home, the commissioner's office, even the office of the CBI. They chased the car when he was picked up, cutting across lanes, to show a glimpse of him under arrest. Rudra remembers how these very people used to wait outside his office for a thirty-second bite, sending him messages so that he would give them 'something exclusive'.

APPROXIMATELY 5 HOURS BACK, 5.15 P.M., MUMBAI

Mumbai Police has not taken kindly to the action against Rudra; there are all sorts of opinions. The commissioner is meeting with the home minister and the state police chief.

'Don't you think we could have handled the media better?' the minister asks.

'You are aware, sir, news has no friends,' Mumbai's Commissioner of Police, Kamal Kant, is being caustic without appearing so. He has the uncanny ability to say the most unpalatable things in the most nonchalant way. The irony is not lost on the discerning few.

'We are the ones who indulge in publicity-mongering, sir,' the state police chief is laconic as always. His depression has not been cured by all the brouhaha.

'I have been in touch with the Union home minister. With an "Opposition" government in the Centre, there are limitations.' The home minister has changed the topic. He is lamenting again. The seasoned player that he is, he knows his officers inside out. He is aware that Kamal has been deeply traumatized by the arrest of Rudra, who is his blue-eyed boy. He is also upset about the issue being blown up by the media, causing perceptions to tilt against the ruling party.

'Sir, we are cannon fodder, always ready to be flogged, so this isn't new for us,' the commissioner quips. The state chief smirks while the home minister ignores the comment.

The commissioner is not content. 'Being an old-timer, sir, I remember what Sir Winston Churchill had to say about sacrifice,' he pauses, casting a glance around to consider his audience. 'I have nothing to offer but blood, toil, tears and sweat.'

The meeting gets over on this note; there is nothing left to discuss.

As they go out, the state police chief expresses his dissatisfaction with the way in which things have unfolded. Kamal gives him a blank look.

The chief is a self-righteous man, warped in his sense of duty and propriety. Over the years, his introversion has cooked him from inside, bringing to the fore a grim exterior.

The media accosts them as they are coming out of the Secretariat building. The state police chief escapes them while the commissioner calmly faces the ambush of the cameras.

'Sir, sir, sir.' 'One minute, one minute, here please.'

There is a rush to place the microphones with channel logos in front of him; he dispassionately observes them.

'Has Mr Rudra Pratap Singh been suspended, sir?'

'What action have you taken against him?' a girl screams.

'Which jail is he being taken to?' someone asks in Hindi.

'Don't you think the credibility of Mumbai Police has taken a beating due to the acts of such rogue officers?' someone is accusing.

The man is as calm as ever, carefully examining his uniform baton (stick) as if it were a rare museum artefact. He then raises his head to take in a full view of his audience.

'I cannot respond to this cacophony. Can someone patiently address me rather than yelling out to each other?' his voice is intentionally barely audible.

There is a hushed silence. The scribes are gesticulating to each other to be calm.

'Thanks, now you may ask me what you like.'

'Sir, this case is a blot on Mumbai Police. It has been proved beyond doubt on national television that your officers have killed innocent people in cold blood. Will you resign, taking moral responsibility for the same?' This aggressive English news channel reporter with an acquired accent always has long questions.

'Proved where? Pardon, I did not follow your question.'

'Proved on national television, sir. How do you respond to this?'

'Two things. I have been too busy with work, so I might have missed watching TV, my apologies for that. Secondly, let's leave the investigation to the agency concerned. Good day, gentlemen.'

He sits in his car and leaves as the reporters scurry to upload the bite, simultaneously adding their interpretations in a tone that gives the impression of a great, impending calamity.

MUMBAI, 10.30 P.M.

The Union home secretary, Anand Tripathi, has just spoken to the Maharashtra home secretary, Satish Kumar. He is now calling the Mumbai commissioner of police.

The operator connects the call immediately. 'Is this the commissioner of police, Mumbai, on the line, sir?'

'Considering that this is my cell phone, it must be,' Commissioner Kant responds in a cold, distant voice.

'Sorry, sir, the Union home secretary would like to speak to you urgently,' the operator is almost apologetic. Kant has this effect on people; he puts others at unease with his no-nonsense approach.

'Please put him through.'

'Kamal, this is Tripathi. I have to share something serious with you,' a heavy, authoritative voice speaks.

'Good evening, sir. If you are on the line yourself, it must be serious.'

'Look, Kamal, the Prime Minister's Office received a call ten minutes back. The call is being traced, but he has warned us of a serious incident in Mumbai.'

'I understand, sir, but we will need more details if we are to do anything about it.'

'That is all we have right now, please bear with me.' There is a hint of anguish in Tripathi's voice.

'Very well, sir, we will do whatever we can. Thank you for the heads-up.'

10:35 P.M., MUMBAI

The control room has been informed; within minutes, roadblocks and checks are going to start. Deputy commissioners have received from the control room terror alerts on their phones. They, in turn, are talking to the various police stations. The commissioner himself is on the prowl.

He growls on the wireless: 'Rex to control, I hope the deputy commissioners have been informed. I expect them to shun their harems and be visible on the streets.'

The control room frantically locates all the senior officers. They hurriedly leave their residences for their respective jurisdictions. The Police Intelligence Branch has also informed the VIPs, asking them to avoid unnecessary travel, a precautionary measure to prevent any possible abduction that could result in a hostage situation.

A LITTLE LATER

Kamal Kant is on his cell phone, his voice more distant and cold than usual. He becomes very impersonal, almost robotic when immersed in work; his family members have learned to avoid calling him up during work hours. In a crisis he becomes less communicative, his mind working like a chess grandmaster's, immersed in the final stages of an endgame

'Quazi, I hope you have received the alert from Delhi by now. In the absence of that rascal Rudra, you will have to coordinate the anti-terror response. I have been informed by some very serious quarters that this is critical stuff.'

He continues, 'Quazi, don't you think we took efforts to defend him? More than your unit, it is a matter of shame for me personally. Now, for tonight forget everything else, just get your act in place right now!'

10:51 P.M., SOUTH MUMBAI

A huge blast is heard, followed by several other small blasts, the sky in the south-east lights up in bright orange for some time. The spot of the blasts seems to be located in the open seas. Cars halt in the middle of roads, people stop in their tracks. There is panic in the air.

10:57 P.M.

Forty-five people are injured in a stampede at Chhatrapati Shivaji Terminus railway station; there are widespread rumours of serial blasts. The railways suspend train movements.

There is a throng of several thousand people outside major railway stations frantically trying to get into taxis and buses. The public address systems installed on the streets by the Disaster Control Authority are relaying messages asking people to keep calm and not panic.

11:05 P.M., OFFICE OF THE COMMISSIONER OF POLICE, MUMBAI

Union Home Secretary Tripathi has dialled the commissioner, Mumbai Police.

'Kamal, I hear of serial blasts in Mumbai, can I get a confirmation?'

'There have been blasts, sir—multiple; locations, casualties and damage are still unknown.'

'Kamal, immediately put your Anti-Terror Cell on the job. Get your tech team to work on this number 9918299823. This is the number from which the Prime Minister's Office received the threat call.'

There is a prolonged pause. 'Kamal, I hope you appreciate that this is a national emergency.'

'I am dealing with it right now, sir, but my ATC is handicapped without Rudra Pratap Singh. He was picked up five days ago by the CBI.'

'This is no time to bargain, Kamal, please go full steam ahead and keep me updated minute by minute. I am in direct contact with the home minister and the prime minister, they both are very concerned.'

There is a long pause. 'I will keep you posted, sir; I have also noted your advice on bargaining. Best wishes to you.'

The commissioner has already declared the city to be in Critical Phase as required by the operations manual.

In Critical Phase, the security of all probable targets is automatically strengthened without waiting for specific orders. All armed units get combat ready, in full gear. All routine jobs like street patrol, combing for criminals and petty-crime investigations come to a halt.

It feels like the calm before the storm, which no one knows for sure will come or not.

11.12 P.M., MUMBAI

'Sir, the number is a fake, it's a virtual number which cannot be traced back.'

'Quazi, you didn't expect the call to come from someone's home number, did you? Anyway, carry on,' Kant's sharp wit never deserts him, even in a crisis.

'Sir, the VoIP number is hosted on a Scandinavian server, in a country which will never part with user details.'

'Expected; since you have located the server, talk to your bandicoots in the wild. See if they can do something for the country other than smoking weed.'

'The network of hackers I have reached out to is at a dead end till now.'

'I am getting the voice file from Delhi, cross-check it with available voice prints of the known devils.'

'Yes, sir. Will keep you posted.'

'I will wait for news. I am up all night.'

Kant has put his insomnia to proper use—he listens to the wireless transmissions on the walkie-talkie through the night, till sleep hits him. It also gives him the advantage of a head start over his juniors; by the time they wake up, he almost always has a first-hand account of the happenings in the night.

11.18 P.M., MUMBAI

The Navy informs the police that there has been an explosion aboard the patrolling vessel *INS Sudarshana*, a 2000-tonne ship, but there is no sabotage suspected right now. Access to navy areas and the dockyard has been blocked to all.

The media has come to know that the blast has been either at sea or in the naval area. They are rushing to the local Navy headquarters.

India-Instant, a leading news channel, has dispatched its helicopter towards the dockyard area to get better shots, but is denied permission. The channel heavily criticizes the government for lack of transparency, and accuses it of trying to hide facts.

The Navy has put up a smokescreen in the sea; several of its helicopters and smaller vessels are seen rushing towards the site. Journalists with cameras are riding in small fishing boats. They are desperately hunting for visuals.

11.30 P.M.

People have been requested to stay indoors. The commissioner has issued a statement to the media, saying that there has been an explosion in a ship and there is no need to panic; people should stay indoors and avoid unnecessary travel until further communication. Rumours are rife; people are discussing the possibility of more attacks by the morning. There is a sense of déjà vu.

12.10 A.M., SUNDAY, 7 SEPTEMBER, MUMBAI POLICE HEADQUARTERS

An emergency meeting of senior police officials has been called at the Police Headquarters. The commissioner starts the proceedings without even waiting for everyone to assemble.

'Listen to this message, I want your immediate assessment,' he says as a hush falls in the room.

A voice file plays:

'Good evening, Mr Prime Minister. This is to remind you to keep the word of your predecessors and complete a small formality.

'There was a commitment given by Indian Prime Minister Pandit Nehru to the United Nations. As his fourteenth successor, it has befallen upon you to make good on the promise. As you have seen from the events in Mumbai just minutes earlier, we are very serious about this. Please declare a plebiscite in Kashmir according to the UN declaration number 47.

'Otherwise you see, we will make you forget 26/11.

Ameen.'

Silence follows.

Joint Commissioner (Crime) Vinay Kasbekar is the first to speak. 'Sir, this does not seem to be like the threats we face on a daily basis. I think we should get more information from the agencies to understand its dynamics.'

The commissioner is unmoved; his stoic face conveys a deeper understanding. Vinay is acutely aware why. He would have preferred a situation in which the danger was clear and present; this seems portentous.

'Any update on the tech, sir? Shall we pool in our resources too?' Vinay says, knowing very well that Kant would have already asked him to do so if the occasion so demanded.

'Won't help much, Vinay.'

The joint commissioner (law and order), Majumdar, pitches in:

'Sir, we are much better placed to handle this than we were on 26/11. We have learned from our failures. Roadblocks, searches and combing operations are on. We have asked our police stations to gather Intelligence on suspicious persons and activities. We will handle this well, sir.'

'Handle what, Majumdar?'

'The threat, sir.'

'Precisely . . .' Kant's upper lip is stiff again.

Deputy commissioner (Intelligence) adds, 'Sir, the Navy is being tight-lipped. To me, this does not seem to be a mere accident. Media is already screaming sabotage. The Union defence minister is likely to visit Mumbai tomorrow.'

'As if we didn't have enough to deal with already,' sighs the commissioner. 'What are the agencies saying? Is it a missile attack, an improvised explosive device or a torpedo?'

'No news till now, sir.'

The joint commissioner of police (crime), Vinay, speaks, 'Sir, we should start a command centre immediately and put all our resources on the job. There is no use in waiting and watching for them to make the first move. They already have a head start.'

'Approved. Locate it at the newly constructed bunker. Ironic that this will be an inauguration of sorts for the facility,' Kant says with a sardonic smile.

Majumdar adds, 'We can call the local Army commander and coordinate with him in case the situation goes out of hand, sir.' The commissioner ignores him totally.

His deep-set eyes turn steely when he is faced with contradiction. Kamal has seen life's twists and turns much more than others. His family had migrated from Pakistan at the time of Partition in 1947; he had grown up in a refugee camp, where daily survival used to be quite a task. From there to being the head of India's most elite police force, he had treaded his path alone. A lifetime of strife has made him ruthless, determined and cold. Crisis situations were not new to him; the thin, short man has always had his ears to the ground and his judgements have a very earthy, practical flavour to them. As always, even today, he is composed, unruffled and conceited.

Kamal Kant looks at the rest of them, and says, 'As all of you understand, no one is going back to their cosy homes till the UN resolution is discussed. The purpose of calling you all here was to inform you about the gravity of the situation.

'Keep your eyes and ears open. You have full authority to act on your own, don't wait for my orders. I will handle it later if the scavengers come sniffing.

'All except Quazi can disperse.'

He waits for them to leave, picks up the phone and calls the control room. 'I want to be updated on the situation every half an hour from now on, come what may, understood? Fine, thanks.'

'Yes, Quazi, from the look on your face I see that there is nothing that you have to share with me right now.'

'Sir, the voice prints are negative, it is none of the known elements.'

'What are the chances that it's just a prank?'

'Then what about the blast aboard the ship, sir?'

'Answer my question first.'

'Sir, we have done a voice-stress analysis on the sample, and it seems to be true to the content.'

'That is not good news then. Quazi, shift your operations to the command centre in the bunker, I will see you there, off and on.'

'Sir, please let me say this much . . .'

'Yes?'

'We are severely handicapped in the absence of Rudra

Pratap sir. He would already have had some serious insight into this by now if he were here. If we have to make some headway quickly, he should be brought in here at any cost. The whole ATC remains paralysed without him.'

'I have heard you, Quazi, you may get back to work now.'

Before Quazi leaves the room, the commissioner's cell phone is ringing. The home minister is on the other end.

'Delhi is very worried, it does not want any embarrassment,' the terse voice informs.

'Embarrassment of what kind, sir?'

'No further attacks. I understand that this one was not preventable.'

'Has it already been established, sir, that it was an attack?'

'Mr Kant, please ensure that the security of my citizens is not compromised under any circumstances.'

'As you are aware, sir, we are doing everything possible, given the limitations.'

'Tell me what you want, Kant, I will speak to Delhi and get it organized.'

'Well, sir, speaking of logical possibilities . . .'

'Will you just spit it out, please?'

'You know his name, sir, I do not need to tell you.'

3

SCHRÖDINGER'S CAT

6 A.M., SUNDAY, 7 SEPTEMBER, MUMBAI

TV channels are quoting 'Navy sources' to say that there are no survivors in the blast aboard the ship. Rough seas, rains and incessant winds have further hampered the 'rescue' operations.

Rear Admiral Mehra is calling the commissioner of police, Kamal Kant.

'Mr Kant, this is Rear Admiral Mehra, I would like to talk to you about the incident on board one of our vessels today.'

'Good morning, Rear Admiral Mehra, I hope your sailors in distress have been rescued. Please let me know if I can assist in any way.'

'Mr Kant, with great shame I have to admit that there are no survivors. We may lose the vessel too. It has listed badly to starboard, it may sink any moment.'

'I am so sorry to hear that, this is more serious than we first thought.'

'The fact is that we suspect sabotage in this incident. You know our protocols; nobody will admit it officially. I have orders to coordinate with you on the investigation. We will give you all possible access, maintaining the confidentiality of our operations.'

'I expected so. Has the admiral arrived?'

'He is landing any moment, the defence minister and defence secretary are also accompanying him. There are orders to constitute a joint investigation team, your officers from the ATC included.'

'Thank you for informing me, my condolences to you and all ranks of the Indian Navy for the loss. I await formal communication from the home ministry regarding the investigation.'

'You will get the orders soon, Mr Kant.'

'Sure, Admiral, we are always there to offer our help and support.'

'Good day, Mr Kant.'

The commissioner picks up the secure line to the Crisis Centre. Vinay Kasbekar answers.

'Vinay, it's on the lines expected, it is definitely sabotage. The Navy wouldn't like this information to be made public for obvious reasons of national security, but they want our "assistance" in the investigation.'

'Sir, we have worked with the forces in the past and it is a very difficult proposition. They don't share anything in the name of confidentiality and yet want all our help.' He continues, 'Sir, if you remember the case of fraud in military supplies, despite the registration of a case, they never gave us any substantial information. The case is still pending.'

'Vinay, we begin our investigations without waiting for any orders from anyone. Investigation into a crime does not need any formal approval. Don't register anything on paper, but ask the ATC to take over the investigation.'

'Sir, the ATC is not in the best shape to take it up. I would rather submit that you give it to the Crime Branch.'

'You may work on it in parallel, Vinay, but let the specialist agency handle it.'

'Right, sir. Quazi is here, you can personally ask him about this.' He hands over the phone to Quazi.

Vinay is an astute statesman, calm and composed, rarely venturing to give his opinion unless asked for; at the same time, he is stolid to the point of being stubborn. His patience has held him in high esteem of his bosses as well as his juniors; two in three times, he has always been proved to be right at the end of many a crisis. He has cultivated the art of waiting and watching into a superior skill, always allowing the other person to make his first move and consequentially the first mistake.

'Quazi here, sir, anything important, sir?'

'Quazi, the ATC takes over the ship blast case. The Union home ministry is likely to send some communication in this regard; regardless, you start your work . . . and please don't give me the drivel about Rudra Pratap not being there or your unit being demoralized. Girdle your loins and fight, this is no time for sentimentality and drama.'

Kant can hear the lack of morale in Quazi and he knows it is a malaise affecting the entire ATC. They aren't just crippled without RP, they are in fact extremely demotivated, and that is going to affect their ability to make decisions and trust their instinct. The commissioner of police is very concerned.

8.30 A.M., NAVY HEADQUARTERS, MUMBAI

The Union defence minister is holding a press conference; he reads out a written statement to the media.

'There was a fire on board the patrolling ship *INS Sudarshana* which led to the explosion of the armament stored in it. I have ordered an inquiry of the highest level into the incident. Efforts are under way to rescue the survivors. While we hope for the best, we should be prepared for the worst.

'It is the greatest tragedy of recent times. There were 189 officers and other crew members aboard the ship when the incident took place. We pray to god for their safety.'

As he gets down from the podium, the media rushes towards him with mikes and cameras. The smart-looking Navy cadets in sparkling white uniforms sternly hold them back. The minister hurriedly sits in his car and the convoy zooms past the barricaded entrance of the Navy headquarters building amidst shouts of the media personnel.

SAME TIME, CRISIS CENTRE

Commissioner Kant has arrived; busy on his cell phone, he gestures to everyone to remain seated. There is no time for protocol and pleasantries.

'We have discussed this earlier, sir—to get results, you have to meet my requirements. Otherwise, I am encumbered.' He hangs up, the few remaining strands of hair on his bald head shine like silver threads.

'Yes, Quazi, do you have any news for me?' he says, adjusting his glasses.

'No news as such, sir, but a hunch.'

'Do you need a formal invitation to begin on it?'

'No, sir, however, I think you might find my ideas a little far-fetched.'

'You're testing my patience, Quazi.'

'All right, sir, please forgive me if I sound dramatic, but my analysis of the number says that there is a hidden symbolism about it.'

'Interesting, go on,' he casts a cagey glance at the others present in the room. All of them are listening intently.

'Sir, I am a devout Muslim, my parents have taught me Arabic and I have read the Holy Quran and Hadith in great detail and depth.' He projects his console screen on the video wall.

'Sir, the number that the caller gave was 9918299823. If we break it up into smaller parts, like 99.1, 82, 99, 82.3, we can relate them to Quranic verses of the corresponding numbers. Is this making sense, sir?'

'Go on, Quazi,' Kant's eyes have narrowed, his fingers are clasped.

'So let's read verse 99 from the Holy Quran.'

When the earth is shaken with its [final] earthquake (Qur al-Zalzala—The Earthquake—Verse 99.1)

And whoever does an atom's weight of evil will see it. (Verse 99.2)

'And now verse 82 from the chapter Bursting Apart:

And when the seas are made to flow forth. (Verse 82.3)

'What are you hinting at, Quazi?'

'Sir, the radicals amongst Islam have been interpreting the holy scriptures to suit their own perverse ends. The religion strictly prohibits harm to the innocent, but these elements have been twisting the sacred teachings to perpetrate violence and war.'

'Quazi, I am aware of the twisted minds which feed upon gullible creatures. It does not require religion; they have been everywhere, in every time and age. I do like your analysis though. What is the message in this?'

'Simply put, it hints at an earthquake which will burst

apart the earth and affect the seas too.'

'Do we have any confirmation linking this to Lashkar?'

'No confirmation yet, sir, but the agencies are reasonably sure it is them. There was a clear mention of 26/11 Mumbai attacks in the threat call.'

'I see your point. Vinay, what's your take on this?' Kant asks, turning to his right.

'If the threat is real, sir, they are the only players who can deliver on it. After bin Laden, there has been nobody big enough in the subcontinent to threaten a country of our size. Moreover, if we go by the "symbolism" that Quazi is proposing, I see a clear reference to Mumbai. Knowing them, they will not stop at symbolism. They will do something spectacular just to prove their point. The ship's blast being a case in point.'

'A little premature to draw conclusions, but you may be right, Vinay.'

Kant knows that Vinay would not venture advice until he was absolutely sure of himself. He does not overtly agree with him, but he has a hunch that Vinay is right in his assessment.

Turning to Quazi, the commissioner says, 'I sort of admire your conjecture, but please don't neglect your work on the ground. Keep your tigers ready to roar.'

'Duly noted, sir, thank you.'

Everyone breathes a sigh of relief as the old man leaves the Crisis Centre.

9.17 A.M., NEW DELHI

The Union home minister has called the chiefs of various agencies for an emergency meeting at his residence. The head of the CBI is there along with the chiefs of external and internal Intelligence agencies; others present are the Union home secretary, law and judiciary joint secretary, Delhi's commissioner of police and the National Counter Terror Centre chief. An important decision is taken after a discussion on the crisis.

10.25 A.M., NEW DELHI

The meeting has ended, the officials are rushing out. Their cars arrive without any order of precedence.

11.05 A.M., MUMBAI, CBI LOCK-UP

The door to the cell opens and ATC officer Kale enters. Rudra is fast asleep on an iron bed, snoring. His muscular, athletic body is curled up like a baby's.

'Sir, good morning.'

'I told you I don't want tea, get lost,' he growls, without even opening his eyes.

'Sir, it's me, Kale.'

Rudra looks up at him with partially open eyes.

'The buggers have arrested you too? You were not part of the operation at all!' He turns to his side and closes his eyes again.

Kale approaches him and taps his shoulder. 'No, sir, I am here to get you out of here.'

'Kale, I have told you before, do not drink in the morning. Now shut up and let me sleep,' he rolls over to the other side and closes his eyes again.

A CBI officer enters. 'Rudra sir, you have been bailed out by the special court. You are free to go.'

Rudra sits up and squints at the officer. 'Oh, I thought you were going to "encounter" me.'

Then a playful smile appears on his face; he springs up from the bed with a bounce in his step, buttons up his shirt and tucks it in.

'Okay, Kale, sorry, I did not believe you,' he says, rolling up his sleeves.

They both come out of the cell. Rudra does not say anything, but casts a quick glance at Kale. Rudra is sporting a thick stubble and is looking unwashed and dirty; his shirt is crumpled, trousers untidy. As they head for the gate, Kale holds him by the arm and subtly directs him to the rear exit. Rudra slows down, but Kale does not explain anything. They keep walking down the road below the agency's office; Kale takes a sudden right turn into an alley. They walk in silence for about five minutes, till they reach Rudra's car.

His favourite driver Savant is at the wheel; he salutes him.

'Savant, is madam okay at home?' Rudra asks as the door is opened.

'She is okay, sir,' the usually chirpy driver is cryptic.

'She didn't want to visit me in custody, isn't it?'

'Sir, we will talk about that later, you need to rest now,' Savant cuts him short. Rudra sits in the car and rolls the window down. Kale is waiting near the car.

'Okay, Kale, you can go now, I would like to rest for some time. The government must have suspended me by now, so no point in going to the office. Thanks for the assistance, will take details from you later,' he stretches and yawns.

'Sir, we are going straight to the commissioner's office,' Kale informs.

'No.'

'Sir, I have orders to escort you there,' Kale is firm in his reply.

'Kale, I am going home, ask the commissioner to relax.'

'Sir, you can't. You have been granted bail in complete secrecy, you know that.'

'I think I was happier in custody. Savant, let's go to the headquarters,' Rudra closes his eyes again as he leans back in the seat.

11.15 A.M., MUMBAI POLICE HEADQUARTERS

Rudra enters the commissioner's chamber and salutes Kant, who asks him to be seated. Tense silence prevails. Kant can feel Rudra's angst at being wrongly implicated in a case and then being left alone and defenceless.

'There is a lot to explain, RP, but we neither have the time nor is this the occasion for it. Something very serious has happened; something more sinister is about to happen. It is you and me between the calamity and the ticking clock.' Rudra has worked for a long time with this man; he has never seen him so worked up.

'Looks like a plan to put me behind bars again, sir,' he is quick to retort. Kant does not miss the sarcasm in Rudra's voice.

'RP, I empathize with what you have gone through. Have you spoken to your wife?'

'From one custody to another, sir, I am not a free man. Haven't had the luxury of a cell phone too. Anyway, all my numbers would be under surveillance, so no point. I know she must be hating me for being arrested; talking to her on phone is out of the question even now.'

'I understand. Anyway, from here you go straight to the Crisis Centre and get back to ATC work immediately. I will brief you en route. Take this VoIP phone, it's secure, encrypted and untraceable.'

'I believe in face-to-face communication, sir. Before I leave, I want to share a Zen story.'

'RP, will you please stop your antics?' a hassled Kant requests, worry lines appearing on his forehead.

'I insist, sir.'

'Go on, please enlighten me.' Kant removes his glasses, closes his eyes as he places his hand on his forehead, as if trying to suppress a headache.

'In ancient Japan, one Matajura wanted to be an ace swordsman. He went to a Samurai master called Banzo.

'He asked Banzo, "How soon can I become an ace swordsman?"

'Banzo said ten years. Matajura asked how long it would take if he tried hard.

'The master replied thirty years.

'Matajura asked what if he tried incessantly, day and night?

'The master's reply was a hundred years.

'That's it.'

The commissioner is silent for some time; then he opens his eyes.

'RP, I get your point. Now can you get back to work?'

'Noted, sir, have a good day.'

'Trust me, can't be better . . . and RP, please take a bath.' Kant breathes a sigh of relief at his exit.

11.35 A.M., MUMBAI CRISIS CENTRE

'Quazi, looks like we have shifted here, lock, stock and barrel,' Rudra enters the Crisis Centre; no one is expecting him there. He is still trying to comprehend the enormity of the task assigned to him.

'Rudra sir! What a pleasant surprise. I knew you would be back, but I didn't think it would be so soon!' Quazi is beaming with happiness and rushes to embrace him; others in the office too rush to greet him.

'Shit happens, and we are destiny's favourite children,' says Rudra, smirking.

'Sir, let me celebrate your return with all our unit members!'

'Quazi, firstly this isn't our office, secondly we have a lot to celebrate already. So why don't we dive straight into the deep waters?

'Noted, sir. I ran a check on all senior Lashkar formations. There is something unusual in this. It isn't exactly their style. They are more into conventional guerrilla tactics. On the outer limit, they are known to explode large vehicle bombs. Their favourite technique being suicide bombers and ready-to-die fedayeen. This threat, if real, seems to be out of their league.'

'I heard about your analysis of the number from which the call was made. I think what you are saying makes sense. How about a further analysis of the time of the call?'

'Sir, the call came at 10.19 p.m. and continued till 10.21 p.m.'

'Any relevant symbolism in that?'

The verse comes up on the wall:

And people are naught but a single nation, so they disagree; and had not a word already gone forth from your Lord, the matter would have certainly been decided between them in respect of that concerning which they disagree. (Verse 10.19)

'This does not seem very relevant, Quazi.'

'Sir, wait, 10.19 p.m. is also 22.19 hours. Have a look at this one:

> These are two adversaries who dispute about their Lord; then (as to) those who disbelieve, for them are cut out garments of fire, boiling water shall be poured over their heads. (Verse 22.19)

> With it shall be melted what is in their bellies and (their) skins as well. (Verse 22.20)

> And for them are whips of iron. (Verse 22.21)

'Interesting stuff, Quazi. Looks like the ship's blast has been predicted here. Hmm, do you have any update on that from the Navy?'

'Sir, Kale has already briefed you, I assume. He is coordinating with the Naval Police and Intelligence. They will never openly acknowledge sabotage, but this is a very serious breach.'

'Yes, Kale?'

Kale replies, 'Sir, they have been trying to make inquiries about a certain Muhammad Taufiq, a smuggler operating on the high seas. No one other than him has the capacity and the reach to execute an operation in the blue waters.'

'How far can they go with their limited resources?' Rudra asks Kale.

'That is why they want our help, that too informally.'

'Keep the commissioner in the loop, don't share anything without running it by us,' cautions Rudra.

'Will keep you in the loop, sir, you can brief the commissioner personally.'

'Quazi, ask the archive section to give me a quick rundown on Taufiq; all his previous cases, informant reports, last-known locations, associates, connections abroad, recent communications and present whereabouts. The last one has to be done by the tech and field Intelligence guys together. I want a surveillance team to tail him starting now. Get me all his numbers, GSM, Satellite, and god-knows-what-else. Just get it done. Kale, you can go and participate in their probe now, pass on anything relevant. And Quazi, ask Mishra from Intelligence to get me details on past threats by the Lashkar in the last twelve months. Also obtain all recent reports of suspicious activity, and load them on to the data-mining engine. Please have them run an instance on my console too.'

12.10 P.M., SOMEWHERE IN PAKISTAN

Ansar Suleri is visiting a hospital where three children, two boys and a girl, all under ten years of age, have been admitted with grave injuries. The poor souls were hit in a cross-border shelling by the Indian Army across the Line of Control in Pakistan-occupied Kashmir. He has tears in his eyes as he leaves the hospital. He instructs his 'volunteers' to take good care of the children. He also reassures the parents, 'Inshallah, we shall avenge this.'

12.45 P.M., BUNKER, CRISIS CENTRE

Rudra is catching a quick nap; his cell phone is on silent, as always. Quazi rushes to him.

'Sir, it is Sana from RAW-External Intelligence. She has been frantically trying to call you. You have not taken her calls, it seems.'

'Quazi, one calamity at a time, tell her I am still in jail.'
For once, he looks worried.

'Sir, you know her. I don't think I can do this, please handle
it yourself. Take care, sir.'

'Quazi! I am here to deal with the Lashkar. Why are you
getting me into more serious trouble?'

'It's your friend, sir, I will not intervene.'

His secure cell has been buzzing continuously; he finally
takes the call.

'This is Head Constable More, sir is busy. Who is
speaking?' he feigns a voice.

His expressions change from irritation to comic dread.

'Okay, okay, peace. Sorry, I was joking. Listen, I am
sorry, can you just stop screaming, please? My cell phone is
on speaker mode.' He seems to be in very deep trouble now.

'Okay, it is not, can you get your breath back and we will
talk in a minute. I have to brief CP sir on something urgent.

'Yes, yes, I was bailed out about an hour and a half back.
I couldn't inform you! It is supposed to be a secret. I will call
you back immediately after speaking to the CP. Bye.'

He is breathless. 'Quazi!' he screams. 'Who told her that I
am out? Wasn't it supposed to be a secret? The fools I work
with, there is no confidentiality in this organization.'

Quazi rolls his eyes. 'Sir, she is Sana. From RAW. Besides,
I have other things to deal with; you will need to handle this
yourself.'

'There is no loyalty left in this world, Quazi, you cannot
be so harsh with me.'

'Sir, I admire your guts, but please keep me out of this. By
the way, have you called home yet?'

'Priya has finally disowned me. She went to her parents'
flat in the suburbs the day I was arrested.'

'Sorry, sir, but you are a deluded man. We have great regard for you, but you are insane. Forgive me for saying this, but everyone is saying it behind your back. Your wife has been visiting every possible temple since the day of your arrest.'

'Yes, I saw god's own signature on the bail bond.'

'You're impossible, sir. I am better off dealing with terrorists.'

Rudra is calling Sana. 'Hi, listen, we are dealing with a huge crisis out here.'

She is belligerent. 'What on earth made you think that I will not come to know that you're out? I have hardly slept a wink in the last five days, you're a bastard.'

'Look, actually I was going to call you up, we need your help here urgently.'

'Rudra, I know the mess you're talking about. Don't you dare take advantage of a situation like this to get out of trouble!'

'Your Majesty, may I be at least allowed to seek pardon for a change?'

'Idiot, have you spoken to Priya? She has been so stressed out. I just spoke to her five minutes back.'

'Should I send you a formal letter of thanks for that or will a text message do? And for god's sake, please don't call her up on my behalf!'

'Rudra, how are you like this? She has a right to be depressed. Do you even realize how difficult a person you're to live with? Can you keep your ego aside for a minute and look at what she is going through, by herself, that too eight months pregnant!'

'Oh yeah, I forgot, another idiot like me is about to arrive. Thanks for the reminder. I hope you didn't act like the jumpy anchor on TV and issue the breaking news of my release?'

'You are an ass, there is no point in talking to you. Bye.'

'Have a goo——' The call has already been disconnected.

Rudra remembers how things soured between him and Priya. A level-headed woman, she was always against his adventures. His posting in the ATC had brought things to a boil; she resented his secretive lifestyle, untimely travels and devil-may-care attitude. The arrest was the last straw, there were other reasons too . . .

4

THE ROLL OF DICE

1.15 P.M., CRISIS CENTRE

Commissioner Kant has called for all the important players in order to get an update.

'RP, may I please be brought up to speed on all the developments so far?'

Rudra stands up. He has a weathered and lost look on his face. He thinks for a while and addresses them. 'Sirs and gentlemen, you are probably aware of Quazi's analysis of a hidden symbolism in the threat call. Going by that, I think the ship's blast was predicted. The next thing it portends is a spectacular event, like an earthquake. This too refers to the sea.'

Joint Commissioner Majumdar speaks, 'The Hilton Hotel blast seven years back in Islamabad had left a 20-foot deep and 70-foot wide crater in the ground. The entire building was wiped out as if it had never existed. A concrete-mixer truck was used for this. It was filled with RDX and concrete.'

'Majumdar, there is no time for long-drawn-out stories.

Can you just come to the point?' Commissioner Kant cuts in. He has never really been known for his patience.

'Sir, I mean to say, there has been no vehicle bomb blast in our country till date. Bombs have been kept in cars, taxis and buses, but a vehicle bomb has never been used. Its use is commonplace in Pakistan though. I think they could target some iconic building and blow it to smithereens.'

'Vinay, your take?' Kant asks the Jt CP (Crime).

'I am yet to form an opinion, sir, I will need more data,' the ever-cautious Vinay informs.

'You can do that after the incident. RP, what is your evaluation?' Kant is getting low on patience, as always.

'Sir, difficult to say right now, but going by the indications, it seems that it is big this time.'

'Be specific.'

'Whatever it would be, it would be much bigger than the 26/11 Mumbai attacks; they are even comparing it to an earthquake if we go by Quazi's theory of symbolism.

'Even to be a series of large blasts, the amount of explosive needed would be impossible to procure and assemble locally. Transporting it from beyond the borders is out of the question,' Vinay adds. He has done his homework properly, as usual.

'Let's not forget that in the 1993 blasts, RDX was shipped in bulk across the sea,' Kant mutters, almost inaudibly.

'Things are different now, sir. After 26/11, the sea route is no longer an easy option.'

'I like your confidence, Vinay,' he smirks. Vinay does not say anything further. He knows very well that Kant has worked with Intelligence agencies in his earlier days and maintains very close ties with them till today. The possibility of the commissioner having some knowledge, which others never had access to, was very high.

'Majumdar, do you think the Lashkar believes we will trade Kashmir for a few buildings?'

'Sir, I have studied every operation of theirs, they cannot do anything more than this.' Majumdar is always cocksure, both his asset and liability.

'RP, you continue to work on the leads. When is the UN resolution coming up in the Security Council meeting?'

'The day after tomorrow, sir.'

'We hardly have the luxury of time, friends.'

Rudra speaks out of turn, 'Sir, do you remember Dr Azam Khan?'

'The father of Pakistan's nuclear programme?' asks Kant, taking off his glasses.

'Yes, sir.'

'How is he relevant to this discussion?' Kant's upper lip stiffens.

'Just a wild guess, sir. The threat has to be sufficiently deterring for us to barter Kashmir. The symbolism talks of "earthquakes", "skies bursting open", "garments of fire", "melting of bodies and skin", seems very ominous, sir.'

'RP, for a change can you condescend to be less cryptic?'

'I think it's a nuclear threat, sir.'

Majumdar goes into a paroxysm of uncontrollable laughter; he cannot stop laughing. Vinay too has a smile that he cannot hide. Kant is pensive. He waits for Majumdar to settle, then addresses Rudra again.

'RP, Dr Azam has been under house arrest for a very long time. The Yankees have him constantly in their cross hairs.'

'Mentioned his name to grab your attention, sir. No harm in considering this possibility.'

Majumdar is still choking. Subtle wit and humour are not his style; he is open and pugnacious on all fronts.

'Sir, Rudra Pratap has become wiser in jail, we should send him there again if he continues this streak of brilliance,' he adds between paroxysms of laughter.

Kant is unimpressed.

Rudra raises his right eyebrow and continues:

'If you agree, sir, can we also work with this as a remote possibility?'

'No harm, RP. Be mindful of the fact that there is hardly any time at hand.'

Majumdar is suddenly serious now; he knows Kant has a very low level of tolerance for errors and aberrations. If he is in agreement, this has to be serious stuff.

1.35 P.M., MUMBAI

Kant is speaking to the head of the Internal Intelligence Agency, which is called the Bureau. He is sharing his apprehensions about the nuclear threat.

'Sir, I believe it would be worthwhile to look into this angle too.'

'Kamal, you must be joking. Lashkar is notorious, but not big enough to lay hands on a nuke. The ISI will not allow its dog to walk the master. They simply do not have the reach or the wherewithal. I keep hearing about them trying to lay their hands on a WMD, but sincerely, I have my doubts. Their linkages with nuclear states are moderated by Pakistan, so don't even bother on that count.'

'Dr Azam was a grim reminder of how theories go wrong at times, sir. The man was touring the world in a government plane selling nuclear secrets.'

'Kamal, these two things are unrelated. Still, I will get it checked out. The prime minister seems a little worried about the threat; I have been contacted by his office five times since the morning. We need to get some clarity on it—decide whether it is a hoax or are we really swimming in a soup.'

'Working on it, sir, take care.'

'You too, Kamal, more than me.'

1.40 P.M., CRISIS CENTRE

Kant is back after his telecon with the Bureau chief.

'RP, the Bureau chief rules out nuclear threat, at least from Lashkar.'

Majumdar is happy. 'Sir, I said that already.' He is beaming.

'I remember, thanks. Tell me what all we have done on the ground.' Kant says, with a finger across his lips.

'Sir, the security of installations has been beefed up. Their managements have been informed about a potential Level-5 threat. The leaves of all officers and men have been cancelled, they are to report for duty immediately. Armed assault teams have been kept ready with weapons and bulletproof vests. Our UAVs (Unmanned Aerial Vehicles) are already in the air giving us live video feed throughout the city. Operations Manual Chapter III has been declared to be in force, sir.'

'You're satisfied with the efforts?' Kant mutters. Majumdar strains to hear.

'As of now, yes, sir. I have also kept sufficient reserves to deal with unforeseen eventualities.'

'I will go catch a quick nap then. I don't know till when this drama will continue.'

Kant retires into a small room beside the main hall. He crashes on the sofa and falls asleep in seconds. This is unusual, as the man is known for his relentless devotion to work and for possessing seemingly infinite energy. Rudra knows at heart that the canny shepherd is conserving his energy for the long haul.

Majumdar has resumed testing Rudra's patience; he asks with a mock-serious look, 'Can you throw some more light on your nuclear-device theory, Mr Rudra Pratap?'

'Sir, I have told you whatever we have deduced. But I have something else to tell you, in case you are interested.'

'What's that, Rudra Pratap?'

'One emperor Goyozei was studying Zen under Master Gudo in ancient Japan. The emperor inquired, "In Zen, this very mind is Buddha. Is that correct?"

'Gudo answered, "If I say yes, you will think that you understand without understanding. If I say no, I would be contradicting a fact which you may understand quite well."

'Isn't that an amazing story, sir?'

'What do you mean by that, Rudra Pratap?' Majumdar is utterly confused.

'Had I known that, I would have been the Buddha, sir.'

Kant has had enough of their conversation which he has been overhearing; he comes out of the room and gives Rudra a disgusting look.

'Buddha, would you mind if I rest for some time? It is going to be a long day for me as well.'

The commissioner has barely napped for five minutes when his cell phone starts buzzing. Kant opens his eyes, they're red with anger. It's the Bureau chief from Delhi calling.

'Kamal, I am coming to Mumbai by the first available flight. There are some disturbing developments,' the man sounds troubled.

'Sir, would you please be more specific about this?' Kant spaces his words in a deliberate manner.

'Will tell you in detail when I arrive. Tell me, do you have any particular input specific to the nuclear-device theory?'

'What are you hinting at, sir? This is sounding all too sinister!' He gets up and sits straight now.

'No, no, don't jump the gun, Kamal, we will find out the truth,' the man suggests in a guarded tone.

'I haven't come to any conclusion, sir, but there seems to be something you want to disclose before you take the flight. Am I right, sir?'

'Nothing so serious, Kamal; Mossad has picked up some chatter about Lashkar.'

'If this is not serious, sir, nothing else is. Welcome to Mumbai, I will see you at the guest house.' Kant has drawn his inference already.

After he finishes the telephonic conversation, he rushes to the Crisis Centre room. 'Vinay, RP, Majumdar, come here quickly! The Bureau chief is arriving in Mumbai on the first available flight. Apparently, he has some input from Mossad about Lashkar trying to acquire a WMD.'

Majumdar is blank, his mouth gaping. Vinay is still. Rudra interjects, 'Every single minute is important, sir. We need confirmation, positive or negative.'

'The Bureau chief definitely knows something; however, he won't share operational details with us.'

'They cannot pull off an operation here, sir,' says Rudra, his lips pursed.

'You know how we all work, no one will share his bone with you,' Kant says, touching his forehead, eyes closed.

'All the crabs will finally go into the same pot of boiling water, sir,' says Rudra, with a sigh.

There is a pause; Kant breaks the silence. 'Since we have

some indication that the nuclear-device threat may be real, let's plan for it.'

Vinay is pensive. 'We have less than two days' time, sir; any major plan would require a lot of convincing and coordination with the administration.'

'What is on your mind, Vinay?' Kant fixes his gaze on him, expecting him to contribute further.

'Sir, if the nuclear threat is real, we will have to consider evacuating the whole population of the city. I don't know if that is even possible. The chief minister will have to be convinced, maybe even the prime minister. In case the device actually explodes, it will lead to a nuclear fallout, and India will target the whole of Pakistan within a matter of minutes.'

'Vinay, any thought of relocating fifteen million people is absolutely absurd; it's simply not an option.'

Majumdar is impatient. 'We are talking as if we are standing on the nuclear bomb. Let us be 100 per cent sure before we start a wild goose chase based on a flimsy conjecture.'

'Majumdar, ask the Centre for additional resources. Send a requisition to the state police chief. If he acts pricey, route the request through the home minister.'

'Yes, sir, I will submit an updated deployment plan in some time. Meanwhile, we have completed search operations throughout the city. Road barricades and stop-and-search still continue.'

'Do it carefully, Majumdar, let's not go overboard.'

'Nothing overboard, sir, we are just doing our job.'

'Do it in a slightly low-key manner. Once the media smells a rat, there will be mayhem; guard against it, please. Also, skilfully instruct the officers not to talk to the media. You may give some diversionary story like the escape of a terrorist from the central jail. They will lap it up. We will complete substantial work in the meantime.'

'As you say, sir.'

'RP, I need a summarized statement on the events till now. Also, include two paragraphs on the further course of action.'

'Surely, sir, that will be done. What is the timeline?'

'The Bureau chief will have boarded the flight, so you have two hours at best. Thanks.'

2.29 P.M., CRISIS CENTRE

'RP, it seems that there was a similar call to the Prime Minister's Office again. This time it was at 2.24 p.m.; nothing special, they just played the tape back.'

'Quazi, can you check on the significance of 2.24?' asks Rudra.

'Checking, sir.'

Verse 2.24 of the Holy Quran is shown on the screen:

But if you do (it) not and never shall you do (it), then be on your guard against the fire of which men and stones are the fuel; it is prepared for the unbelievers.

'Sir, this seems to be in line with the earlier message. Quazi, what do the voiceprints say?'

'No match with any of the known ones, sir. Checked with linguists also, they can't place the region of the speaker.'

'Quazi, talk to the data-mining unit, check for profiles. If the voice belongs to the man who is actually orchestrating this, we need to form a picture of him. He seems to be deeply religious, yet not from the madrasas. He seems to be well informed about UN resolutions and the history of the

Kashmir issue. Ask them to do a quick check on blogs and websites in Pakistan. See if we can find something similar in content or style online.'

'RP, I will head off to meet the Bureau chief, he will be arriving soon. Vinay, I need you to tag along with me when I speak to him. Majumdar, you're in control on the ground; any operation cropping up, you deal with it independently, you have full autonomy to do so.'

Majumdar gets going. 'Sir, I am in touch with the team at the Atomic Energy Department, they are ready to supply us with portable detectors.'

'Detectors to detect what, Majumdar?'

'Geiger counters, sir.'

'So, you too are coming round to accept the nuclear-device theory?'

'The risk is too big to ignore, sir. We will get the devices from the Atomic Energy Department in an hour if you approve it.'

'You have complete authority. From now on, you are the commander on the ground.'

'Right, sir. I will inform you of the developments from time to time.'

'Provided we have time for that, Majumdar.'

Kant and Vinay leave, Majumdar rushes out to handle things on the ground.

3.45 P.M., MUMBAI CITY

Majumdar has procured the Geiger counters; they have been installed at checkpoints. He has sought the help of the Disaster Management team of the Atomic Energy Department. Two choppers equipped with Geiger counters are also at his beck and call.

Airports and ports have been sounded off to enforce very strict security measures. Cargo is being put through the severest checks; all containers are being physically inspected by airport security. Customs has pitched in to help—it has put in use its advanced scanners to locate explosives and other dangerous materials. Mobile gantries have also been provided to the police to be pressed into service for checking trucks and other vehicles on the move.

Majumdar has always been a field man, leading from the front in times of crisis. The force still remembers how he had stormed inside the CST station during the 26/11 attacks and had nearly gotten killed. He had rushed in without a bulletproof jacket and fired at the terrorists, getting hit in the right thigh in the return fire. Before he could retaliate, they had fled the building.

He has been flaying the deputy commissioners over the wireless; Kant has been listening to his tirade, mentally taking note of the preparations while reading Rudra's brief on the situation. He will be meeting the Bureau chief in a few minutes. Vinay is accompanying him in the car. He has been talking to his sources and 'assets' in a low tone, taking care not to disturb Kant.

'Vinay, this RP may be jumping the gun, but the cop in me says that he has his finger on the pulse. What do you say?'

'Let us see what the Bureau chief has to say, sir.'

'Do you think he is coming here to bring tidings of great joy?'

'I am acutely aware of the situation, sir, in case you are entertaining any doubts on my account.'

'Vinay, come to the point straight, add value, or else, keep your trap shut.'

'In that case, sir, even if we consider the worst-case

scenario, while Rudra seems to make sense there is no need to be so pessimistic.'

'Hmmm, let's see what the messenger of truth has to reveal, considering the fact that he is descending from the skies in such a hurry.'

'I submit that we keep the home minister informed, sir.'

'First, let me get informed, Vinay.'

'Right, sir.'

'Any progress with the ship's blast?' Kant's eyes narrowed.

'Not yet, sir.'

'What is the Navy saying?' He removes his reading glasses and looks out of the car. The traffic is sparse.

'They are trying their best, sir,' Vinay says with a hint of sarcasm in his voice.

'Wasting time. Investigation is not their forte. They have to step out of their little citadel,' he says, as if to himself.

'They have been very secretive, rightfully so. Although I suspect they will end up chasing their own tail, sir.'

'Bring it up in the discussion with the Bureau chief; no orders have been received yet about the investigation of the case. If they do not issue orders, we will take it up suo motu.'

'I see no legal hurdles, sir. It would be worthwhile to keep Delhi and the state police chief in the loop.'

'Yes, pearls of wisdom we strive for, my dear, those guys are our only ray of hope.'

3.55 P.M., OUTSIDE CRISIS CENTRE

Rudra is on the cell phone. 'Why on earth do you think I can come out now?'

Sana is on the line. 'Liar, you are already outside. Now stop the drama and meet me quickly.'

'Sana! You're impossible. You can share the input with me on the phone. You know I will literally be rogered if I am found roaming around like this.'

'You know, R, I like these little hide-and-seek games with you. And you sound so cute when you're irritated.'

'Irritated? Who's irritated? I am just being professional.'

'And I am the one who is playing games, right?'

'Sana, we can do this later, just tell me where to come.'

'Cross the road. Do you see a taxi approaching from the right, an old one, with dark windows?'

'No, I can't.'

'What kind of a cop are you, you can't locate a beautiful girl in a taxi, a girl who's completely crazy about you.'

'Crazy yes, right now I am going crazy. If I find you and shoot you, don't blame me.'

A taxi screeches to a halt just beside Rudra; he is startled. Sana is laughing her guts out at his reaction. She opens the door and pulls him in. Wearing a maroon dress, she seems to be going to an afternoon party.

'Broadway, when will your drama end?'

'My love, it seems you don't like my company nowadays. Who is the new muse? How old is she? Is she beautiful? Is she good in bed?'

'Sana, will you please shut up, else I'll jump out of the taxi.'

'Oh my god, what have we come to? The love of my life hates me . . . I should commit suicide now! Hahahaha,' she enacts a jilted lover.

Rudra holds her by her shoulders, and says, 'Evil spirit, tell me how to propitiate you? Here I am, out of my little crisis, but dealing with this mega disaster. God, what did I do to deserve this?'

'Okay, R, on a serious note, take me out for a cup of coffee, please. You know, I have started to drink that poisonous black brew because of you, but I sort of like it now.'

'Driver, please stop at the next Fresh Roast shop.'

'Ah, now my boyfriend is making sense.'

They get off; Rudra attempts to pay the fare, but retracts looking at the irate girl. She pays, takes his hand and walks into the coffee shop. She struts like a ballerina on drugs.

'I hope you're not going to propose to me now,' Rudra is acting cocky.

'R, shall I call your wife right now and tell her that you are flirting with an innocent girl?' she says, fluttering her eyelashes.

'Okay, peace; tell me now.'

'R, I have some very bad news.' She is finally serious.

'I wasn't expecting anything else from you,' says Rudra, sighing.

'Shut up and listen now, you idiot. The Mossad has been closely following the current crisis. They have sent a message warning us that the threat is real. They have asked us to deal with it in all seriousness without wasting a minute.'

'Means what, Sana?'

'They were not specific, but I think the Bureau chief has some input on the subject. He would have arrived by now. You know that they will not share any serious stuff with RAW. We are like stepsisters, always jealous of the other's frills and vanity.'

'What do you want me to do, Sana?'

'Sherlock, I want you to save the world. Will you do it for my love?'

'Oh man, will you ever get serious?'

'Idiot, can it be more serious than this? Bastard!'

'Damn it! Give me something specific. This is of no use to me.'

'Ass! Don't be oversmart. I have told you all I could. Now for my pound of flesh, give me feedback after the Bureau chief's meeting. I too need to be seen working.'

'I haven't heard anything, you haven't said anything. Now if you permit me, Your Majesty, can I get back to work?'

'You are such an ass, you leave your date alone in a cafe like this? What happened to chivalry? Who will protect me from the goons, the innocent little girl that I am?'

'God save them if they try to mess with you. I will pray for the goons. Bye, devil, take care.'

'You too, bastard. Bye,' she is giggling as he leaves.

SOME TIME LATER, POLICE GUEST HOUSE, MUMBAI

The state police chief is already there, in serious conversation with the Bureau chief. They both have been colleagues in the past, working as young superintendents in the Bureau.

Kant smartly salutes the Bureau chief as he enters the room, and then in his characteristic style, asks, 'Am I intruding into something confidential, sir? I can wait outside till you finish.'

'Kant, come, please sit,' the Bureau chief says in a plain but serious voice.

The state police chief does not acknowledge their presence; he keeps reading some papers from the file in his hand. Kant clears his throat, and addresses his glum colleague, 'Ahem, good afternoon to you too, sir. Vinay was just suggesting a while ago that we seek your guidance.'

The man slowly looks up, his lips pursed as if he has just had a gulp of some bitter medicine, then goes back to ignoring them.

Kant continues, 'So, sir, can we talk business now?' he addresses the Bureau chief.

'Any luck in the ship blast case, Kant?' the man asks in a flat voice. Kant is mindful that the Bureau chief would be aware of everything, but will still question him like a novice. He feels his defences rise up.

'Not anything that you're unaware of, sir.' Kant is now diligently cleaning his reading glasses with a tissue paper that he picked up from the table.

The Bureau chief looks quizzically at Vinay and then at Kant, who casts a reassuring glance indicating that it is okay to talk in his presence.

'Sir, this is my joint commissioner, Crime Branch, Vinay. Very bright boy, sir, knows his nuts from bolts.'

The man seems reassured, and he addresses Kant, 'You know, Kant, this threat seems to be concrete.' Clearing his throat, he continues, 'The Israelis have somehow come to know about it, they too seem to be concerned.'

'How are they concerned, sir?' asks Kant, leaning forward.

'They track every major Islamist action minutely all over the world.'

'That still does not answer the question.' Kant is cold and stubborn.

'The Mossad has been worried about a missing nuclear warhead, the CIA too confirms it.'

'Are you indicating that this is related to the current scenario, sir?' Kant's eyes have a steely look.

'I am stating facts, Kant, you may join the dots.'

'Pardon me, there is no time for such an intellectual exercise, sir. Give us the bitter pill if you have brought one.'

'There is nothing concrete, Kant,' the old man begins with his eyes closed.

Kant looks at Vinay, who, almost on cue, says, 'Am I permitted to raise a query, sir?'

The old man slowly opens his eyes, looks at Kant who looks away; he then closes his eyes again. There is a strange silence slowly filling the room.

'Shoot,' the old man says.

'Sir, the Navy has been requesting for help in the ship blast investigation. They had told us that orders will soon be issued from Delhi to form a joint team,' Vinay says hurriedly.

'So?' the old fox is noncommittal.

It's Kant's turn now. 'Vinay, doesn't the Indian Penal Code apply to the whole of India? The seas are Indian territory, do I have to remind you?'

The state police chief who has been silent till now warms up—polemics are his staple diet. 'These are basics. We have already registered an offence. I don't know what is wrong with the training of these later batches,' his latent bitterness now turns acerbic.

Vinay looks down, casting a short, disgruntled glance at Kant. 'Not to worry, sir, we have been investigating it,' Kant tells the state chief. 'Vinay will share with you the crime number and sections under which the case has been registered against unknown persons.'

The Bureau chief has now taken out his tobacco pouch; he is rolling the paper diligently. He then takes out a pinch of tobacco and rather delicately places it on the paper, slowly rolling it to perfection as if it were a delicate piece of art. He appears to be playing the part of a sushi chef at a Japanese restaurant.

Finally, he licks the end of the paper to seal the cigarette. He then looks around to check if someone else wants to smoke, without intending to share his treasure.

Kant is barely able to suppress his laughter; he is somehow reminded of his Delhi University days when they would roll marijuana joints at the tea stall outside the hostel gate during cold evenings. He suddenly misses those days. 'Alas,' he sighs to himself, 'being a policeman is no fun.'

He remembers the state chief as a grumpy and involuted senior who never smoked a joint or had a girlfriend. He pitied him then too. When he had cleared the coveted Indian Police Service exam, Kant had prophesied that this man would be the saddest sadist who would ever wear the uniform, little knowing that it would be his lot to work with him; thus, he helplessly watched his prophecy unfold.

His reverie is broken by the smell of raw tobacco, emanating from the filter-less rolled cigarette. The old fox has finished reading Rudra's report and the state chief's files.

'Interesting perspective,' he says as he gently extinguishes his half-smoked cigarette, as if it were an injured butterfly being safely put aside, out of harm's way.

'But you know,' strangely he addresses the state chief, 'only Kazakhstan was suspected to do this after the Balkanization of the USSR in 1991. It tried to sell four warheads to Iran.'

The CIA had carefully watched Belarus and Ukraine as they handed over their nuclear stash to Russia, with Kazakhstan following suit. By 1996, Russia had deactivated and destroyed more than 1300 launchers which had more than 4000 warheads collectively. Not a single warhead was lost or untraceable.'

The state chief quips in agreement, 'I feel these flights of fancy should not direct operational priorities. Unless and until we have concrete proof that there is a nuclear threat, we should not go that way. This conjecturing is a sheer waste of time and effort.'

Kant removes his glasses and rubs his forehead, eyes closed; Vinay is looking at the TV, which is running some news channel in mute mode. Kant has had enough; he picks up his glasses, then takes his baton from the table and puts on his cap, indicating a readiness to leave. 'Hope you're comfortable here, sir. Vinay has unobtrusively kept armed men in plain clothes here for your security. Now if you permit, we will take your leave.'

Vinay gets up hurriedly; Kant is still seated. The old man looks at Kant, and then indicates to Vinay to leave.

'If it is there, you will have to find it and dispose of it too,' the Bureau chief says, picking up his half-burnt cigarette.

'The "if" is your specialization, sir, my men are already on the ground; Majumdar is supervising operations. Please share anything else that comes your way which may help us get rid of the "if". One more thing, sir, we may need a lot of assistance from the Centre, for which I trust you would have already made arrangements.' Kant cannot help being acerbic now.

The old man nods in agreement, yet Kant does not get a feel of solid confidence. He knows that this battle has to be fought on his own.

'Kant, you know, Lashkar has never been on the scanner for trying to acquire a nuclear weapon. It does not have the bandwidth. At any rate, spending upwards of $50 billion is not within their range. Al-Qaeda was different, it was very near to acquiring a nuclear weapon; he seems to be weighing his words carefully now.

'Yet there are disturbing signals. We cannot ignore them

totally. I hope you get my point, Kant. This is all that I can share at this moment.'

As they talk, Vinay knocks on the door and requests permission to enter. The old man asks him to come in; he whispers something in Commissioner Kant's ear.

'Something on TV, sir, Vinay just got an SMS from the press.'

He picks up the remote and searches for a particular channel, then stops at News India. An anchor is screaming hoarse over a new WikiLeaks revelation. The state police chief is startled at the disclosure; he gets off his seat; Kant and Vinay are focusing on the TV; the old man is unfazed.

'We should shut down our Intelligence branch now,' says the police chief; he is twisting his chin between his index finger and thumb in a rather harsh way.

Kant looks at the Bureau chief, and says, 'So you knew this already, sir. Thank god the media was at least generous enough to let us know.'

'Now that it is out in the open, you can get down to brass tacks.'

'Obliged over your indulgence, sir. We expect your generosity to be unabated.' Kant gets up, crisply salutes and leaves.

5

HELP FROM HEXAGRAM

7 P.M., CRISIS CENTRE

Quazi has brought a printout of the WikiLeaks revelation;
he shows it to Rudra.

It reads:

*When Lashkar's No. 2 leader, Ashraf, called off a
planned chemical attack on New Delhi's subway
system in 2011, he offered a chilling explanation: The
plot to unleash poison gas on New Delhi was being
dropped for 'something better'. This message of Ashraf
was intercepted by US eavesdroppers.*

*The meaning of Ashraf's cryptic threat remains
unclear more than two years later, but a new report
warns that Lashkar has not abandoned its goal of
attacking the Indian state with a chemical, biological
or even nuclear weapon.*

*The report, by a former senior CIA official who led
the agency's hunt for weapons of mass destruction,*

portrays Lashkar's leaders as determined and patient, willing to wait for years to acquire the kind of weapons that could inflict widespread casualties.

The former official, Ron Michaelson, draws on his knowledge of classified case files to argue that Lashkar has been far more sophisticated in its pursuit of weapons of mass destruction than is commonly believed, pursuing parallel paths to acquiring weapons and forging alliances with groups that can offer resources and expertise. It has also recently given a call to all Pakistani nuclear scientists to provide nuclear weapons, materials and technology to the Lashkar in its fight against India.

Evidence from Lashkar documents and interrogations suggest that the terrorist leaders had settled on nuclear weapons as a choice and believed that the tools for a major attack were now within their grasp, the former CIA official said.

'What is the source of this WikiLeaks revelation, Quazi?'

'Sir, it quotes a report by the Statham Foundation, which was taken from an article carried by an obscure daily in Israel. I have the original source with me too.'

'How recent is this?'

'The secret report is said to be a week old. The WikiLeaks revelation came up today.'

'Quazi, I am left with no doubts about your theory of a nuclear threat. We should talk to Kant sir at once; Kale, connect me to commissioner sir's line, please.'

Kant has just reached the office; his PA has answered the call, informing Rudra to wait for some time.

Kant comes on the secure line. 'Yes, RP, any breakthrough

on the ship blast?'

'Something more serious, sir, please check your mail immediately. I have also added my comments and analysis to it at the end. I suggest that you talk to Delhi without delay, sir.'

'I have just come from a meeting with the Bureau chief. He is already here to help us, RP.' Kant sounds concerned. 'Please hold the line till I check your mail.'

'I am very sure you must already be aware of it, sir.'

'Yes, RP. I see your mail now. It's all over the media already, but good you could lay hands on the background documents too.'

'Is it too early to call it a national emergency, sir, or is it too late?' Rudra asks starkly.

'RP, there is nothing concrete in hand yet. No one will trust us without any tangible evidence. Still I will brief the powers that be, let them take a call.' Rudra hears Kant exhaling deeply.

'Sir, this reminds me of a Zen story.'

'RP, I admire your guts.'

'Shall I begin, sir?' Rudra is adamant.

'Do I have a choice?' asks an exasperated Kant.

'So sir, there was this old Zen monk who was on his deathbed. He declared that evening that he would be no more. Followers, disciples, friends, lovers started coming . . . are you listening, sir?' Kant does not bother to answer.

Rudra continues, 'When one of his old disciples heard that the master was going to die, he ran to the market.

'Somebody asked: "The master is dying in his hut, so why are you going to the market?"

'The old disciple said: "I know that my master loves a particular type of mandarin fruit. I am going to purchase it." It was difficult to find the fruit, but by evening he had somehow managed to get it. He came running in with the fruit. Everybody had been worried—it was as if the master was waiting for someone. He would open his eyes and look, and close his eyes again. When this disciple came, he said: "Okay, so you have come. Where is the fruit?"

'The disciple produced the fruit, and the monk happily started eating it.

'Somebody asked: "You are so old and on the verge of dying. The last breath is soon to leave you, but your hand is not trembling." The master replied: "I never tremble, because there is no fear. My body has become old, but I am still young, and I will remain young even when the body is gone." Then he took a bite and started munching the fruit. Then somebody asked: "What is your last message, Master? You will be leaving us soon. What do you want us to remember?"

'The master smiled and said, "Ah, this fruit is delicious."'

Rudra paused, and then asked, 'Excellent story, sir?'

'If you're done with it, am I permitted to disconnect?' Kant sounds jaded.

'By the way, RP, I hope you are not hinting that I am the old monk?'

'These are only ancient stories, sir, but they have a message for each one for us. I tell them as they occur to me, never on purpose. You know that.'

'I seriously want to have a heart-to-heart talk on your Zen stories, RP. But at a later time,' Kant sounds seriously pained.

'Appreciate it, sir, I will look forward to it.'

'Scoundrel, go back to work now.'

'Good day, sir.'

On internal orders of the commissioner, his ATC team has taken up the ship-blast case. Information has started to trickle in; somehow the oil mafia kingpin Muhammad Taufiq is not to be found, he has gone underground. So have his associates Zafar and Nazar, the twin sharks of the sea. Field officers report that they have suspended their operations for the last fifteen days. Rudra finds this very suspicious—were they aware of the impending ship blast? Rudra has instructed the data unit to run checks on all relatives of the oil mafia gang members, as the main players have suddenly gone off the radar. Mishra has come up with the results.

'Rudra sir, just have a look at the profile of this girl, something seems out of place. She came up in a second parsing of the database. Although not directly related to these criminals, she has a credit card trail running to her.'

'It better be important, Mishra. Bring it here.'

He examines the report, then takes a pencil, and draws circles at various places, marking words. 'Looks interesting indeed. Develop it further, find out if she is using any other credit cards, check her cell phones, put her on surveillance immediately.'

7.45 P.M., GADDAFI STADIUM, LAHORE, PAKISTAN

Hakim Mohammed Sheikh has just finished the *isha* namaz and evening sermon at the mega rally held at the Gaddafi Stadium. He has spoken with passion about the 1965 war between India and Pakistan. His Punjabi-accented Urdu has struck a chord with the audience. Ansar Suleri, who has finally been seated on the stage with him, has tears in his eyes.

The audience hails him with cries of 'Allahu Akbar' as he calls for the liberation of Kashmir and destruction of India. He challenges the President of Pakistan to take action against him for his patriotism and love of Islam.

Hakim gets down from the podium, as his tall, bearded, stoic bodyguards keep scanning the audience with stern eyes. As Hakim boards the car, he beckons Suleri to accompany him. The posse of bodyguards hurriedly sit in the convoy vehicles. As they leave the red brick walls of the stadium by the Hafiz Kardar Road towards the Liberty roundabout, a sea of black-and-white flags carried by their supporters greets them. Hakim has been very careful of his movements after the announcement of a 20-million-dollar bounty on his head by the United States government.

The iconic Liberty Fountain is lit green as jets spout water high in the air. Hakim addresses Suleri, 'This is the place where the Sri Lankan cricket team was attacked; unfortunately, six policemen were killed, but we demonstrated to the world what we could do. The President of Pakistan had announced presidential security for them.' He laughs, his eyes beaming with pride through his spectacles.

Suleri's pleasant face flushes red with excitement; he is handsome in an effeminate way.

'Mashallah, Amir, I saw it on TV in London,' he says with admiration.

'Wait for more, Ansar. Inshallah, we will be victorious. Blessed are your parents who have given you this name. You have helped us today like a true Ansar.'

'O, Amir, do not put me to shame, this is the least I can do,' his eyes are glistening with happiness.

'It is a matter of hours before you see the cowards bow to our feet and beg for mercy or meet the wrath of Allah,' Hakim roars.

'Ameen, ameen!' all the occupants of the car cry.

7.15 P.M., GARIB NAGAR SHANTIES, BANDRA, MUMBAI

An ATC team has reached the residence of the oil mafia member, Nazar. It is a three-storeyed concrete house built in a ghetto. The team is pretending to be repairmen from the state Electricity Board. There is a small garment workshop in front of the house; the old owner is sitting at a desk with a glass display beneath, showcasing his finished goods.

'Where have these people gone?' the officer masquerading as the leader of the repair team asks him.

The shop owner is chewing paan; he comes out of his shop, spits a mouthful of red juice on the black road and tells them that they all left some time back.

'Left for where, Chacha?'

'God only knows, my son, they aren't good people. How many times have I heard of their illegal activities. But some people will not be happy with their going.'

'Why do you say that, Chacha?'

'Why? My son, these people used to distribute a lot of free gifts to the riff-raff of the area. As a father of three daughters, I was always worried about their visitors. They would come and go at all odd hours. Godless rascals, never saw them performing namaz at the mosque. Their women also were useless. I never allowed my daughters to mix with them. I am so happy that they have left the place now, good riddance.'

'How do you know that they have left for good, Chacha?,' the officer digs deeper; he has gotten a very cooperative source now.

'What do you mean how do I know? I was here when they loaded all their belongings in the trucks. They filled up five trucks for a family of twelve! I think they must have had ten televisions, those large-screen ones,' he widens his arms to show the dimensions, 'and six refrigerators! How much does a family need?'

The officer has lit a cigarette, but looking at the disapproval on the face of the old man, he drops it and extinguishes it with the toe of his shoe.

'Thank you, Chacha, please remember us if you have any electrical fault in your workshop.'

'God bless you, son, we do not need anything by god's grace.'

The officer has a smile on his face as he looks at the illegal electrical connections around, which have been made by attaching wires to the street lights.

The team casually makes an exit; the officer walks with his men for a hundred metres through the narrow lanes bustling with people, virtually brushing against each other. An open sewage gutter nearby makes breathing difficult. There's a foul smell mixed with the stench of sweat and whiff of alcohol from the jostling locals passing by.

He is calling his chief, Rudra.

'Sir, Kale here. We just checked the house of Nazar. He has disappeared with his whole family from here, left with all his belongings.'

'Where has he gone?' Rudra seems disturbed at the news.

'No idea, sir, his neighbours say that he left for good. Did not make further inquiries as it would have aroused suspicion.'

'Kale, come back from there, put a surveillance team on the job, and see if we can break in at night and search the house without alerting anyone.'

7.20 P.M., CRISIS CENTRE

Navy Intelligence has informally asked the Mumbai Police to help trace the oil mafia kingpin and his associates, suspecting them to have had a hand in the ship blasts. Rudra has already sent a team to the residence of Zafar, the other henchman of Muhammad Taufiq, while one team has already reached Taufiq's place. They report that Taufiq and Zafar have also left, a week back, with their families. He asks Inspector Mishra of the data branch to get the passport details of the suspects and their family members. He has already contacted the deputy commissioner of airports and the immigration department head; they have been requested to check on the departure of the oil mafia family members and associates. These characters have been well known for their illegal enterprises, but never for anti-national activities. It is also true that no one else would be able to operate in the sea waters without their consent or knowledge. The Navy feels that their sudden departure from the scene seems to contain a sinister design.

DCP Lokhande is in charge of the Airport Zone; he has been tasked with checking if any of the members of the oil mafia families or their associates have left the country through the international airport. He is on a call with Rudra. 'Sir, I have personally met the officer in charge of the immigration department. There has been no departure from the Mumbai airport of the suspects. Airline records also do not show any bookings in the names of anyone from the list you have sent.'

Rudra seems to be lost. 'We should also check on departures from other airports, sir. The immigration people can also tell you if there was a departure by ship from the port,' the DCP adds, seeming to be rather relieved about the fact that some dangerous suspects did not escape through his jurisdiction.

'Lokhande, thanks for all the help, do let me know if anything important comes your way.'

Rudra is at sea now; he finds it difficult to comprehend any other reason for the sudden disappearance of the oil crooks. They virtually have no business competition; their relations with all the significant players have been very 'warm and cordial'. There has been no sudden development on the law enforcement or business fronts that has made them abandon a business worth hundreds of crores annually. The very fact that they have suddenly left with families torments him deeply; they definitely know something that he doesn't. 'Well, someone linked to them must still be around,' he thinks.

Quazi has been waiting to talk to him; he senses that something is amiss.

'All well, sir? You look preoccupied.'

'It's my birthday, Quazi. I am waiting for cake and candles. Would you like to celebrate with me?'

'Didn't mean to disturb you, sir, I just wanted to update you on the ship-blast investigation.'

'Go ahead, please.'

'Taufiq, Nazar, Zafar—untraceable, families gone too. They all left via the illicit sea route aboard fishing boats, it was easy for them. Their domestic belongings have been shipped in containers heading for the Khlong Toei Port in Bangkok. We should ask the Interpol to help us, along with the Thai Police, to track the recipient of this cargo.'

'Quazi, Mishra was working on a girl connected to this mess. I want her here in the interrogation room ASAP.'

'Sir, what is the connection of this girl with the oil mafia?'

'Quazi, this girl was using a credit card which is linked to Taufiq's account. It turns out that she is his niece, and an air hostess with Qatar Airways. Records do not show much interaction with the family; her own father died many years ago.'

7.35 P.M., SANA'S FLAT, TARDEO, MUMBAI

'Yes, I know you were in Tehran. Are you still of some use to us?' Sana is virtually screaming on the phone. 'Why didn't you share this with me earlier? Everyone waits till it is out on WikiLeaks. Damn you all . . . Yes, I am calming down, now shut up and listen.'

She pours her drink down the drain. It is not of the right temperature. She has preserved her obsessions and compulsions over the years, and they are sacred to her. She makes a face at the glass and continues: 'So you're saying that the friendly neighbourhood Spiderman was seen in Tehran? Doing what?'

'. . .'

'Uh-huh, and we thought that they were at loggerheads owing to the whole Shia–Sunni thing. Yes, I am aware of the ferry crossing at Bandar Abbas Port from Iran to Sharjah for $50. All our deluded boys go to Dubai and then cross over to Iran from there, then they complete their crash course in Pakistan and return by the same route from Dubai; no visa needed.'

'. . .'

'What were the Lashkar guys up to there?'

'. . .'

'Yes, you idiot, do you want to see it on TV and then you are going to tell me?'

'. . .'

'Now don't get offended, this is the way I talk. You have

not spoken to me for months, that's why you are feeling offended. Now hang up and go to hell.'

'. . .'

'Bye.'

She immediately calls up Rudra, 'Listen.'

'Yes, Your Majesty, what has happened now? Just so you know, I do not have the time for a long story.' He has a tired smile on his face.

'Bastard, if you don't want to speak to me right now, tell me clearly.'

'Highness, the commoner is always at your beck and call; tell me.'

'No.'

'Listen, Sana, for old times' sake, tell me what made you call.'

'I understand, it is probably the new girlfriend, I am sure about it. Does your wife know about her? Is she prettier than me?'

'Oh my god! Not again Sana, can we talk business?'

'Okay, okay, listen. My batchmate, who is now posted at Tashkent?'

'The one who has a crush on you?'

'Idiot, you always have it wrong. Yes, he is the one at Tashkent, but he never had a crush on me. Even if he did, how the hell do you know about it? You think you are really smart?'

'Sana, business, please . . .'

'Yes, so my batchmate, who does not have a crush on me . . .'

'Ahem . . .'

'Says that Lashkar guys were found loitering in Tehran.'

'They must have gone on a weekend picnic, Sana, like

people go to Lonavla on Friday evenings.'

'Did I ask for your opinion, idiot? Listen . . . our guys didn't notice that; in any case, we do not have much strategic depth in Iran; the Mossad was monitoring someone whom they recently met.'

'And who was that? You know hundreds of these meetings take place all over the Middle East every day.'

'Yes, my love, if I am telling you this, it must be important, don't you get it?'

'Then give me the whole deal, please, don't do this striptease.'

'What? You can go to hell, you idiot. I don't want to talk to you any more.'

'Oh my dear, stop the Broadway Show, tell me the crux of the information, please.'

'This is all that I know.'

'And what am I supposed to do about it?'

'Idiot! We are working on it, you just do a check to see if it rings a bell for you somewhere.'

'Right now my head is ringing all right.'

'You are incorrigible, now I know why your wife has left you.'

'Has she? Haven't heard from her lately.'

'Rudra, you hopeless rascal, go to hell, bye.'

8 P.M., CRISIS CENTRE

Kant has arrived, looking distressed. He indicates to everyone to be seated as they get up to greet him, and then takes a seat near Rudra. Rudra notices underarm sweat stains on Kant's uniform as he sits. He looks at his own clothes and realizes that he too has been wearing the same set of clothing since the CBI took him into custody. Rudra has been intensively working on the information available to them, planning operations, scanning through data and connecting the dots. He knows that Kant has just met the domestic Intelligence chief of the country, the Bureau chief.

'How did it go, sir?'

'You know them, RP, they play this nice game of riddles. If you don't know even one answer, you are blamed for negligence.'

'What did he come here for, sir? Did he discuss the WikiLeaks revelation with you?'

'He knows something that we do not, RP. My hunch is that he is supervising an operation here personally. He hails from the operational wing, a very hands-on man, so I wouldn't be surprised if he really pulls out a rabbit from his hat.'

'So nothing concrete yet, sir, we deal with it like other generic threats?'

'Majumdar is taking care of the generic aspects, Rudra. I am rather concerned about your nuclear hypothesis. As time is passing, there are signs leading us in that direction. How large is a mid-sized nuclear bomb?'

'As far as I have gathered, sir, a plutonium bomb is very compact, requiring less than 10 kilograms of the material, while a uranium bomb may require thrice the amount of fissile material. Which means that the devices need not be very large, any box approximately four feet by two feet can hide a nuclear weapon. It can nicely be accommodated in the boot of a car, sir.'

'More like a large suitcase?'

'Yes, sir.'

'Strange situation we are in, RP, by all accounts this threat seems to be real, yet we only have theories and pointers. Even if we go by your nuclear hypothesis, how the hell do you search for a suitcase-sized object in a city of fifteen million people?'

'It makes no sense to go looking without the relevant Intelligence, sir.'

'RP, has there been no development in the ship-blast case either? The sudden disappearance of these oil thieves needs to be urgently investigated. Pick up anyone who has any connection to them; get to the root of it. It is inexplicable that none of the agencies noticed their vanishing act; we too were caught napping.'

'I am on it, sir, will give you something soon.' Rudra then leans over to say something in Kant's ear; Kant is listening intently, he then seems lost in thoughts as if he is making some calculations.

'Not an impossible thing, RP, let me try and get them to make a request directly to the Israeli government.'

As they talk, Rudra's cell buzzes. A text message on his cell reads:

'Hide-and-seek, wanna play?'

Rudra has a smile on his face now. He has finally got engagement.

8.15 P.M., NEW DELHI

Acting on a tip-off, the Special Cell of Delhi Police has laid a trap in the Karol Bagh area. Three terrorists of the dreaded Lashkar are expected to be there any moment; these men have been reportedly tasked with a major terror attack in Delhi. A roadblock has been organized by the local police station at D.B. Gupta Road to check vehicles. There is a severe chill in the air; visibility is pretty low due to the fog. The Special Cell personnel have positioned themselves nearby in plain clothes, waiting for the targets. Assistant Commissioner of Police Satbir has been through many such operations; he has a good network of informants and sources. It is rumoured that he runs sources deep into Pakistan too.

He sits across the street in a civilian car, engine running, pretending to be talking on the phone, while his eyes are riveted on the side-view mirror. His trusted source has given him very reliable intel. He has grown to be dependent on this informant; he has twice given him arms and explosives dumps and once a fugitive.

His chain of thought is suddenly broken by a loud screech, followed by a melee. A car, which was asked to stop, halted and then sped on, breaking away from the roadblock. Satbir sees a red Maruti Alto 800 speeding away towards Khalsa College. He immediately takes a turn and follows. Three members of his plain-clothes team also have started on their motorcycles. He catches up with the car by the time they have crossed the D.B. Gupta Market and has a fleeting glance of two young men sitting in the front seats.

His informant has given a matching description of the car. Satbir follows them vigorously as they dodge cars. Suddenly, the Alto takes a sharp turn to the right at Prahlad Market and zooms past the red light towards Maharana Pratap Road. Satbir and his team are hindered by the flow of cars from the opposite direction, but they too jump the signal and follow; they momentarily lose sight of the 'target'. Head Constable Malik is in the lead on a bike when the Alto swerves and crashes against an electric pole near the Ayurvedic and Unani Tibbia College. The car stops, doors open and two figures followed by two more run towards the college boundary wall. As they are trying to scale it and alight on the large lawn, Malik fires from his service revolver in the darkness.

One gets hit. Visibility is too low and, by the time the other policemen reach, they hear firing. They open fire at the targets, fearing retaliation. In seconds, all the targets are down; Satbir reaches there to find two men and two girls badly struggling with multiple gun-shot wounds.

He immediately informs the control room that crossfiring has taken place near the Ayurvedic and Unani Tibbia College at Karol Bagh. He calls for an ambulance with critical-care facilities. Then he tells the control room that two of his constables have been injured and that there may be more casualties.

9.15 P.M., DELHI

Media has flocked to Ram Manohar Lohia Hospital; ACP Satbir is about to address them about an encounter with the dreaded Lashkar terrorists. As he comes out of the casualty ward, cameras start flashing, and TV journalists jostle with each other to get the first bite. The constables on duty from the local police station stop the mob of reporters from surging ahead. Satbir has known most of them for years now; he also knows the questions they will ask. He comes near them as they gather mikes in a large bunch in front of him.

There is a cacophony of sounds as each journalist tries to ask a question. Satbir indicates to them to calm down, and tries to concentrate on the questions.

'Yes,' he says, 'what were you saying?'

'When did you get the information about the terrorists, sir?' a bearded journo in the front asks urgently.

'This morning we received information from a trusted source that four terrorists of the Lashkar are planning an operation in New Delhi. We stationed our team to check the suspects and apprehend them. At around 8.20 p.m. this evening, as informed, a Red Maruti Alto 800 broke the *nakabandi* (blockade) at D.B. Gupta Road. When the police personnel present tried to stop them, they fled away towards Maharana Pratap Road. There when our team members accosted them, they began to fire from the car. When we returned the fire, they lost control of the vehicle, collided with a lamp post and tried to abscond. Two members of the Special cell have been injured in the crossfiring, four terrorists have been declared dead on arrival, two of which are women. Their identities have not been confirmed yet. We have recovered three automatic weapons and Rs 10 lakh cash along with 45 rounds of ammunition from them.'

'Sir, sir, what were they planning to do?'

'According to the tip-off received, they were wanting to orchestrate a major terrorist attack in a metro city.'

'Sir, was any warning given to them for surrendering before opening fire?'

'Yes, we gave them ample warning, but when they fired at us, we had to fire back in self-defence.'

'Do you think these four people were working in isolation or is there some deeper conspiracy behind this?'

'These things we will come to know with further investigation only, thanks,' says Satbir, leaving the hospital premises.

9.30 P.M., NEW DELHI

A video clip has been uploaded on YouTube, showing the real sequence of events outside the Ayurvedic and Unani Tibbia College. The media has picked up the clip from YouTube; it is completely in contrast with the official version. The clip also gives the identities of the deceased; they are students of the AUT College. There is an uproar in the public as demands for booking the Special Cell personnel are made by religious leaders and some political formations. The Union home minister suspends ACP Satbir and his team.

In Mumbai, Rudra gets an SMS on his cell phone:

'Strike Two.'

Rudra calls Quazi: 'Contact Advaita Sharma. I am getting text messages on my cell phone from a Web portal. Ask him to track the IP address and the location of the sender. Do not share any information with him or any outsider; do not tell him that I am getting these messages.'

'Sir, he has been busy on a project these last few weeks. I will still request him.'

'Quazi, he is a nice patriotic boy, use his services; there is nobody in the force whose skills even remotely matches his; we do not have an option here.'

'Roger, sir, will be done.'

SAME TIME

Majumdar is reporting on the phone to Kant.

'All compliances in place as per the operations manual, sir. We have asked our VIPs to remain indoors till further communication. I have liaised with the Navy and coastguard to safeguard the shores; they have also commenced helicopter patrolling of the coastline. Our SWAT teams are armed, ready for intervention any time. Hotels, lodging and boarding houses, inns, brothels, bars, shanties, everything is being checked for suspicious activities and persons. I would also request you to activate the Self-Defence volunteer force, sir, they will come handy.'

'Yes, Majumdar, I can see that a lot of work is being done on the ground. Keep your vigil; let the men not slacken. Wherever they are required to be on continuous static duties for many hours, send food from our mobile canteens.'

'Noted, sir, will be complied with.'

'And yes, any information, howsoever insignificant it may seem pertaining to the ship blast or the current threat, should be directly relayed to me and RP at the Crisis Centre.'

'The police station officers are in touch with their sources, sir, anything that is relevant will be passed on immediately.'

'Majumdar, forget the relevant part for now. I want no filters! Bye.'

SAME DAY, A FEW HOURS EARLIER, TEHRAN, IRAN

Yaseen Al-Majali, a Jordanian businessman in his late fifties, lives on Hessabi Street in the plush northern district of Elahiyeh. He has just left for Imam Khomeini International Airport. He does not want to park his car at the airport and has called for a taxi; he intends to spend some days abroad. The last few days of his life have been very hectic; he intends to relax and have a good time at a nice, sunny, tropical location. Not that he is just going on a trip of leisure. There is much work at hand, yet he is looking forward to this sojourn.

The driver is going at an easy pace. Yaseen puts on his earphones and listens to Mansour playing 'Shirin'; he starts swaying to the music with his eyes closed as the car enters Niayesh tunnel. Within no time, the constant hum of the vehicles in the tunnel and the soothing music lulls him to sleep.

He is awakened by a sharp burning pain in his neck; startled, he opens his eyes to see that he is still in the tunnel, but a small dart with a sharp needle is stuck in his throat. As he removes it with his fingers, he feels that he is being rapidly sucked into a dark void, and then loses consciousness.

9 P.M., PARK PLAZA HOTEL, LAHORE, PAKISTAN

Ansar Suleri is playing a MMORPG (massively multiplayer online role-playing game) on his laptop. *Dinosaur Hunt* has been his favourite one for years. He likes this one particularly because he was a part of the development team of the game as a young rookie. Now that the game has taken the world by storm, he admires its real-life graphics, 3D rendering and breakneck action. The best thing about this game is that it allows one to collaborate with other players online and form teams.

'Jibreel! Assalam alaikum,' he exclaims on his headset. 'I have been waiting for you, where have you been?'

He is voice-chatting inside the game with a player whom he calls 'Jibreel', the archangel of Allah.

'I have been busy, brother, doing a lot of work, carrying out your instructions.'

'Alhamdulillah, keep up the good work, bhai.'

'How is the enemy reacting?' Suleri says, filled with a childish sense of exhilaration.

'They are scared to death. It is not yet out in the open, brother. They are tightening security, picking up innocent brothers and questioning them. It is only a matter of a day or two before we have our first major victory.'

'Ameen, my dear brother, inshallah, we shall emerge victorious. What is your prime minister planning to do?'

'I am surprised that there has been no reaction till now. I request you to seek further directions from the Amir about what should be done next.'

'The Amir is very happy with our work. I met him recently

at the big rally held at the Gaddafi Stadium. I will speak to him immediately.'

'Khuda hafiz, brother, we meet here online again tomorrow morning at the fixed time.'

'Khuda hafiz.'

7 P.M., A YACHT ON THE CASPIAN SEA

The sun is setting on the beautiful Caspian Sea off the Iranian Noshahr coast; deep-orange clouds are turning red and then purple as the big ball of fire sinks in the sea. The air is cold, yet tolerable. The sea is calm.

Yaseen Al-Majali is regaining consciousness; he feels that his arms and feet have gone cold. A sense of heavy pressure on his chest has made breathing difficult.

Two men are sitting beside the bed brewing Persian tea in a traditional Iranian teapot.

'You Indians murder the tea.'

'Darius, you Persians marry it and make love to it. I can see the rose petals too. Seems like a honeymoon.'

They both have a hearty laugh.

'Kumar, I will brew another cup for you, with cardamom, no rose petals.'

'I was just joking. Let's offer some tea to our guest too, he is waking up.'

'Yes,' says Darius, 'General, would you like your tea with rose petals or cardamom?'

He then picks up a sugar cube, places it between his teeth and sips his well-brewed tea from a glass cup.

'Kumar, you don't even try drinking it this way, it will destroy your teeth.'

'I have already put my sugar cube into the cup.'

'One more cup of tea has been murdered.'

They both laugh again as Yaseen sits up. He has a confused expression on his face, but does not say anything.

'Sorry, General, we broke protocol during your travel, but you see, we had such important things to discuss with you that we couldn't help it. I hope you don't mind,' says Darius in a very polite voice.

'Who are you, Mossad, CIA or MEK?'

'Do we have to have a formal introduction, my dear sir? We are your friends, as long as you are ours.'

'I have nothing to give you. I am no general. I am a businessman. You can check my company profile. If you allow, I will show you my business card.'

The Indian speaks now, 'We know your business too, General, and the 50-billion-dollar deal you did some weeks ago is also known to us. Do you still wish to go through the formalities of an introduction?'

Yaseen is silent. Darius is at ease; he gets up to brew another cup of tea. His shoulder-length, salt-and-pepper hair gives him the look of an artist more than that of a Mujahedeen. He is a member of the banned MEK. The Mujahedeen El Khidmat has been declared counter-revolutionary by the Iranian government. They have been operating from Iraq with the active support of western agencies. He has been an old contact of Kumar's, the Indian Intelligence agent stationed in Baghdad.

'I will not speak to you unless you tell me who you are and you guarantee my life.'

No one reacts, Kumar and Darius do not even exchange glances, they keep sipping their tea.

After some moments of silence, Kumar speaks again.

'Coming back to the topic, General Badi, who was your customer?'

Darius has closed his eyes; he is reclining on the chair, as if he is relaxing after a long journey. He slowly turns his neck first to the left and then to the right, relieving some of his stress.

Kumar continues, 'General, it is getting dark. We will leave the yacht soon; it has been rigged to sink in some time, along with you, leaving no trace.'

'What is the assurance that I will remain alive if I give you the facts?' the general's voice is trembling.

'You are endangering the lives of millions, how can you ask this question, sir?' Kumar is laughing sarcastically.

'You will not get anything from me.'

'If we know your real identity and we know about your financial dealings, there is not much that you can tell us. This is your chance to redeem yourself. We can allow you to transfer the money to your heirs if you so wish.'

'Just guarantee my life, I will help you out.'

Darius now opens his eyes. 'Kumar, I told you before, the general is a good man.'

9.45 P.M., CONFERENCE ROOM, SOUTH BLOCK, NEW DELHI

The Union Cabinet has met for an emergency meeting at the Secretariat building in South Block. The corridors of the red-and-cream sandstone building are silent. Only security personnel and some personal staff of the ministers are present at this late hour. The large empty corridors are echoing with hurried footsteps as the ministers pour in. Their convoys line up on the virtually empty Rajpath Road. The drivers and bodyguards question each other about the nature of urgency as they share cheap cigarettes and tobacco.

The senior Cabinet ministers sit close to the prime minister as he awaits the arrival of others. Tea has already been served to prevent interruptions later. They speak in hushed tones with each other as they guess that some very serious issue is at hand. The chandeliers on the roof emit a milky-yellow, diffused light from the high ceiling, adding to the seriousness of the atmosphere. The walls are lined with wooden panels while the floor is covered with an exquisite Persian carpet, primarily red, with designs woven in golden-and-white threads.

The prime minister starts when the quorum is complete; there is a hushed silence before he speaks.

'Today is a day of national crisis, when the very existence of our beloved country is threatened. The terrorist group Lashkar, responsible for the recent Mumbai attacks, has acquired a nuclear weapon. It has threatened us with "never before" consequences if we do not declare a plebiscite in Kashmir at the discussion in the United Nations Security Council on this issue day after tomorrow.

'I have called you here in this moment of reckoning, to help me make a decision. If we declare plebiscite, we may lose Kashmir, which has been an integral part of India since time immemorial. If we don't, we lose Mumbai and with it, millions of lives. This is a lose–lose situation; we have a Hobson's choice here.

'You are all senior and experienced people; you have seen and handled serious calamities and disasters. I lay my trust in your judgement on this day; whatever decision we take, the country and the people will never forgive us. It is our great misfortune that it has befallen upon us to take this decision today.'

No one speaks, the air is heavy, there is complete silence in the room, and it looks like there are thirty-two mute statues.

The prime minister is reminded of a tale from his childhood, narrated by his late grandmother. The great King Bhoj finds the throne of the legendary King Vikramaditya. The throne has the power to make the occupier see the truth, but every time he attempts to sit on it, a statue has a tale to tell. At the end of the tale, it asks him, 'Are you worthy enough to sit on the throne of the great King Vikramaditya?'

The prime minister feels that the question is echoing in his own head: 'Are you worthy enough to sit on the throne?'

Defence Minister Raghavan has been around in South Block on earlier occasions. He was the defence minister in his earlier tenure when India and Pakistan had come to the brink of a major war following the overzealous overtures of a hyperactive Army chief. He is in his sixties, an astute man of few words, very serious, yet decisive and assertive in a cold way.

'I suggest we call a meeting of the Nuclear Command Authority (NCA),' he says. 'Now.'

The home minister is a considerably younger man, always full of energy and enthusiasm.

'Should we not pick up the Red Phone and dial the Pakistani prime minister right away?'

'Saxenaji,' Raghavan addresses him, 'we have avowed a No First Use policy on nuclear weapons. The threat is not from the Pakistani Army this time. If we decide to go for a retaliatory strike, we should not alert them about it.'

Finance Minister Mishra speaks, his voice failing with emotion, 'Sir, we have to prevent this nonsense at any cost. Millions of people will die in both the countries. I do not know if we would be alive to see our retaliation.'

The prime minister is pensive, as Raghavan interjects, 'No one wants a nuclear war, yet if it is thrust upon us, we will respond resolutely. With finality.'

'Why are we not talking to the Americans? They can definitely help us. We should come out in the open about this, it will defeat the very purpose of the ultimatum as there would not be any discussion on Kashmir in the UN after this,' says Raosaheb Kadam, the agriculture minister. He is an astute statesman who has risen from the Cooperative Societies Movement of Maharashtra. He always makes sense and gives practical, workable solutions.

'Mr Kadam, if we do so, Lashkar will detonate the bomb before the deadline. In the other unlikely scenario, if we consider giving in to their demands of a referendum, it will be Tamil Nadu tomorrow declaring independence, followed by Punjab and then the whole of the North-East—there would be no India left,' says the prime minister. 'Another thing is that this is an issue of terrorism, not a bipartisan issue between two countries.'

The home minister is getting impatient. 'What if we do a surgical operation to take down the head of Lashkar, the way the Americans killed Osama in Abbottabad?'

'You think he is waiting for us out in the open after delivering a nuclear threat?' quips Raghavan. 'We are talking about the most powerful terrorist group in the world today.'

The prime minister is instructing the Cabinet secretary to call an urgent meeting of the NCA. He also asks him to include the heads of the three armed forces along with the National Security adviser.

'I need to urgently apprise the President of India about this situation after the meeting,' he says.

The meeting continues as the prime minister waits for the NCA to convene.

10 P.M., CRISIS CENTRE

Sana has arrived at the Crisis Centre; she asks Rudra to accompany her for a confidential briefing. Rudra is bewildered. She is attired as if she is coming straight from the gym, a purple T-shirt over black track pants. She seems to be in a terrible hurry, as always.

Looking at the lack of patience on her part, he accompanies her to a small room.

'What now, Sana, why are you here?'

'Now who is catastrophizing? Tell me, tell me . . .' she raises her eyebrows, which makes her look even more beautiful.

'Sana, we are in the deepest shit here, the commissioner may land up any moment. This is no time for romance!'

'Do you think I'm dying to meet you, idiot? I am on work here,' she adjusts her apparel as if it were formal wear.

'Oh, then it's okay.'

'Why, I can't come to meet you without work? You have lost all feelings for me. See how men behave once they have achieved their goals.'

'Which goals are you talking about, Sana?'

'So I too was a conquest. Now that I have been clinched, you do not care about me,' she feigns anger.

'Please, my dear, spare me today, I do not understand a word of what you're saying.'

'Bastard, I am joking. Such a dud you have become, you don't get my jokes any more.'

'Broadway, can we talk business, please?'

'Yeah, man, I forgot what I had come for! You always talk about irrelevant things, never let me concentrate!'

'Please oblige me now, my dear.'

'Okay here we go, so R, after we spoke about the

information my Tashkent batchmate gave me about the Lashkar guys, there was a joint operation between the CIA and our chaps. They got to the high-value target the Lashkar chaps were meeting with.'

'Amazing, your agency has started to work? That too in the Middle East, not bad, not bad.'

'Shut up and listen.'

'Majesty, at your service. Please continue.'

'The target that was captured with the help of the Iranian rebel Mujahedeen El Khidmat chaps, turns out to be a deposed Syrian general called Adbel Badi, who was the architect of their nuclear programme.'

'What was he doing in Tehran?'

'He was leading his life under the alias of Yaseen Al-Majali, as a Jordanian businessman. He had escaped from Damascus in March 2011 after the eruption of the Arab Spring there. Being close to the ruling leader Hashem Qabbani-II, he was likely to be hunted down by the rebel faction of the Army. He escaped from there and landed in Iran, to lead a secret second life as a businessman.'

'Why was Lashkar meeting him then?'

'You dimwit, have some patience, I am coming to it. So this General Badi had a nuclear weapon in his control. A small plutonium device, which he had been trying to sell to the highest bidder.'

'Since when did Syria have nuclear weapons? I have never heard of it.'

She now takes his hand in her hand, caresses it sympathetically, and says, 'Sherlock, the beauty of it is that nobody was aware of it, except the CIA and Israel.'

He takes away his hand, trying to really concentrate on the information.

'If they knew it, why have they been silent about it? They would have made such a hue and cry about it that even school kids in Congo would have known that Syria has nuclear weapons.'

'It is a long story, suffice to say that Mossad and the CIA were tracking him when he made a fifty-billion-dollar transaction. This was from the sale of the nuclear weapon.'

'Fifty billion dollars is one-fourth of Pakistan's GDP; no one in the world would allow the ISI (Inter Services Intelligence, the Pakistan Intelligence agency) to sell that much worth of drugs for Lashkar's nuclear weapon.'

'I do not know where they got this money from, to hell with it. There has been a completed transaction worth this amount from a Lashkar front to General Badi's account.'

'So, Lashkar has a nuke now? Where is it?'

'Yes. Now you want me to tell you the geographic coordinates? Like latitude and longitude?'

'Oh, Sana, be serious sometimes at least!'

'My love, you be serious, you are the one supposed to be saving the world.'

'Look, I do not have words to thank you for this input. This confirms Quazi's theory of the symbolism behind the messages. He decoded the messages which hinted that there will be a Zalzala—an earthquake, seas will flow, god will send garments of fire for people, boiling water and what not.'

'Well, then, if you are not able to save the world, I meet you up there.'

'I can deal with Lashkar, but surrender before you, Sana? Go now!'

She turns haughtily and dashes for the door. There is a hint of sadness on her face.

'One minute,' Rudra says. 'If the world is really going

to end soon, there is something urgent that needs to be done.'

She has a confused look on her face as he comes near her, puts his arms around her waist, holds her close and brings his lips close to hers. Close, but not touching. She feels the fire rising up from her stomach; he keeps breathing, holding her close. She is not one to relent or make a move; she holds her ground, her hands holding him tight in embrace. Rudra closes his eyes in anticipation; he feels her body against his own, warm and soft. She is breathing fast now, yet not kissing, slowly turning her head so that Rudra is breathing on her neck. She turns her head again, virtually brushing her lips against his; Rudra feels as if he is about to relent, just then his cell phone rings.

'Shit!' she says. 'What timing, man. Shoot the bastard calling right at the most inopportune moment. Bye, I am leaving.'

She rushes out, leaving Rudra burning with passion. He looks at the cell phone angrily; it's Commissioner Kant. Before he takes the call, it gets disconnected. He notices that Sana has left a piece of paper behind. He lifts it up and reads:

Top Secret

Israeli Air Force's Bombing of the Syrian Nuclear Reactor

Operation Eden

Israeli Air Force conducted a top-secret operation in the Syrian desert region of Deir ez-Zor on 6 Septembr 2007. This operation, nicknamed Operation Eden, resulted in the total destruction of a Syrian military facility, suspected to be an undeclared nuclear site.

Syria has vehemently denied these charges, claiming the attack to be a violation of Syrian sovereignty. Later, investigations by the International Atomic Energy Agency (IAEA) found traces of uranium and graphite at the site; the agency also complained of lack of cooperation from Syria regarding the investigation.

The White House and CIA have confirmed that the complex was indeed a nuclear facility.

Reports further state that the 69th Squadron of the Israeli Air Force carried out this operation with great success. F-15s and F-16s equipped with AGM-65 Maverick missiles, 500-lb bombs and external fuel tanks participated along with an ELINT aircraft. It is also reported that elite Shaldag commandos had arrived at the site a day before to highlight the targets with laser beams; other reports state that Sayeret Matkal special forces had carried out the preparatory work.

Rudra is stunned: 'Is this the missing piece of the puzzle? So Syria produced a nuclear weapon, the general controlled it, and when things got too hot for him, he flew away with the device, only to offer it to the highest bidder.'

He reads and rereads the paper, his hands are trembling; he has never been so sad at being proven to be correct.

'The Arab Spring has had such a domino effect that no one could have foreseen,' he thinks; scenes from his engineering days flash in his mind when the sexy lady professor used to say: *The beating of a butterfly's wings in Brazil can cause a tornado in Toronto*, and they all used to laugh; ironically it seemed so prophetic now . . .

6

MOLE IN THE HOLE

The ATC team has reached the ninth-floor flat in a Lokhandwala complex. Inspector Mahajan is leading the team. He rings the doorbell and waits. His five colleagues have positioned themselves at the upper and lower floor landings on the staircase. One team has blocked the lifts, while another backup unit is waiting in the basement parking area in case things go wrong.

There is no response, he rings the bell again. After a long wait, he knocks; still no response. He then listens carefully for noises inside the room. Realizing that the air-conditioning unit is running outside the window, he knows that the inhabitant is inside the room.

He beckons to his colleagues who back him up, arms drawn. They count up to three, breach the door open and rush in, warning the inhabitants to drop their weapons. The lights are on only in the bedroom. A strong stench greets them. It smells like puke mixed with urine and excreta. Mahajan

91

covers his nose with a handkerchief and cautiously enters the bedroom.

The bed is full of dried vomit, while the floor is still wet with what appears to be urine and human faeces. The smell is unbearable. The air conditioning is recirculating the foul smell over and over again. As he moves further, he sees the body of a young girl on the floor, covered in filth. He feels like puking as he approaches the body. It seems to be lying still. He checks for breath and pulse, and registers no vital signs. Her hair is matted with body fluids, her skin parched dry, her beautiful face contorted into the horrible grimace of death. The terrible stench prevents him from staying inside the room for a minute longer. He calls for the mobile forensic van to collect samples, and transport the body.

He is disturbed at the extinction of the single lead they had in the ship-blast case. All the other people connected with the oil mafia have disappeared, and this girl had been the only ray of hope. He calls Rudra to brief him.

'Rudra sir, Mahajan here. We have reached the flat of the girl, but she is not alive.'

'. . .'

'No . . . not shot dead. There are no signs of violence in the room.'

'. . .'

'Not strangulated, sir, she seems to have been very sick. The body is lying in a pool of vomit, urine and faeces. The poor girl has died a very painful death.'

'. . .'

'Approximately three days, sir, not more than that. She had last been seen entering the flat with her boyfriend on Thursday evening.'

'No landline, sir. She must have used a mobile phone. I

will get that for analysis.'

'Yes, sir, we will conduct a thorough search before leaving. The local police officer in charge, Shinde, is my batchmate; he will arrive soon to take over the scene. I am posting a plain-clothes watch at the flat after they seal the premises.'

'Right, sir, good night.'

His colleagues are carefully searching the room for clues when the local police station team arrives with Inspector Shinde.

10:15 P.M., SOUTH BLOCK, NEW DELHI

The Nuclear Command Authority is meeting, and both the political and executive wings are participating. In a breach of precedence, the prime minister has involved the chiefs of the three armed forces as well as the Cabinet secretary. The National Security adviser, Gopal Rao, opens the deliberations.

'Gentlemen, we are now well apprised of the situation. The vital question to be answered here is whether we go for a retaliatory nuclear strike in the likely event of Lashkar attacking us with a nuclear weapon. If so, the modalities, targets, modes of delivery and logistics will have to be discussed.'

Army Chief General Malhotra responds, 'If we are attacked, we finish them. No two ways about it. Most important would be to take off their retaliatory strike capability. They also have a Nuclear Umbrella Treaty with NATO, which will bring the USA in. Hence, when we attack, we need to finish them once and for all.'

Air Chief Marshall Fernandes is contemplative; after a while he responds:

'I second the opinion of my worthy colleague.'

Gopal Rao takes the discussion forward. 'We will require a total of twenty-four warheads to totally destroy Pakistan beyond redemption. If we intend to use more than 25 kilotonnes of yield bombs, the Air Force would have to do it. In case we use Agni missiles, we can cut down the risk of detection and failure by reducing the delivery time substantially.'

'I propose to use a combination of delivery methods. Karachi and other coastal locations can be targeted by medium-range missiles launched from our submarines, while distant cities like Peshawar can be covered with ICBMs, and the rest can be taken care of by the Air Force dropping the payloads,' suggests Fernandes.

'We go this way then—any city of five million or more population will require three bombs of an average 25-kilotonne yield; those having one to five million population will require two, whereas any city with a smaller population can be effectively finished with a single bomb,' Gopal Rao continues. 'Thus, Islamabad, Peshawar, Quetta, Hyderabad and Rawalpindi will need one each, while Lahore and Faisalabad two each and finally Karachi will require three bombs. If we approve of this, the delivery mechanisms will have to be carefully mixed and matched.'

Defence Minister Raghavan looks at the prime minister's face. 'I do approve of it, sir. A nuclear attack leaves us with no choice but to respond with a nuclear weapon. There is no point in waging conventional warfare with a nuclear neighbour after we have been hit by a nuke ourselves.'

He then turns to the National Security adviser. 'Mr Rao, what about the US and China? How would they react?'

'If the US gets the slightest hint of our plan to annihilate

Pakistan, it will use everything in the book to stop us, including threatening us with nuclear consequences. As far as China is concerned, it will posture, but not react after the strike. Secrecy is of utmost importance to us.'

Gopal Rao pauses, gauging the reactions of others in the room, then proceeds, 'Russia used to be our ally at one time, now we cannot bank on it. I am not sure if it is in any condition to honour the Nuclear Umbrella Treaty that it has with us. Thus, as a good strategy, we should not leave any options for anyone; if there are any, they will be used against us.'

Raghavan has a determined bearing now, as if he has come to a conclusion. He addresses his chief, 'Mr Prime Minister, it is time to take a decision on this.'

There is a hushed silence as the prime minister stares into space. He seems to be tormented from inside. Raghavan can imagine the whirlwind of emotions that is passing through the man even though his face remains unperturbed.

Finally, the prime minister speaks: 'Our nuclear doctrine has been one of peace. We have never intended it to be used as a weapon of offence. We are aware that with great power comes great responsibility. We are never going to abuse it.

'We have a policy of "no first use". This does not mean that we are weak; if attacked with nuclear weapons, we will decimate the opponent. I assure you, gentlemen, at this historic moment that grass will never grow on Pakistan. It will be a desert forever. *I, the Prime Minister of India, hereby authorize the full and effective use of nuclear weapons against any adversary who chooses to attack us with one.*

'Let my words go down in history thus.'

No one speaks; one can hear the breath of the people in

the room, and no one looks at the other. A decision to take away millions of human lives has just been taken, collectively by them. Their conscience is never going to forgive them, nor will history . . .

10.35 P.M., CRISIS CENTRE

Rudra Pratap Singh is furious; he is looking for Inspector Mahajan.

'I will clobber him to death if I see him. Where the hell is he? Unprofessional, stupid clod.'

'What happened, sir? I have never seen you so angry,' asks Quazi.

'Quazi, this joker had gone to get the girl who was linked to the oil mafia. He informs me from there that the girl is dead. He then searches the flat and finds nothing of significance.'

'So what happened, sir, why are you so angry?'

'Shinde, of the local police station, who took over the scene from him reports that the girl is alive, though comatose. How the hell did he leave the place before confirming whether the girl was dead or alive? Shinde also found her cell phone that she had dropped in the bathroom. She must have been very sick before she lost consciousness. This character of ours has returned empty-handed from such an important scene.'

'That's highly unprofessional, sir!' Quazi too is agitated now. 'He is not a raw recruit just out of the academy. He is a seasoned officer, this is totally unacceptable.'

'To hell with him, the worst part is that the girl has been probably poisoned with a slow-reacting substance. She is in a very critical state at City Hospital.'

'We should not lose this thread, sir. I have a feeling that she will lead us somewhere in this case.'

'Which case, Quazi?'

'Why, sir, the ship-blast case?'

'Ah yes, the ship-blast case. Hmm, arrange for unobtrusive security at the hospital for the girl. Let the media know she is alive. The one who has tried to kill her is bound to react.'

'Yes, sir, I will personally ensure. Do not worry, please.'

'Let me know if she regains consciousness. I need to talk to her at any cost. And yes, Quazi, what happened to the messages I was getting from the Web portal? What did Advaita do about it?'

Quazi takes out his tablet, and reads out a mail. 'Sir, Advaita says the messages are difficult to trace as the sender is using a VPN which gives his IP address as California. All the log-ins to the SMS portal have been through the Virtual Private Network Server.'

'Can we talk to Bose in the National Cyber Reconnaissance Organization? Put him on the task too.'

'Roger that, sir, doing it right away.'

As Quazi retreats to his cubicle, Rudra retires to his temporary office cabin. His coffee is cold, but he still sips it. 'Bitter, lousy coffee,' he says to himself. 'But does all this matter when everything is about to be destroyed? The taste of bad coffee, hierarchies, aspirations, love, relationships, dreams, possessions . . . everything will just evaporate.' He looks at the video wall showing feeds from the city, people going about their lives, unaware of the fact that it may very well be their last days on this planet. Buildings, roads, monuments, bridges, malls, theatres, schools would all be destroyed forever. A city with its history, its soul, its essence, architecture, society, web of relationships would simply vanish.

He suddenly remembers his unborn child and his wife. The

poor woman had suffered much due to his eccentricities; he felt that his unborn child was moving, floating before his eyes.

He sees it floating mid-air, black and white, like a sonography image made of grey dots, merging and separating, swarming to form the face, hands, toes and nose, going in and out of focus like the static TV dots in the olden days when there was loss of signal. Buzzing grey dots, now combining to form shapes, now dispersing into noise.

In a flash, he feels the formless child crying out loud. He opens his eyes, but cannot move, cannot breathe. The dots before him turn white and then yellow. Before he can realize what is happening, they light up into flaming orange and dissipate into the air. He feels like he is choking, he struggles hard and finally he can break free of the apoplexy and breathe. His cell starts ringing while he lapsed into this reverie. It's Commissioner Kant again.

'RP, on the personal front, I have asked for your wife to be shifted to interior Maharashtra. To be precise, I have asked for her to be relocated to Nashik Rural near Igatpuri, if that's okay with you. Or you could enlighten us about the alternate plans you have made.'

'No, sir, you will not do this! What about your family? What about those innocent fifteen million people, most of whom are going to evaporate like you and me?'

'RP, you have not spoken to her once since you came out on bail. How dare you decide whether she lives or not?'

'You told me, sir, that my release on bail was a top secret. How could I breach your faith by talking to my wife?'

'No time to discuss that, RP. The girl at City Hospital is gaining consciousness. They are trying their best to revive her. Haemodialysis has been performed on her; she was poisoned with ice cream laced with ethylene glycol. The poor girl could not get medical help in her emergency. We have registered a case of attempt to murder by poisoning. You had better proceed to the hospital. I will send Vinay as your replacement till then at the Crisis Centre.'

Rudra calls up the tech unit.

'Raghu, Inspector Shinde of the Lokhandwala police station has sent the details of a cell phone; it belongs to a girl who was on our scanner for links with the oil mafia. Now quickly get me the last dialled, frequently contacted or texted numbers, do the location tracking for the last one week, and figure out any SIM or instrument changes. You know the drill well.'

'Rudra sir, the preliminary analysis is complete. There is a number that has been dialled repeatedly in the last three days. I ran a check on that number too, it has been unavailable. The instrument is also off air; the most interesting thing about the number is that it has outgoing calls only to the girl's number. No other number has been contacted by the person.'

'Subscriber details?'

'Sir, the SIM is registered in the name of a labourer, Rameshwar Prasad, in Ranchi, Jharkhand. The address seems to be false. The details on the girl's phone are accurate. The first SIM has been active for the last three months only.'

'Location trace?'

'Something interesting here, sir, for the last one month before it went off air, the instrument has been at the girl's flat.'

Rudra's mind is running fast. 'Is the number set to call-forwarding?'

'Sir, yes, it has been set to forward all calls to a VoIP server.'

'Oh, if the person is bouncing calls, then he must be using a spoof caller ID to dial. Scan the gateway for the incoming calls to the girl's number, I am holding the line.'

'Please hold, sir, getting it now.'

'This is a smart person,' Rudra thinks, 'and damn good at his job. Knows his tech very well. Most likely her boyfriend, but why did he intend to kill her, why did he poison her and leave her to die? Was it revenge over some quarrel? No, it does not seem likely. This person has a plan. Most likely he has been using her, but using her to achieve what?

'And her connection to the oil mafia . . . what was that?

'Was her task over? Was that why she needed to be killed?

'What was the task?'

He felt lost, there was no clarity, no ray of hope, no clue.

'Sir,' Raghu is back on the call. Jolted out of his thoughts, Rudra takes a second to respond.

'Yes, Raghu.'

'You've guessed it right, sir. This person has taken care to hide all trails, he has covered his tracks successfully. No useful information on location, subscriber details, other numbers contacted or anything else can be gathered. It is a dead end, sir.'

'Give me details on the VoIP server, Raghu, although I have a feeling that this also may not lead anywhere. We are dealing with a devious mind here.'

'The VoIP server is an open source server, sir, lean and thin, but hosted on a cloud, the details are unavailable.'

'Cul-de-sac.'

'Pardon, sir?'

'Nothing, Raghu. Ask Bose from the NCRO to help. Don't tell him that you have already worked on it. Ask him to speak to me as soon as he gets anything worthwhile. Bye, take care.'

His driver Savant has been driving quite fast, aiming to reach City Hospital as soon as possible.

'Savant,' Rudra says, 'take me to Lokhandwala.'

Without a word, Savant takes a sharp right turn at the next signal. He is now heading towards the girl's flat. Rudra has updated the destination on the car navigation system from his cell, it is not very far.

The city is awake, vibrant with the celebrations of Ganpati. He passes by pandals lit with coloured lights, modelled on famous temples and mythical locations, depicting scenes from folklore and contemporary life.

'One day more for the immersion ceremony, millions of people will be on the streets. Men, women, children carrying Ganesha idols on trucks, cars and carts. There will be festivity in the air, processions playing drums, people dancing in the streets . . .

'Couldn't we simply tell them to run away to a different location, empty the city? No, the enemy will be watching, they will detonate the bomb if this happens. There is no way out . . .'

He gets a text message on his cell, again from the Web portal. It reads: 'No light at the end of the tunnel?'

Rudra mutters, 'Even in darkness, I will find you . . .'

The car halts at the building entrance. Savant goes and talks to the security to let them in. Rudra takes the lift to reach the girl's flat. It has not been sealed yet, there is a sub-inspector of police and two constables completing paperwork there.

Rudra asks the Crisis Centre to inform them of the arrival of an ATC team at the crime scene. He does not disclose his identity. When they get the message they salute him; he asks to be allowed to have a look at the premises.

He goes to the bedroom; it smells putrid, with drying fluids all over the place. He can figure out how badly the girl suffered before she lost consciousness. She must have writhed in extreme pain, unable to seek medical help, knowing each moment that she is dying. She must have tried to call her boyfriend or relatives . . .

Rudra thinks of something; he dials Raghu of the tech team.

'Raghu, how did the first cell phone go offline?'

'Sir, the connection was cancelled at the request of the subscriber.'

'Find out when, let me know ASAP.'

'Yes, sir, getting it.'

Rudra's mind is racing again. 'How did the cell phone show continuous location at this flat for three months? This means the instrument must be here! He would have kept the instrument hidden here, forwarded all the calls to a bouncing network, used a spoof ID of the same number to call her back. Brilliant! She would have never thought that the cell phone was at her place, passively forwarding calls. But where is it?'

'Raghu, are you there?'

'Yes, sir, getting the details in a minute from the service provider.'

'Listen, Raghu, ask him to activate the number again, immediately.'

'But, sir . . .'

'Tell him to do it now!'

'Sir, he is saying that it cannot be done, it needs subscriber verification, only after that they can activate the number.'

'Give him this option—will he do it now, or within the next ten minutes with a gun to his head?'

'Sir . . .'

'Now!'

'Telling him, sir.'

'Text me as soon as the number is active, ask them to cancel the call-forwarding on it.'

Rudra calls up Savant, asks him to bring up to him an instrument from his briefcase. When Savant reaches and hands him the instrument, Rudra switches it on. It is a portable handheld bug scanner which tests for radio frequency emissions at all spectral ranges and wavelengths.

In a few minutes, he gets a text from Raghu, saying, 'Done.'

Rudra texts back. 'Now continuously dial the number.'

He starts scanning with his device, he picks up a signal near the living room; it's coming out of a cupboard. He opens it to find a cell phone.

It is not ringing, its battery is almost dead.

Rudra thinks, 'If the phone has been hidden here for months, it must be connected to a power source through a charger; it cannot be lying somewhere it can be located.'

As he nears the bathroom, he picks up another signal. In the bathroom the signal is strong. He opens all the cabinets one by one, but nothing is found there. The signal is still strong. Rudra rushes to the kitchen, gets a knife and scrapes the sides of the electric outlet board. He then carefully pries it open.

Inside, he sees an object wrapped in black cellophane tape. He carefully removes the wires from it without touching the tape. He brings the object out—a stripped-down cell phone, without a dialler or screen, just the battery, connected to a small transformer-charger, and the bare essential circuitry. It is a cheap, disposable Chinese phone.

Rudra stands there in the bathroom looking at his own reflection in the mirror, lost in thoughts.

Meanwhile, at the building gates, media persons have flocked with their outdoor vans and cameras. Savant has driven the car into another lane. He messages Rudra to come out through the back gate; Rudra quietly makes an exit and sits in his car.

'City Hospital, Savant.'

'Yes, sir. These camera people are there also. You will have to use the doctors' entry. I have kept a person ready there, he will take you up.'

'You are a champ, Savant.'

SOMEWHERE IN MUMBAI

A young man in a funky T-shirt prevents a waiter from changing the channel. He has been sipping on a large cup of chocolate milk when the channels break the news of an air hostess admitted to City Hospital due to poisoning. He wipes the beads of sweat emerging on his forehead with his left hand. The correspondent is screaming himself hoarse about the lack of safety for women in the city. Soon, they are showing statistics of cases, demonstrating that there has been a steep rise in crime against women. The correspondent is demanding the immediate arrest of the accused. They are repeatedly showing shots of the building where the girl lived and scenes from the hospital main gate.

The man gets out of the cafe, and sits down on the pavement outside. He takes out a seven-inch Android tablet from his bag; the cafe Wi-Fi is still connected.

His tablet is a special one. Rooted, hacked and modified to his specifications. It has a default connection to a VPN that protects all his communication from being tracked. He then types a message and sends it across.

Rudra's cell buzzes as he is about to enter the Intensive Care Unit where the girl is recovering. It is a text message that reads:

'Welcome back, you get one more life.'

Rudra looks at his phone and takes a deep breath. His eyes narrow as he pauses before he opens the door. Before he steps in, he gets another message on his cell. As he opens it, the message shows up as 'malformed content, cannot read message'.

The young man outside the cafe puts on his headphones and mic, and logs in to his account of the mega game, *Dinosaur Hunt*.

In the next twenty minutes, Rudra comes out of the hospital room; he is in a hurry.

11.05 P.M., COLABA, MUMBAI

An ATC team is searching a flat. It's a small 300-square-foot bachelor's accommodation in an old building on Second Pasta Lane in Colaba, South Mumbai. They do not find much except programming books and a few personal belongings. The neighbours inform that the occupant, a young man, is rather reclusive. He has hardly ever interacted with anybody. Rudra asks them to pick up fingerprints from the objects in the room; he gets them to retrieve combs used by the man to get hair samples for a DNA match if required.

A trace is run on the fingerprints, no record emerges. Rudra asks the forensic wing to match it with the fingerprints found on the SIM card of the stripped phone found in the girl's apartment. There is a perfect match.

The same young man is sitting on Marine Drive, looking

at the lights of the Queen's Necklace, over the beautiful horseshoe bay when his cell rings; the text message reads: 'FGSQTC' (For gosh's sake, quit the crap). He is startled, looks around carefully, people seem to be watching, staring at him. His heartbeat races, he can hear his breath now. He fumbles as he takes out his tablet from his bag. When he logs in to *Dinosaur Hunt*, there are three pending messages from Suleri. They read:

'Government acting funny here, going underground.'

'Keep the switch with you at all times, wait for my orders.'

'You will be received properly in Dubai, inform me before boarding.'

He hurriedly checks for available tickets to Dubai. There are none available for the next twelve hours; he books the first available one; his hands are trembling. After years, he has a strong urge to have a drink, something which he had renounced long back.

11.15 P.M., MUMBAI

Vinay gets a conference call signal. Kant, Majumdar, Rudra are already online.

'Any development, Vinay? You picked up those Pakistan-trained boys, are they saying anything?'

'Sir, three sleeper cells which had been on long-term surveillance have been apprehended. They are being interrogated. I understand that the ATC has also picked up a couple of them independently as they too are investigating it. Nothing of use till now, sir.'

'Majumdar? What is happening at your end?'

'Watertight security, sir, nothing can move in or out of the city without being seen by us. The media has inadvertently helped us by spreading rumours. There are very few cars on the road. People are also largely staying indoors. The problem will be tomorrow when the Ganpati immersion processions start. Millions of people on the streets; no idea about what to do then.'

'RP?'

'Nothing concrete, but we are on the right path, sir.'

'Okay, I have news for you people. The President of India has taken a decision to inform the USA about the current crisis. He has asked the prime minister to appeal to the United Nations if the crisis is not resolved.'

'So it is escalating now, don't know if that will help the cause, sir.'

'RP, I will get your opinions conveyed to the President of India. Now would you please shut your trap and listen to me? The Bureau chief has his teams working day in and day out. If they conduct an operation in our territory, I will skin you all alive.'

Rudra quips, 'It's not only about our prestige as a force, sir, this is the biggest test we have been put to in the history of the nation. We will not let you down.'

'I don't know what that means, RP. Hardly twenty-four hours are left for the UN resolution on Kashmir, barely a day left for doomsday.'

There is silence, moments pass, no one speaks.

Kant ends the call. 'All except RP to disconnect.'

'Yes, sir?'

'My dear magician, now tell me, what's up your sleeve?'

'Sir, you know how to earn this; I will tell you only in exchange of a Zen story.'

'RP, patience has never been one of my virtues, you test it to the hilt. Go on.'

'So it goes, sir:

'A young man came to a Zen master to learn about meditation. The master asked, "Are you capable of waiting?" The young man said, "Of course, for how long?" The master said, "How long is long enough?"'

'RP, if we survive this crisis alive, I wouldn't mind putting you back in jail.'

'Obliged, sir, will get some respite from work.'

'It's been "long enough" now? Will you tell me what's happening?'

'Yes, sir. The air hostess, the one who was poisoned with the sweet antifreeze agent, was related to the oil mafia. Actually, a bit distantly related. We were looking for her in relation to the ship-blast investigations. Her "boyfriend" it seems came to know of her "connections", he then asked her to get an expensive server delivered to him via the sea route, bypassing customs. The fishermen who were to deliver this consignment offloaded it from a ship on the high seas, but have gone "missing" with the expensive package.

'We have got the boy's fingerprints from her room. We have also located his bachelor's pad in Colaba. Gotten fingerprints and DNA samples for a match later on. He seems to be deeply entrenched in this Lashkar business. I have other things too, but it is too nebulous right now.'

'How sure are you, RP, of this leading to the nuclear device?'

'This is our only hope right now, sir. One more thing, he is in a way known to me.'

'Seriously? How is that possible?'

'He is the one who arranged for me to be sent to jail in the encounter case. I walked into his trap, so did ACP Satbir of Delhi Special Cell. He led us down his path, leaving breadcrumbs for us to follow. Giving small reliable inputs till we walked into something major.'

'How do you know that?'

'He has been text messaging me, sir. I have never met him. After Satbir was put under suspension, he had text messaged me: "Strike two", meaning one was me. He was successfully crippling the anti-terror formations in the country. First Mumbai, then Delhi.'

'Seems interesting, don't let the trail go cold, warrior.'

'He is playing a game, sir, we too have joined him.'

11.45 P.M., CRISIS CENTRE

Advaita Sharma has been called to the Crisis Centre. He has helped the ATC on countless occasions. When Mumbai Mujahedeen, a local terror group, was on the rampage, Advaita would help track their locations using the IP addresses of the threat emails sent to the media and the government. His hacking skills are unmatched. Bespectacled, tall and fair, he is soft-spoken, reliable and trustworthy. Through many operations, the ATC has come to rely on him heavily for his skills. He is ever willing and amiable, helping them just for the love of his motherland.

Rudra has had to disclose his release from jail to Advaita as there is an emergent situation. Advaita has been assigned a workstation at the Crisis Centre; he is now working on tracing the location of the man who has been texting Rudra. He is submerged in cables connected to a number of strange devices, pieces of open circuitry, blinking small LED lights . . .

Rudra is happy to see him; he greets him with a chuckle.

'Advaita, I really need to track and hunt this bastard out, he has been taunting. I know he is somewhere in the city, waiting for me. Don't know who will get there first.'

'Chief, just leave it to me. He is leaving his footprints all over. He may be smart, but we are no less. Rudra sir, are you aware of the cyber war that happened six months back? Indian and Pakistani hackers bringing government sites down on either side. I disfigured the Pakistani Air Force site and put a GIF animation of an Indian tricolour flying high! It was hailed in my circles as an epic achievement.

'I then attacked the Lashkar website, it was a breeze to bring down, just an SQL injection did the trick. It took them seven days and a change in the host server to be up and running again. Now they have patched up a lot of vulnerabilities.'

'Advaita, we can chat at peace later, can we get down to business now?'

'Oh sorry, forgot, sir. I get so excited with this work that I cannot tell you,' he heads back to his workstation.

'One thing, my apologies for calling you here so suddenly. I hope you have no other pressing assignments.'

'Nothing today, sir, except that my father is ill, I may have to go and see him. He is old now, something or the other keeps happening to him. He fell down in the bathroom this evening, don't know if it is a fracture or not.'

'Oh I am so sorry to hear that, you may leave as soon as you complete this task. Please let me know if I can do something about it. Anyways, if you have to leave tomorrow, would it be possible for you to keep working on it there?'

'Chief, what makes you think that I am not going to complete the task given? We're a team here, so chill.' He turns and gets back to his devices and the labyrinth of cables in front of him.

Rudra returns to his cabin when Bose of NCRO calls up on

the secure videoconferencing line. Rudra fails to understand why this fat soul with a goatee is beaming when the world is about to collapse.

'Rambo, your X-man may not be far. We have our bug on him. He won't escape us for long!'

'Bose, how the hell do you have a bug on a man whose identity is unknown? What have you been smoking lately?'

'Fighter, how can you forget the joint operation we conducted eight months back?'

'Which one? We have done many things together.'

'The one in which we modified the Chinese SIM cards which had a data back-port, to send a stream to us. Remember, we had flooded the black market with such cards? You had said that the bad guys are always on the lookout for cards in the underground.'

'Yes, I remember. My team had placed them in the black market.'

'He is using one of our doctored SIM cards! We have identified it, it is connecting to a California-based VPN, using highly encrypted communication protocols. Another smart thing that he has done is that he has ported the writeable SIM card to a foreign service provider. Getting data from them is next to impossible.'

'Then you must be having his location at least? Where is he now?'

'He is smart, bossy, the critter is using a location obfuscator, which gives fake locations.'

'So all the king's horses and all the king's men couldn't put Humpty together again.'

'Van Damme, there is a piece of good news for you.'

'And that is?'

'The California-based VPN is our honeypot. It is a long-standing operation that we have been conducting with great success. People who want to do illegal transactions hunt for these services, we offer them for free, ha ha.'

Rudra now understands why the fatso has been incessantly grinning.

'Give me the juice then, genius.'

'There is a little problem here. We have a dump of all his communications, but he is using an encryption of his own. A whole team is sitting here working to break the encryption.'

'Bose, pass on the data card details to me, I will also work on it simultaneously.'

'Why not, captain, it would be fun to crack this one. Bye.'

Rudra comes out of his cabin to the operational area; weary-eyed operators have been working on camera feeds from the city, running video analytics on accumulated feeds; there is interrogation going on in the lower basement; data-mining teams have been analysing travel patterns, financial transactions and cell phone records to ferret out any nugget of information that would be remotely useful.

Advaita comes up to Rudra.

'Your man is in Colaba, sir, I am getting into his VPN connection. Your chaps at the ISP have given me access to the gateway.'

'Where in Colaba, Advaita?'

'There has been a repeated log-in from somewhere near Second Pasta Lane, it may be a residential location. Log-ins are at late night, meaning the villain must be at home.'

'What is his current location? Can you get that?'

'I am trying my level best, sir. He is using an app to give confusing location signals.'

'Work on it, man, we don't have much time.'

'Post-haste, sir, post-haste.'

11.59 P.M., CRISIS CENTRE

Sana has called just as Rudra had dozed off in extreme exhaustion; she has dialled three times before he picks up.

'Bastard, where are you?'

'Is this a bad dream? Am I having a nightmare? Where am I?'

'R, shut up. I have called you three times, idiot.'

'Come to the point, princess.'

'Listen, I am actually on my way to Pakistan. Bosses think that I can pull off an operation there with the help of my old contacts.'

'God save them, poor little terrorists. My sympathies are with your victims.'

'You know, R, you talk too much. You should listen sometimes, for a change.'

'All ears, Your Majesty.'

'I am getting the Syrian bomb specifications from my Middle East contacts. After the Israelis bombed Al-Kibar, the North Korean connection began to emerge. Once it became clear that they had supplied the technology, the design specifications were not too difficult to get. It will come to you as soon as I lay my hands on it.'

'I am not a nuclear scientist, why do I need it?'

'Genius, in case you find it in your backyard, the design will help you practise for your car electrician practicals.'

'Are you serious? I was thinking of taking it to dinner.'

'Get lost, bye.'

'Hey, Sana, tell me, what are you up to in Pakistan?'

'Confidentiality clause, my friend, need-to-know basis. You have no access to this.'

'Righto, Your Majesty, send me the bomb recipe.'

'Idiot, say thanks at least.'

'Obliged, Highness, bye . . . Sana, on a serious note, do come back, please, even if nothing exists here when you return . . . Please.'

'I will get bored without you, you idiot. What will I do all alone? Let's do something different, why don't we both survive this? Nice idea?'

'Bye for now. I think the government has been really harsh towards the poor terrorists. They just sent us a nuclear bomb, they don't deserve this in return!'

'Shut up. Bye.'

As he disconnects, Rudra notices that tears have welled up in his eyes. He is surprised at himself; the world as he knows it is about to get annihilated; he hasn't been able to speak to his wife, and ask about his unborn child, about the trauma she underwent after his arrest; he has been working mechanically.

'The heart has far more deeper connections to the being than to the brain; its illogical wisdom rests on some bedrock of obscure truths,' he thinks.

'Que sera sera, back to the crisis at hand, no time to die!' He laughs at himself.

Meanwhile, the ATC team that has gone to the fisherman's village at Colaba reports that four fishermen have not come back since a week. Their disappearance had been reported to the police after two days. The police has obtained their mobile numbers in an attempt to track their present locations.

Their mobile phones are presently not reachable. Rudra requests Raghu to get the last cell tower location and other details about the phones; he has come up with an analysis.

'Rudra sir, bad news, all the mobile phones went off air at

the same time. This means that they have not been manually switched off; it also rules out battery draining off. Most likely it is an accident,' says Raghu as he is peering at a printout in his hands.

'This means they were in the same cell tower range when they disappeared?'

'Yes.'

'One cell phone company or many?'

'Two service providers, sir.'

'Can you triangulate and get me the exact location of their position at the time of their disappearance?'

'In a minute, sir. I have the dump data from that cell site. Position within fifty metres can be accurately mapped.'

'Pass on the coordinates, Raghu, good job.'

He has gotten a message from Sana in the meantime; he quickly reads it, and his mind goes into a whirlwind.

Rudra is now dialling Commissioner Kant.

'Rudra Pratap here, sir, how soon can we meet? There is light at the end of the tunnel,' he says, realizing the irony of the remark.

He moves into the conference room. He has to jot down his points before he can give Kant a concrete plan. His cell buzzes, it's the adversary again, the text reads:

Hickory, dickory, dock,
The mouse ran up the clock.
The clock struck one,
The mouse ran down,
Hickory, dickory, dock.

Rudra now loses his patience, he rushes to the control room where Advaita is still working on the details provided.

Rudra feels a rage bubbling inside him. He shows the text to Advaita, who bursts out laughing after reading it. Rudra does not find it funny.

Advaita immediately apologizes, but Rudra is really upset. He asks Advaita to go home. He profusely apologizes, but Rudra doesn't budge. He drives him out of the Crisis Centre. Quazi and Raghu try to intervene, to no avail. Advaita goes with a heavy heart.

'We just lost one of our best resources, sir,' Raghu is lamenting.

'I neither have the time nor the patience for jokes and jokers, Raghu. We will do it on our own. Let him use his skills elsewhere.'

Raghu and Quazi are sad and hurt at Rudra's outburst. All through this crisis, the usually edgy Rudra has been unusually calm. Quazi is perplexed at the sudden outburst.

Within minutes, Kant arrives with Vinay, while Deputy Commissioner (Intelligence) Majumdar is expected any time.

Rudra requests them to accompany him to the conference room. A visibly worried home minister is already online on videoconference and so are the state home secretary and the state police chief with his sad face. They hurriedly take their places as Rudra asks Kant's permission to start. Kant nods, signalling approval.

Rudra takes a deep breath before he starts.

'Our worst fears have come true, sir. There is a nuclear bomb, right now, ticking away in Mumbai. We have hardly a day before we discover it, locate it and defuse it.'

A stunned silence follows; the state chief sports his trademark twisted smile; Kant's eyes have narrowed, and he has an intense studious look; Vinay seems pensive.

'How are you so convinced about this, RP? You are

speaking as though you have already located it.'

'Very near to locating it, sir, it's a small plutonium device, containing around 5 kilograms of weapon-grade plutonium from the Syrian Al-Kibar reactor, destroyed by Israel in September 2007.'

The home minister is aghast. 'Rudra Pratap, where did you get this information from? Why have we been kept in the dark about it till now? Explain this to me right now!'

'Respected sir, I got this information from my overseas contacts barely five minutes back, and the first thing I am doing is to inform you all. The External Intelligence had been tipped by Mossad about Lashkar men trying to procure a nuclear weapon from the deposed Syrian General Abdel Badi in Tehran for a sum of 50 billion dollars. I will give you the details soon, first we have to get the help of the Atomic Energy Department. Only they would know anything about stopping this bomb. The information with me suggests that the bomb will give around a 15-kilotonne yield, which would be almost 120 per cent of the Hiroshima explosion.'

'How did it come into our country, Commissioner Kant? Have we been caught napping again? Why don't we learn from our mistakes!'

Kant does not answer; the state chief of police replies instead, 'If they had read my circular about coastal security issued two months back, this situation wouldn't have come.'

'Absolutely right, sir, you are always so prophetic,' Kant says, grinding his teeth.

The home minister ignores the comment and now addresses the state home secretary.

'Satish, call the Disaster Control Authority, announce a Grade 1 Emergency. I will talk to the Union defence minister and the Union home minister about taking immediate help of the Atomic Energy Department.'

'So, RP, where is the bomb now?' Kant asks with deep concern.

'It is in the sea, sir, just a little off the ferry line in the Back Bay, not very far from here. Its exact coordinates are 18° 56.028', 72° 48.493'. We obtained the coordinates by getting the last location of the mobile phones of the poor fishermen who were carrying it.'

'How did it get there in the first place, RP?' Kant's voice is cold and matter of fact.

'That is a long story, sir, not a Zen one. Zen stories are short, you know.'

7

DOCTOR, DOCTOR

12.40 A.M., MONDAY, 8 SEPTEMBER, MUMBAI

The incessant ring of the landline phone wakes Disaster Management Secretary Ida Fernandez. She checks the clock, it has barely been an hour since she slept.

'What calamity has befallen now? Last time it was the government's main administrative building catching fire. This had better be serious or the caller dies,' she thought.

The chief secretary of the state is on the other end, his voice failing with distress. 'Your cell phone is not reachable, Ida, even the chief minister is trying your cell number.'

Fully awakened by this jolt, she knows that this is major; nonetheless, she maintains her composure.

'My apologies, sir, somehow there is no signal in this part of the house. I will talk to the cell company tomorrow. What is it about, sir? You seem to be very stressed.'

'Ida, you had informed me last month that you hold these regular drills and tabletop exercises with various departments

119

to assess their disaster preparedness. When did you hold one with the Atomic Energy Department?'

'It was fifteen days ago, sir. Is there anything critical, sir? I have good contacts with the head of the department and their other staff.'

She suspected that there might have been a leakage of radioactive material somewhere near the nuclear reactors. She knew what would happen now. The media will scream itself hoarse, panel discussions will be held cursing the government, self-styled experts will discuss the effects of radiation . . . the whole charade will continue for a week.

'There is a nuclear emergency, Ida. This is no drill, you should immediately come to the State Disaster Control Room.'

'What are you saying, sir!?'

'Please treat this as most confidential.'

'How do I activate the Nuclear Disaster Response Scheme if we have to keep it confidential, sir?'

'I am reaching the Disaster Control Room, you come there first. On the way, please talk to your Atomic Energy Department contacts, and ask them to send their people there, with all their equipment.'

'I am leaving right now, sir.'

She rushes out in casual clothes, trying to call the driver. When the lift reaches the ground floor, the watchman tells her that the driver has gone home, but the keys are with him. She hurriedly takes the keys and sits at the wheel.

She is driving crazily fast, suddenly remembering the days when she used to take out her father's car for a spin. When she was discovered, she used to get a terrible scolding, but it was fun.

She is now overcome with this eerie feeling of impending

doom. 'What is it that made the chief secretary so jittery? Normally a composed man, why was he so distressed on the phone? What is this nuclear threat thing? How can I ensure the safety of around fifteen million people? How can I protect my own family?' She tries the numbers of the Atomic Energy team, but nobody is responding. She sends a group text, urging them to call back immediately.

She reaches the State Disaster Control Room, it is locked. Not a soul is in view. She checks the cabin of the guards, they too are absent. Fortunately, she has an all-access contactless card. A dog with a half-eaten ear lazily barks at her, barely getting up from his place on the stairs. She opens the Control Room, tries to locate the switches in the dark, finally locating one as she almost trips over a tangle of cables.

When she finally turns all the systems on, she hears the chief secretary's car entering the premises.

'The man is too agile for his age,' she thinks, 'that's why, unnoticed, he surged ahead of everybody in the race for the top post, ha ha.'

The boss hurriedly wobbles in. 'It's quite a sight to see this 110-kilogram man moving at such a pace. He looks like a top spinning out of control, tottering before a fall. Only, this one never falters.' She has by now sent alert messages to everyone on the list. The chief secretary has also got it en route.

'Ida, good to see you here, where are the others?'

'I have sent messages to everyone on the list. They will be reaching in some time. Can you tell me now what has actually happened, sir?'

'Commissioner Kant has told me that a nuclear bomb has been planted on the shores of the city! They are trying hard to locate it. It may explode in the next twelve to twenty-four hours.'

'Oh my god, sir! How can that be true? How do we evacuate fifteen million people in a day? No agency would respond in the night, everyone must be sleeping. What do we do now?' She is trembling with emotion.

'Ida, calm down, I know that we have an impossible job before us. That is why we are here. All those drills, you see, were for this day. Now compose yourself, and do your best. I will be here the whole time till the crisis is over either way.'

'Either way means, sir?'

'Means whether we live to see another day, or die here, Ida . . .'

She has tears welling up, but today she has to be the mother of fifteen million people. She feels a strange resolve building up in her. Even as her tears keep flowing, she activates the steps of the Standard Operating Procedure.

Other members of the State Disaster Control Authority have started pouring in now. Automated messages had been delivered to their cells, offices, homes, assistants, and other access points.

The Atomic Energy personnel are on their way too.

12.45 A.M., MAHIM, MUMBAI

The young man sitting in the taxi is playing *Dinosaur Hunt* on his Android tablet. He gets an in-game chat message.

'Jibreel, where are you in the name of god? The Amir is worried about you. It is time that you leave that land of infidels.'

'I have been working, brother. Inshallah, we shall be victorious.'

'Nothing can stop us from victory, bhai. I had to shift to the mountains. Things have heated up here too. The Amir has been advised by the ISI colonel to lie low for a few days. He too has disappeared, heeding the advice.'

'I could not book an early flight, brother. The ATC has also raided my flat at Colaba, I have nowhere to spend the night.'

'I know that, Allah will take care of you, bhai, do not worry.'

'Brother, I have a feeling that I am being tracked. That police officer Rudra Pratap Singh is out of jail. He is handling the operations at ATC again. I had successfully put him in jail, as I did with ACP Satbir. God only knows how he has come out.'

'Where are you going now, bhai?'

'One minute, brother, how do you know that my Colaba flat has been raided?'

'Ah that, you just told me a minute back. Why, bhai, any problem?'

'No, nothing, you take care, brother.'

'Khuda hafiz.'

The young man has approximately eleven hours before the flight.

The taxi driver is driving at an easy pace, humming an old Bollywood tune. The amiable old Muslim strikes a conversation with the young man.

'Sahib, look to your left, this is the tomb of the Sufi Saint Makhdoom Ali Mahimi. Every year on 12 December, a two-week urs is held here. Hindus, Muslims, Christians, other people, everyone comes here to his durbar,' he says, gently caressing his white beard.

'Why do others need to come here to the grave of a Muslim saint?' the youg man asks with sarcasm. 'Aren't their thousands of gods enough?'

'Tauba, tauba, my son, do not speak like that. You will

be most surprised if I tell you that the saint is the patron of the Mumbai Police. An officer of the police has the primary right to offer the first chaddar to the saint. All others come later. In the urs procession, two officers each from the ninety police stations of Mumbai participate.'

'That is very surprising, Chacha.' He is growing fond of the old man. It pains his heart to think that tomorrow, if Kashmir is not liberated, this poor man, too, will die with the others.

'Son, the Mumbai Police believes that two saints and two temples have been taking care of the city since the olden days. The Haji Ali dargah, Siddhivinayak and Mahalaxmi temples are the other protectors of the city, but nothing equals the fame of the Saint of Mahim. Police officers come here to seek blessings when cases are not solved,' the old man is now in a chatty mood. They pass two police checkposts in a short time, cursory questions are asked, and they are allowed to proceed. The driver slows down after some time.

'Will you mind if we stop here for some tea?' he asks. The young man has no objections, he has all the time in the world to kill.

The old driver comes back with two cups of tea from a roadside vendor at the Kala Nagar junction on the Western Expressway. He is also carrying some snacks.

'I've the night shift, the wife was a little sick, so I could not eat dinner. Did you eat something in the evening, son?' He offers him some of his food.

The young man realizes that he is terribly hungry. Through this entire mission, he has not been eating properly. He takes a morsel from the old man's plate, and then has a sip of sweet roadside tea. It seems to soothe him, calm him down. Yet he feels that his heart is growing heavy, as if he is slowly choking.

'Everything all right, son?' the driver asks with concern.

'Yes, Chacha, just remembered my parents.'

'May Allah keep them well, where do they live, son?'

The man points to the sky, indicating that they are no more. The driver silently reads a dua for them.

'Everything will be all right, son. Have faith in Him. Did they die recently?'

'No, Chacha, they were killed in the 2002 Gujarat riots.'

The old man again reads a dua to their souls.

'I am so sorry to hear that, son. Human beings can be worse than animals. Mumbai also has seen riots, in 1992. Allah should never bring such a day again. We had lost faith in humanity at that time.'

'Then what happened, Chacha?'

'Better sense prevailed, son, now no one wants a riot ever in this city. We have learned our lessons.'

The man is thinking of the orange ball of fire when the nuclear bomb explodes tomorrow, consuming this city, its buildings, inhabitants, temples, mosques and dargahs. 'How will the Saint of Mahim prevent this?' he thought.

'Did you say something?' asks the driver. 'I am an old man now, cannot hear like in my younger days.'

'Absolutely nothing, Chacha, thanks for the tea,' says the young man as they sit in the taxi again.

1.20 A.M., STATE DISASTER CONTROL ROOM, COLABA

State Home Secretary Satish Kumar has also arrived, he is sitting with the chief secretary, having a serious conversation. Sreedhar Padmanabha Nair, an expert at the Atomic Energy Department, has been briefed about the impending threat. He now addresses the group about the impact and effects of the probable nuclear explosion in Mumbai.

'For a 15-kilotonne-yield plutonium bomb, the casualty figures will be around two lakhs. The mortality will also depend upon the place of the explosion. If it takes place high up in the air, like an air drop, the damage will be more widespread than a surface explosion.' He has a distinct vernacular accent to his English, which makes it very difficult for the others to understand him. They listen to him, straining their ears to catch every word.

He continues, 'Everyone within 500 metres of the site of explosion will die in an instant. Eighty-five per cent of the people within one kilometre radius will also meet the same fate, 50 per cent of those within 1.5 kilometres will also surely die. Survival rates for those beyond three kilometres will be more than 90 per cent. But they will suffer other effects in the course of time. Around three lakh people will be injured; they will require immediate hospitalization, without which they will find it hard to survive.'

Satish Kumar is visibly upset. 'You have scared us enough, Mr Shridhar. Please tell us what can be done?'

'My name is Sreedhar, not Shridhar, please pronounce correctly,' Nair is peeved at the mispronunciation of his name. 'You may call me Mr Nair for the sake of convenience.'

Satish is losing patience. 'Will you please, Mr Nair, tell us what are the possible options in this scenario?'

'Beyond the radius of three kilometres, anyone who is not outdoors has a fair chance of survival from burns, but the radiation effects will continue for two days more, at a conservative estimate. Collapse of buildings, secondary fires will be the major source of casualties. People on the ground and basement floors are relatively safe. They will be saved as other structures will act as shields for them,' Nair explains.

The chief secretary interrupts now. 'Yes! We get that. Now tell us what to do!'

Nair looks lost. 'How can I tell you what to do, you have to decide what is to be done.'

It's Ida's turn. 'Please have a look at the Disaster Response Manual, Sreedhar. We have done this tabletop simulation exercise of a nuclear explosion in Mumbai three times in the past.'

'Yes, Mrs Ida, we have done that already,' Nair speaks in a matter-of-fact manner.

'We just have to implement that,' Ida explains to the scientist.

'I see no problems with that, let us go ahead.'

The members of the Disaster Response Committee seem to be a bit relieved now.

The Disaster Management department has been mandated with preparation, mitigation, recovery, and response to all possible kinds of disaster. They have ready plans for all possible scenarios, a nuclear attack being one of them. An operations manual has been prepared for each scenario, detailing resources, responsibilities and response strategies. Ida has painstakingly coordinated with various departments and agencies in order to precisely prepare for such a day.

'What is the plan, Ida?' Satish Kumar asks.

'Not much that can be done, sir. Mass evacuation is next to impossible, still, if we have time, I suggest we attempt it.'

'Ida, you are talking of fifteen million people.'

'Sir, we do not have to move everybody out. As the location of the bomb is known, people from a radius of five kilometres should positively be evacuated.'

'This means we move out people from the areas of Cuff Parade, Colaba, Marine Drive, Malabar Hills, Bhuleshwar,

Kalbadevi, Mohammed Ali Road, Bhendi Bazaar, Byculla and Haji Ali. These are the most densely populated areas of Mumbai, but there is no way in which we can accomplish this. Even if we evacuate, where do we take them, Ida?' the chief secretary questions.

'Sir, I have already compiled a list of strong structures like schools and large halls which can accommodate people on a short-term basis. It will be needed for twenty-four hours only. The advice to all the others is to remain protected indoors for a minimum period of twenty-four hours. Once the radiation fallouts are over, we can think of bringing them back,' she explains earnestly.

Suddenly, Ida notices something interesting on the television; she asks her assistant to un-mute the large TV screen near the projection wall.

It's all over now, someone has leaked the information to the media. They have announced the presence of a hidden nuclear bomb in Mumbai, which can go off at any time. Terrified, people have started to come out on the streets.

'Look, sir, this is exactly what the terrorists must be wanting, people coming out on the streets. If it explodes now, I cannot imagine the death toll. Why doesn't the media act a bit more responsibly? During the 26/11 attacks, they unwittingly provided the terrorists live feedback of the security forces' operations. It will be extremely difficult to implement anything now,' Ida tells the chief secretary.

'I will ask the chief minister to come on air. He should make an appeal to the people to stay indoors. What do you say, Satish?' the chief secretary asks the home secretary.

'In order, sir. This is the right time for him to directly address the people. I will call up his secretary now. We should keep a speech ready for him, detailing what all is to be done and what efforts are being taken from our side.'

On the streets there is mayhem. People are trying to escape in cars, taxis, motorcycles, and even on foot. Mobile networks are jammed. Suddenly, hundreds of thousands of cars are on the streets. It is minutes before the roads get completely clogged. Thousands of stranded people are honking, abusing, fighting on the streets. People rushing out of buildings—some in nightclothes, some half nude, some wrapped in whatever they could get. There is a virtual stampede all over, babies are crying, women are screaming, while the old and infirm are being left behind, begging for help.

Media cameras are still capturing the chaos that they have partially created, accusing the government of a total failure to respond.

1.30 A.M., CRISIS CENTRE

Kant is looking at the CCTV feeds in awe, and his hands go up in despair, as if cursing god. Others too are looking at the screens in total bewilderment as they see chaos, stampede, streets full of stranded cars, and loot and mayhem in the city.

'This was the only thing left for me to see in my lifetime, RP,' Kant says with resignation in his voice. 'Now that the cat is out of the bag, let's hunt it down openly.'

'The Navy chopper is landing in a few minutes, and my team is ready to board any time. We will get the Atomic Energy expert en route to the site from the State Disaster Control Room,' says Rudra as he gets into his black combat overalls.'

'RP, this may be the last time we see each other. I don't want to miss listening to a Zen story before that.' Rudra can't help but notice tears in the tough man's eyes. He smiles at him with affection.

Everyone waits with tears in their eyes as Rudra narrates a Zen story.

'A Zen master endeavoured all his life not to be attached to anything. As a wandering mendicant when he was twenty he happened to meet a traveller who smoked tobacco. As they walked together down a mountain road, they stopped under a tree to rest. The traveller offered him a smoke, which he accepted, as he was very hungry at the time. "How pleasant this smoking is," he commented. The other gave him his extra pipe and tobacco, and they parted. The master felt, "Such pleasant things may disturb meditation. Before this goes too far, I will stop now." So he threw the pipe and tobacco away.

'When he was twenty-eight he studied Chinese calligraphy and poetry. He grew so skilful in these arts that his teacher praised him. The master, who was a student then, mused, "If I don't stop now, I'll become a poet, not a Zen teacher." So he never wrote another poem till he died at the age of ninety-five.'

Kant gets up and hugs him. 'I wish you live till ninety-five, my son, take care.'

They hear the flutter of the rotor blades of the chopper landing on the roof, and one by one the team members rush out of the Crisis Centre.

1.30 A.M., INTERNATIONAL AIRPORT, MUMBAI

Flights are still on; large numbers of people have gathered outside the airport. The security has installed heavy steel barricades to prevent people from breaking in. Only those with valid, confirmed tickets are being allowed inside the premises. There are people who have come to the airport in the hope of purchasing tickets there, but the airport administration has taken the decision of not issuing any new tickets at the counters.

The young man is already inside the airport building, sitting in the lounge. He finds it fortunate that the airport's free Wi-Fi is still working. He logs on to his favourite game. There are five pending messages from Suleri.

'Jibreel, bhaijaan, watch TV now!'

'Return to the site, they may try to defuse it.'

'The Amir has asked you to detonate it if they find it.'

'Jibreel bhai, please reply immediately.'

'Are you all right, the switch is still with you?'

Suleri is offline; he sends him his reply.

'At the airport, there is anarchy here. The media has disclosed that a nuclear bomb has been placed in Mumbai. People are fleeing in panic. I will monitor it from here on TV; if they find it, I will detonate it.'

Suleri suddenly comes online on the text chat.

'Bhai, it's time that you get ready for martyrdom. Go to the site now. The Indian government has banned the coverage of operations by TV. The Amir is really worried.'

There is a long pause, then Suleri asks, 'Bhai, what happened?'

'Leaving for the site, *alvida*,' he types.

He is now going out of the airport, the security personnel at the gate questions him. He seems to be in a daze; brushing the guard aside, he exits.

There is bedlam outside, as he looks around. People are running helter-skelter. He feels a sense of pride in what he has caused. 'Infidels, this is the Day of Judgement, all your sins will be answered today. Ask your thousand idols to save you, but they will fail.'

He finds an abandoned bicycle, he takes it. Cycling against the flow of the people on the footpath, he soon takes a turn to reach the internal roads; they are relatively empty, except for the odd person left out of the exodus. He pedals fast through the bylanes of Bandra East.

He is out of breath already, a huge cloud of dust is in the air as people flood the main Western Expressway. He still pedals hard; when he reaches Mahim, he witnesses the same scenario: cars abandoned on the road, people running helter-skelter. With great difficulty, he enters a bylane.

Soon he is before the Mahim dargah, its beautiful gate standing tall in the ghostly light. He is startled to see a demented beggar standing outside the gate and singing:

Walewalio me wali makhdoom
Kadam kadam pe kya hona hai, tujhko hai maloom,
ya baba makhdoom
(What will happen at each moment in the future
O saint, you know already.)

As he passes the beggar, the glare in his eyes catches his attention, the glare of insanity.

He reaches Dadar in a few minutes; he sees men and women trying to climb on to the roofs of stranded cars to move forward. In the internal lanes, hooligans are breaking shop windows to loot goods. He sees a slum dweller running away with a mannequin. At Prabhadevi too, the same chaos prevails, crowds running on the road, vehicles abandoned, noise, dust, and cries. It seems like a Hollywood movie to him, and he waits there for some time to watch the fun. He cannot believe that he has caused this wholesale frenzy. It feels like an episode from *Dinosaur Hunt* where the hunters herd the smaller herbivorous dinosaurs to death. When he reaches Peddar Road, most of South Mumbai has already run away, leaving their belongings, automobiles, and the old and infirm behind. Old men and women are screaming from balconies, crying out for help. Dogs are barking incessantly, confused about the mayhem. Then he takes the internal road from Girgaon to reach Marine Drive. He abandons his cycle, and starts walking hurriedly through the lanes between old houses, to reach the sea front.

There is heavy police presence there; they are not allowing anyone to come near the shore.

1.45 A.M., STATE DISASTER CONTROL ROOM

Ida has put in place the nuclear threat response protocol. The commissioner of police has informed her that a team of the Anti-Terror Cell will be reaching there soon to assist the experts in locating and attempting to defuse the bomb. The local Army unit has also offered to help with their Bomb Disposal Unit. She knows that the ATC has defused several bombs in the past, but this is the mother of all bombs. She is still deeply confident in her heart that the ATC will be able to live up to the challenge.

When she sees off Sreedhar and his colleague Kulkarni to the chopper, she meets the ATC team. Rudra greets her, she wishes them luck. Barely anything is audible as the chopper blades have not stopped yet. There is no time for any delay now. The experts, along with the ATC members, take off for the sea. There is so much noise in the chopper that nothing is audible; Rudra suggests that they stop somewhere for a few minutes to plan the whole location-and-disposal operation. The pilot obliges, they get down at the Brabourne Stadium cricket ground, then walk towards the sea front. When they reach the promenade, the scene is epic: thousands of abandoned cars on Queen's Necklace Road, some with their engines running, some chirping, tweeting alarms and sensors in various shrill tones, a lone horn continuously blaring, while smoke accumulates in the dense air making the whole place look like a ghost city.

As they walk, Kale spots Advaita Sharma behind the barricades, arguing with the policeman on duty there. Kale gestures that he be allowed in. Advaita rushes to join them. Rudra introduces him to the Atomic Energy Department experts.

'Mr Sreedhar, here is a very bright young man, who has been of great help in many, many operations. He is a whiz-kid who breathes technology. I am very sure that he would be of great use to us.'

Nair looks at Advaita and nods, but does not show much interest in him. Advaita greets him with a faint smile.

A constable in the team that handles tech comes and whispers in Rudra's ear that the adversary, who has the switch to the nuclear device, has been electronically spotted in the vicinity. Rudra smiles.

He then concentrates on the job at hand. 'Advaita, sorry for the outburst some time ago, kindly bear with me, the circumstances are such.'

Advaita is amiable. He says, 'Sir, I fully appreciate the problems about working with very tight deadlines. Happens often in our software industry. I will render any help that is required, please allow me.' He smiles sweetly.

'I am so grateful to you that you could make it here, despite all odds. I will be personally obliged to you,' says Rudra, beaming.

Rudra gets an extra set of combat gear from his team for Sreedhar Nair, who refuses to wear them.

'Where is the bomb, Mr Rudra?' Sreedhar asks, as he lights up a beedi. Sreedhar and Kulkarni sit down on the embankment at the promenade. Rudra looks at them in amazement; he wonders if these people would be able to do something if the bomb is actually discovered. They might as well be sitting in the department canteen, in their half-shirts and slippers fretting over an office file.

'Mr Sreedhar, these are the device specifications. It is a small plutonium device, capable of a 15-kilotonne yield. It is somewhere in the sea, we have the coordinates with us.' He hands him the printout of the specifications sent by Sana.

Two more choppers have landed now with more equipment from the Atomic Energy Department. The assistants have come to Sreedhar, who is now setting up his shop. Rudra has been officially designated to be in charge of this operation, and the Atomic Energy personnel are to work under his supervision. He has been given at his command almost infinite resources.

'Mr Rudra Pratap, the bomb cannot be in the sea.' Sreedhar squints as he approaches Rudra, his breath smelling of raw tobacco smoke.

'Underwater is not possible, would have no thermal effect, and the radiation would be negligible,' adds Kulkarni, a short, bald man with spectacles.

'Means what?' Rudra does not understand the communication.

'It means, Mr Rudra, that the terrorists will waste a nuclear weapon if they explode it underwater. All the heat of the explosion will be absorbed by the water, most of the gamma rays and neutron radiation as well. Only a tsunami-like wave of water will be created, which will not cause substantial damage. We can effectively withdraw the operations now,' Sreedhar informs, as if conducting a lecture for undergraduate students.

'This means that either this is a decoy and the bomb is elsewhere or it will be brought up to the surface before the blast,' Rudra reasons.

'There are no communication systems which work underwater, sir, except a sonar or a wired electromagnetic signalling system. Wireless and radio frequencies cannot travel effectively in seawater, so how will they activate it?' Advaita adds.

'This means that they may have retrieved it from the sea to plant it somewhere in the city; but that seems highly unlikely. The risk of exposure of such an operation is very high. It will require specialized teams, local support and stuff, which they may not have here,' Rudra reasons.

'Sir, the only way one can communicate with the device is through a floating antenna wired to it,' Advaita reasons.

'Which makes our job a little bit easier,' Rudra smiles and pats Advaita on the back. 'You're a champ! Keep it up!'

'Anything for my country, sir! I will lay down my life when the time comes.'

'Patience, Advaita, patience, the time has still not come,' Rudra reassures.

'Okay, team, we go for our first sortie. Sreedhar, Kale and I go first, constables Kamble and Karjatkar are to come with us. We will fly very close to the water, looking for a floating antenna. At the site, I will lower an underwater camera probe into the water, its feed will be available here as well as at the Crisis Centre. Anyone who does not know how to swim?'

'I cannot swim, neither do I like water,' says Sreedhar in disgust. 'It is also very dirty.'

'Please give Mr Sreedhar a life jacket to wear,' Rudra commands.

'Advaita, you want to accompany us?' he asks.

'I too cannot swim, sir, I will observe from here,' he grins sheepishly.

The chopper has been called to the promenade now, it hovers in the air before landing.

'Jibreel' is feverishly messaging Suleri, who is offline on the game now.

'They are going to find it! What should I do now?'

'Should I detonate it?'

'Please guide me, brother!'

He himself has never seen the bomb, but feels attached to it. He has been told that once the signal is given, a floating antenna connected to the device case will transmit it down; a small unit which has a chemical capsule embedded in it will fill the four stabilizing pontoons which will then bring the bomb slowly to the surface. A second trigger will detonate it, causing a mushroom cloud. As the explosion would be on the surface, it would cause maximum damage, with steam clouds carrying the radiation fallouts to large areas. With convectional rainfall, there will be a black rain of death everywhere in the city.

'Jibreel' knows that he would die that instant. He fortifies his determination, tells himself that the cause he is fighting for is much larger than his own martyrdom or the lives of all these people. He also wants to punish them for their sins, for the atrocities they have committed on his brethren all over the world, and avenge the death of his parents too.

He witnesses the chopper taking off with Rudra Pratap

and the ATC team. The machine flies close to the water, meandering through its way slowly. A strong seaward wind has made it fly at a strange angle. It goes towards the horizon for some time after which the only activity visible is the reflection of the searchlights on the sea surface. They keep searching for some time. 'Jibreel' is very restless.

8

NOWHERE TO GO

No one, not even the Lashkar, has ever estimated the power of the idiot box. It has thrown a spanner in the scheme of things that everyone's calculations have gone awry. The Amir of Lashkar had never thought that this information would go public and would lead to the fleeing of their targets. Their bargaining power has been reduced to zilch. The Pakistani 'establishment' has asked them to lie low for now.

2 A.M., RASHTRAPATI BHAVAN, NEW DELHI

The prime minister has come to meet the President of India. Meanwhile, in the Cabinet meeting that just concluded, when it was disclosed that the nuclear device had already been planted in Mumbai, it was unanimously decided to declare war on Pakistan.

President Charanjeet Singh is waiting for the prime minister in the north drawing room. Over the last few hours, he has had a fair idea of what has been happening. He has been a governor of two states; after having held many portfolios in the last several government terms, he had decided to retire when out of nowhere his name was proposed for the post of the President of India. He remembers that he had gone to request the senior leadership of the party to excuse him from this responsibility as he intended to lead a peaceful retired life. He had to finally give in to the pressure and accept the post as they felt that the nation needed him. They said that his experience, sagacity, vision and forthrightness were the need of the hour. What was most surprising was that the opposition too voted for him. Hence, when there was a change of guard, he still enjoyed a rapport with the new prime minister. The tall Sikh had jet-black hair and had never looked his age, yet he was always taken seriously throughout his life. He knew that the Cabinet decision was a fait accompli, but he needed to have a word with the prime minister before the subcontinent was engulfed in war.

The prime minister is ushered in, while the defence minister, home minister, external affairs minister and the finance minister wait outside. Charanjeet Singh gracefully gets up to greet the prime minister, who hurriedly comes forward to shake hands with him. The President asks him to take a seat and indicates to the staff that they will have this discussion in private. The staff promptly retreats.

There is a prolonged silence. Charanjeet Singh is watching the prime minister's body language. His composure is reassuring; the prime minister breaks the silence.

'Your Excellency, President sir, we are faced with a calamity of untold proportions today. As you know, Lashkar has threatened to detonate the nuclear bomb if we do not declare plebiscite in Kashmir before the upcoming UN resolution tomorrow. We have an avowed policy of non-negotiation with terrorists, and there is no time left for diplomacy.

'The issue was discussed in the emergency meeting of the Union Cabinet. The members were of the unanimous opinion that we will use the nuclear option in retaliation if we are subjected to it. The Cabinet also felt that we have repeatedly failed to respond to repeated acts of aggression by Lashkar, which has the open support of the Pakistan government. The Parliament attack, Mumbai attacks, several instances of bomb explosions all over the country claiming lives of innocent people have gone unpunished. This proxy war has to stop; it has hence been decided to declare war on Pakistan and resolve the issue once and for all. I have come with the declaration, Your Excellency, you may go through it and sign it.'

The prime minister hands him a Cabinet Note, stating in terms the intent of a declaration of war. Charanjeet Singh reads it carefully, then keeps it aside.

He looks intently at the prime minister, and starts to speak. 'I have very faint memories of Partition. I remember travelling hidden under bales of cotton in a bullock cart for days before we crossed over into India. Such scenes of death and destruction! We are still reaping the poisonous fruits of that hatred.'

'We will have nothing left to respond after Mumbai is nuked, Your Excellency.'

'We still have time, this can be averted. Do you think Pakistan will be so irrational as to allow Lashkar to actually start a nuclear war?'

'It has already happened, Your Excellency, it is a matter of time before Mumbai is reduced to ashes.'

'I differ with you on this, Mr Prime Minister. I am aware that I am supposed to sign on the dotted line, but I will ask you to exercise restraint. I will not sign this until you have spoken to your counterpart in Pakistan. If that is not possible, I will personally speak to the Pakistani President. If the issue is not resolved, then we will go for a full-fledged war.

'In that scenario, you will have to use the nuclear weapon first, as a pre-emptive strike. If you carefully read our nuclear doctrine, it says that we have a "no first use policy", but we can exercise the nuclear option when we are threatened with one.'

'I did, Your Excellency, consider the option of a dialogue. When we discussed it in the Cabinet, it was vociferously rejected. I had to abandon that idea.'

'Their anger is understandable. You and I stand as the guardians of the people, we have to practise restraint. Anger cannot be the basis for rational decisions.'

'I do not know if we have the time for this.'

'I will sign this document and give it back to you. I expect a gentleman's promise that you will promulgate it only after speaking to the Pakistani premier.'

The prime minister is contemplative, he then gets up, greets the President, and as he leaves, says, 'You have my word, sir.'

1.50 A.M. [PKT], ISLAMABAD

Pakistani Prime Minister Aziz Ahmad has just returned from a diplomatic dinner. He has been worried about the buzz in diplomatic circles that India and Pakistan may be at the brink of a war.

He sits on the bed as he removes his socks, and wiggles his toes as he finds the chill of the room comforting. The feeling of sweat drying off his feet offers him relief. 'Long day,' he yawns.

The bedside telephone rings. Begum Aziz, his wife, gets up startled and then on seeing him, turns over to the other side, attempting to sleep. She has stopped waiting for him now. 'His responsibilities cannot have the better of my sleep,' she thinks.

The operator is almost breathless. 'Wazeer-e-Azam, please forgive me, the prime minister of India wants to speak to you urgently.'

His heart misses a beat. 'This is no good,' he thinks.

'Please connect immediately.'

The Indian prime minister comes on the line. 'Mr Aziz, apologies for the late-night call. I hope you are doing well.'

'Thank you, I am perfectly all right. I hope everything is well at your end too.'

'No, Mr Aziz, I have to inform you with great regret that we have been driven to the brink of a war with you.'

'What happened now, I don't think anything has happened in the recent past which makes you take this stand. However, you should realize that we too are a nuclear country and a very proud people. We do not take kindly to threats, we will respond with our full might.'

'I talk to you in full awareness of that, Mr Aziz. What has prompted us to make a declaration of war is a nuclear bomb placed by the terrorist outfit Lashkar in the city of Mumbai. I promise you that grass will never grow on Pakistan if anything happens in Mumbai. We will obliterate you from the face of the earth.'

'Mr Prime Minister, we have absolutely no connection with Lashkar. We cannot be held responsible for their actions. But if you threaten us, we are ready for a fight till the finish.'

'Mr Aziz, let not the dog walk the master, rein in Lashkar,

144   BRIJESH SINGH

hand over its Amir to India, deactivate the nuclear weapon in twenty-four hours, or else, goodbye.'

'You first . . .' But before Aziz completes his sentence, the line is disconnected.

Begum Aziz is up now. She takes away the receiver and puts it back on its cradle.

'Who was it?' she asks.

3.45 P.M. [EST], CAPITOL HILL, WHITE HOUSE, USA

United States Secretary of State Ashley Skinner has barged into the President's office. President Warren Waters has just come back from a press briefing about the efforts taken to mitigate the effects of the North Dakota pipeline oil spill. One look at Ashley's face and he knows that there is something very urgent she needs to talk to him about. He leaves his table to accompany her to the adjoining room.

She barely waits for him to settle down, and then blurts out, 'War about to break out between India and Pakistan.'

'When did this happen?' He gets up from his chair.

'Apparently, Lashkar has placed a nuclear weapon in the city of Mumbai, which is likely to go off at any time. India has directly threatened Pakistan with a full-blown nuclear attack if this happens. Pakistan has been asked to defuse the bomb, hand over the Lashkar chief or face nuclear Armageddon.'

'Have they gone nuts! This will be the start of World War III. Why have they not spoken to us till now?' He pounds his fist on the table in exasperation. 'How did the CIA miss the run-up to it, were they napping when this was building up? Get me the CIA chief right now.'

'Aziz has spoken to me three times, Mr President. He is in a foul mood too. If we do not intervene now, China or

Russia will, taking away our initiative. India has a Nuclear Umbrella Treaty with Russia, which the Russians may choose to honour, prompting China to react. It will start a chain reaction of sorts.'

'Ashley, this madness has to stop, NOW!'

2.45 A.M., CRISIS CENTRE

Commissioner Kant has been monitoring the operation from the Crisis Centre. The Bureau chief has also joined him there. Three more chopper sorties have been conducted, but no trace of the weapon yet. Raghu has requested permission to show a new video uploaded on YouTube, ostensibly by Lashkar.

He runs it on the video wall.

A man, face covered with a chequered scarf, barely hiding his black curly beard, is holding an AK-47 rifle. A green backdrop with Quranic verses written on it is also visible. He threatens in a determined voice, 'People of Hindustan, now we demand not just plebiscite, but the total freedom of Kashmir. If in twenty-four hours from now, the governments of India and Pakistan do not liberate Kashmir, we will destroy the city of sin, Mumbai. So be forewarned, you will not escape the wrath of Allah.

'We also warn the Indian government to not attempt to touch the bomb. If you are found anywhere near it, inshallah, it will get detonated. Withdraw all your operations to trace it now, or lose the city of sin, ameen.'

'He is serious, Kant. Call the choppers back,' the Bureau chief says, matter-of-factly.

'Trust you on that one, sir. Quazi, ask Rudra to withdraw all operations immediately.' Kant is serious but composed. The lines on his forehead have taken up permanent residence;

he remembers that he has not gone to the washroom for the last many hours, his groin is aching with a full bladder. He excuses himself for a washroom visit.

As he is relieving himself, his cell keeps buzzing. Once done, he answers the call, it's Rudra.

'Sir, how on earth can you take this decision to withdraw operations at this stage?' he is screaming into the phone.

'RP, it will be plainly counterproductive. Lashkar has an eye on the operation, they will not let you locate and defuse their Adam's apple. Come back now, it's a command.'

'How can you do this, sir, this is going to be disastrous. I have actually traced the bomb. I know that Lashkar is watching the operation, therefore I have not disclosed the information to anyone!'

'Report to the Crisis Centre, RP. The Bureau chief is also here. Come back now, it's an order.'

'Very well, sir, best wishes to you and the Bureau chief.'

'Keep your trap shut, RP, and come now.'

3 A.M., INDIA

The prime minister has appeared on national television to address the nation. The look in his eyes is steely, his voice firm. He begins without a prologue.

'My fellow Indians, I have to address you at this odd hour because the nation is under attack. Pakistan-based terrorists have threatened to destroy the city of Mumbai with a nuclear weapon. We are not going to take these threats lying down, we will do everything in our power to pre-empt these attacks.

'These are difficult times, demanding sacrifice from our armed forces, police, security agencies, civil defence, and citizens as well. The President of India has declared a state of Emergency in the country on the unanimous advice of the Union Cabinet. I have personally warned the prime minister of Pakistan against any kind of adventurism.

'We have demanded that Pakistan surrender the chief of Lashkar to us, defuse the nuclear bomb placed in Mumbai and make immediate amends for its mistakes; otherwise, we will have to attack and destroy Pakistan as a measure of self-defence.

'The Army, police, civil defence and district administration in your cities and towns will help you prepare for all contingencies, even a nuclear attack. Please cooperate with them in protecting you. I am very sure that you will all stand united in this hour of crisis. Our great country has faced many challenges in the past, this too shall pass. We will emerge stronger and better through this ordeal by fire. Jai Hind!'

Panic has gripped the country all over. Telephones are ringing incessantly. District collectors and superintendents of police have been asked to report to their offices immediately. They have been asked to arrange for dissemination of information to the public about the measures to be taken in the event of the nuclear attack. The district administration at most places has a ready-made Disaster Response Plan, one component of which is nuclear war. Hospitals, health department officials and doctors have been asked to be prepared for the treatment of mass casualties. Some people are digging deep trenches to hide during the probable attack, stocking food and other provisions that would last them for days.

Something similar is happening in Pakistan too . . .

2.30 A.M., ISLAMABAD

The prime minister of Pakistan, Aziz, has just delivered an address to the nation, informing them how India has unilaterally threatened them with a nuclear war. He has asked them to be prepared for the war of their lifetimes, comparing it to the Day of Judgement. He has appealed to them to follow instructions given by the Army and the civil authorities. He has reiterated his faith in Allah, and has reassured them that god is with them.

The ISI chief has been summoned to meet him. Aziz's eyes are burning with anger and indignation. He does not even ask the spy chief to be seated.

Lieutenant General Mukhtiar Chaudhary heads one of the most efficient and deadly espionage organizations in the world. He is rumoured to have charmed several snakes at one go. The Taliban, Lashkar, Al-Qaeda—everybody in the business knows that they cannot function without his guidance and support; even the Americans have developed great respect for his prowess. He has learned to play one against the other, give 'results' whenever required, play to the gallery when needed and successfully divert any allegations directed at him or his agency. A career Army officer, he was identified and picked up early by his masters—a desk job suited him as he had been battling a severe leg injury caused by an Indian shrapnel during a border skirmish in his rookie days.

His thinning hairline, dyed in a very orange henna makes him look more like a singer than an Army man. But his neatly trimmed moustache gives him away. He is renowned to be as sharp as a razor blade, as adaptable as a chameleon and as sly as a fox. Successive prime ministers have hated him, but each of them soon came to depend upon him and his ways. A man of action who never fails. The ISI under him has virtually become an independent entity, a 'state within a state', as observers call it. His analytical and operational capabilities are unmatched; such is his expertise that he rarely keeps the political executives in the loop on operational matters.

'You think a mullah and a soldier can declare war in this country, Mr Chaudhary?'

'Wazeer-e-Azam, I do not understand. What are we talking about?' Mukhtiar picks up a glass of water from the table.

'If you continue feigning innocence, I will put you in jail and try you for treason. I should have never relied on you. Many people told me to be wary of you; it was my fault to have reposed my faith so blindly in you.'

'I am a loyal servant of Pakistan, Aziz sahib. I will not think twice before laying down my life for this country. Even if you try to put me in jail, my love for my country will remain unaffected.' He sips water as the prime minister begins speaking.

'Mukhtiar Chaudhary, that does not give you the right to put Pakistan in such danger that its very existence has come into question.'

'I am not responsible for any of the happenings in India, Wazeer-e-Azam. Neither am I an irresponsible person. I have nursed the organization with my sweat and blood for four decades. I will not do anything which harms the interests of Pakistan,' he says, getting up. There is a silent defiance in his posture, which worries the prime minister.

'I will put you under arrest right now if you do not tell me the whole story!' Aziz is speaking with so much anger that he has started slurring.

Mukhtiar is as calm as ever. 'There is no story to tell, Aziz sahib.'

3.10 A.M., MARINE DRIVE, MUMBAI

'Why are you calling the search operation off? We will discover it very soon. I am not tired, Kulkarni is also fresh, we can continue for three to four hours more,' Sreedhar Nair objects.

'I have orders to withdraw,' Rudra says in a sullen voice. He takes the cup of tea handed to him and sips it, sitting on his haunches on the promenade.

Advaita Sharma approaches him. 'Rudra sir, I hear that the operation has been suspended, why? What happened now?'

'Lashkar does not want us to play with its toy, so they are playing with us again,' he checks his combat gear as he talks; his pistol holster is on the left side. He is reminded of the last operation, which turned out to be a trap; his mind flits to the genius that had got him. Had it not been for the text message after the botched-up operation of the Delhi Police Special Cell, he would have never figured out the conspiracy behind it.

'What does Lashkar know about this operation, sir? How are they getting the information?'

'Right now, they know everything, my friend. This very moment, they have eyes on the ground here. Someone has been reporting to them each and every move of ours,' says Rudra as he suspiciously looks around.

'You mean a mole, sir? The kind they show in the movies?'

'Yes, my dear, the mole in the hole needs a hole in the mole,' Rudra smiles.

'What does that mean, sir?'

'Dear Advaita, don't you fuss over such things. Come, let

us go back to the Crisis Centre to catch up on some sleep.'

Rudra gets up and stretches; he realizes that his whole body is aching. He has barely slept a wink for the last twenty-four hours. He hasn't had a bath either. 'Kant will not like this,' he laughs to himself.

He has been updated that India has made a declaration of war on Pakistan. It's not a single nuke lying in the sea waiting to be defused. It's hundreds of warheads, on short- and long-range missiles.

'Before the world ends, let me have a cup of coffee,' he thinks.

What must his wife be doing now? Watching the drama unfurl on TV or travelling somewhere out of Mumbai with his unborn child? Cursing him, tears flowing down her cheeks...

His head seems fogged. 'I had better return to work. The demons of my thoughts will eat me before the world ends.'

'Why aren't you ready? Come inside the chopper with me. Sreedhar and Kulkarni will be coming with the others in the second and third birds.'

Advaita is very hesitant, he is finding it difficult to entertain the idea of riding in a chopper, that too a military one.

'I am afraid of heights. I cannot even travel in a glass lift!'

Rudra holds him by the arm in a friendly way and drags him to the helicopter. Advaita is trembling, breathing hard; he has never seen a helicopter so close. He holds on to his bag tightly as they climb into the machine. Kale hops in from the other door, commandos Pai and Kamat also join them.

Advaita is startled when the rotor blades start swirling; the commandos sitting beside him are laughing at his torment. Rudra is seated on the opposite seat with Inspector Kale; he looks as if he will fall asleep any time. The noise is deafening as the helicopter lifts off, swaying from one side to another as it gains height. Advaita's body is stiff with fear, he sees the dust raised by the blades rise as others run for cover on the ground, holding their ears, protecting their eyes. The noise considerably reduces when they turn right to fly over the sea. Kamat hands over a red headset to Advaita. He is relieved as soon as he puts it on; it cancels noise very well. The helicopter takes a U-turn and flies southwards towards Cuff Parade.

As they are passing above the World Trade Centre buildings, Rudra is fiddling with his cell. Advaita, too, feels that his cell is buzzing. 'Maybe, networks have been restored now,' he thinks.

He takes out his device from the bag, and looks at the message: 'Game Over'. Startled, he looks up. Rudra is looking straight into his eyes. Before he can fully comprehend the situation, Rudra snatches his device from him. The constables sitting beside him tie a rope around his waist, the side doors of the helicopter are suddenly flung open and he is thrown out of it.

Advaita ties to grab something as he is flung out. His breath stops. He is petrified. He falls and swings dangerously under the landing gear; the chopper tilts badly, then stabilizes, with Advaita swinging like a pendulum under it. He does not even scream; gripped by extreme fear he can hardly breathe.

The chopper is now gaining height, Advaita has regained consciousness, he is reciting verses from scriptures for his protection. He sees that Rudra is looking at him from the floor of the chopper, lying flat on his stomach, holding the rope.

'Rudra sir, pleeeeeease,' he cries out, his voice drowning in the flutter of the chopper blades. 'Pleeeeease don't!' he begs again.

Slowly, he feels that he is being pulled up. He feels the

blast of air on his body as he is brought up. Rudra holds his hand as he is pulled in.

Once again, he is seated in between the commandos; the red headset has been put back.

He hears Rudra speak, 'Jibreel, where is the switch?'

2.45 A.M., BHIMBER, AZAD KASHMIR, PAKISTAN

Suleri has already reached, he is waiting for the Amir. Using a satellite phone for the Internet, he has set up a small VSAT terminal. It is a clear moonlit night. The hills are looking rather ghostly in the white light. The air is crisp, with a hint of chill in the air. The rains stopped barely three days ago. The wind is laden with the smell of pine trees; it is blowing in spurts creating a fluttering sound in the tall poplar plantations.

The facility is a training camp for mujahedeen of various shades. It has even had the distinction of training women mujahedeen in the recent past. The facility was almost totally destroyed in the 2005 earthquake. It was later rebuilt when NGOs and foreign aid agencies went back. The 2005 earthquake has been of great strategic advantage to Lashkar. Their charity wing did a much better job than the government in rescuing the people, delivering first-aid and providing financial assistance to the needy. This has left it with a great deal of goodwill and strengthened the local support base. There has been a spurt in the number of 'volunteers' coming to Lashkar to assist in the cause of Jihad.

The Amir has started after him from Lahore; the journey will take him around three hours. They have decided to travel separately for safety reasons. Suleri travelled in a Pakistan Tourism Development Corporation Bus carrying two heavy sacks full of instruments. The Amir has his own means of travel, about which much is not known to anyone.

Suleri is tinkering with his instruments when three SUVs come to a grinding halt near the building. The main building is a single-storeyed, flat brick structure with nine rooms, seven of which serve as bedrooms for the mujahedeen under training. There is no training going on right now; one batch of thirty-five fighters has left the camp only three days back. The building is tactically camouflaged in a plantation of trees—almost nothing is visible to an observer perched in the hills.

Hakim Mohammed Sheikh is looking tired as he gets down from the SUV. His bodyguards fan out in the area, searching with flashlights for anything suspicious. The Amir is happy to see Suleri, he rushes to greet him with an embrace.

'Ansar, I am so proud of you. Today you have done what the whole Pakistan Army and ISI could not do in fifty years! You have tamed that mad elephant India.'

'Amir, it is only with your blessings that I have been able to make this contribution. Jibreel is there in Mumbai, he is doing a very good job.'

'We have now extended the deadline. We have given twenty-four hours more to India to declare the independence of Kashmir; we are no longer satisfied with plebiscite.' He settles down on the mattress laid on the floor and straightens his back. He smells the kahwa served to him with eyes closed, and continues:

'India has threatened Pakistan with war. I believe it is an empty threat. They do not have the guts to attack us. You saw how the Indian Air Force was frozen with fear during the Kargil war when our Army shot down two MIG aircraft? They suspended all air operations, cowards they are!'

He is now washing his hands in the stream of water being poured from a spouted metallic jug, covered with floral designs. He then wipes his hands and face with a soft white cloth; he now feels energized and fresh.

Suleri has set up his command centre, it is now up and running. 'I have been out of touch with Jibreel for the last hour or so. The roads to Bhimber have very bad network connectivity. Thankfully, I have my own Satellite Internet here, it's a bit slow, but the connection is fail-safe.'

'Ansar, have you prepared Jibreel for *shahadat*, martyrdom?' asks Hakim in a sombre voice.

'Yes, Amir, he was hesitating initially, now he is there, ready for everything.'

'May Allah accept his martyrdom.' Hakim turns his palms upwards as he says a prayer for 'Jibreel.'

'Ameen, ameen,' say the others present in the room.

3.15 A.M., NAUSHERA, JAMMU, INDIA

Sana has just landed at the Naushera airstrip in a small military aircraft. An armoured troop carrier is waiting to take her to a forward station in the hills. She can hear the distinct sound of crickets as she boards the troop carrier, with two seasoned commandos from the operations division of RAW accompanying her. She gets into black combat overalls designed for night use. These special outfits are designed not to leave any heat signatures, thus making them invisible to night vision or thermal-tracking devices.

A fifteen-minute rough-and-tumble ride takes her to a forward command post near the Line of Control (LoC). It is strategically located in a ravine, away from any prying eyes, and difficult to approach. It is housed in a snow tent, camouflaged so well that she is not able to locate it even when they are quite near it.

Once there, a team of Army Intelligence, communications experts and a backup-cum-rescue squad greets her. Colonel Dogra, a very fit and stylish gentleman from Army Intelligence, receives her. He comes to the point straightaway.

'The distance from here to Lashkar's Bhimber camp is around twenty-five kilometres, as the crow flies,' he says, moving about in a rather non-soldierly manner. His body language doesn't betray his service background. He appears to be more a vice president of a corporate firm than an Army official. He has a gentle, polished bearing, which successfully conceals a sharp and determined mind. He has been the backbone of many operations in this area. Never shy of courting trouble, he is completely aware of the terrain, risks involved, the capabilities of the adversary and the pertinent tactical considerations. 'So you think we are going to just fly over the hills to reach there?' Sana is sarcastic.

'Yes,' he says plainly. 'Let me introduce you to Gopal.'

A scrawny man with matted curly hair is standing beside a strange-looking contraption. 'This is your flying machine,' Gopal grins happily. 'You can try it right now.'

She is sceptical about getting into it—these experimental aircraft are somewhere between a toy and a man with wings. Simply put, these are like 'wearable helicopters', running on battery power. The Indian Defence Scientific Establishment has been secretly working on them for the last three years. These ones are actually the beta models, for testing purposes. Gopal Srinivasan, its inventor, tries to convince Sana that they are fail-safe, but she does not find his words reassuring.

Gopal tells her that he has personally flown one of these for sixty kilometres at a stretch and back, but she still has doubts on its stability and power. The worst part being that these suit-like contraptions, once taken off, are folded and carried in a backpack. The research into these metamorphing flying craft has seen a convergence of many technologies: super-efficient fuel, cell batteries that last up to sixty hours in operational conditions, ultra-light materials, stealth surface finish coatings, modular scalable structure, and miniaturization.

When unfolded, the suit contains a set of two rotor blades, which spin opposite each other, tied to a bare-bones metal frame carrying a seat for a single person. A joystick control panel allows steering, and an on-board GPS with a comfortable backlit display gives coordinates. Gopal gets into one for demonstration purposes; he starts the engine noiselessly like an electric fan, rises up in the air with the ease of cotton fluff, manoeuvres like a dragonfly before landing effortlessly. It is more like a toy helicopter managed by game controls, the only problem being that one has to sit in it.

It is Sana's turn now, as she is strapped into the harness of the contraption. Gopal lowers a panel which contains very simple controls: up–down, right–left. It can be operated simultaneously with both hands; the display is a palm-sized panel with maps and an overlay of controls. A headset-mounted miniature camera relays live feed to the control. Once fully harnessed, she feels like she is back to her training days, carrying a large backpack on those gruelling exercises, tired to the bone. She laughs to herself when she remembers an exercise with Rudra in the RED team, while she led the BLUE team which hunted the RED for hours. It was early morning when she heard the inescapable laughter, only to find him perched high on a tree in a makeshift hammock! The bastard had been sleeping there like a prince all night.

She hated him for that, yet admired his freakish antics. She had beaten him up with her fists after the exercise was over, while he rolled on the floor laughing. She sort of misses him at this moment.

She presses the start button on the panel; with a little buzz, the rotors at the top start spinning, gently lifting her into the air. She tests the directional controls, they are working flawlessly. Sana takes a larger round of the valley. Already feeling comfortable with the machine, she asks her other team members to get into their harnesses while she stays aloft. The communication headsets are working on encrypted frequencies with fail-safe peer-to-peer connectivity.

Within minutes, the group of four is airborne. Colonel Dogra says on the channel, 'You will fly south–south-west for eleven kilometres to reach Baghsar, then go thirty degrees westwards to reach Bhimber in a thirteen-kilometre flight.' He seems to be making some calculations.

'This should take you around forty minutes in total. You will fly in an arrow formation, maintaining a constant distance of thirty metres from each other.'

'What is the update on the target, Colonel?' Sana asks on the channel.

'Both guests arrived a short while ago. I have a surveillance drone stationed 300 metres above the structure. By the time you reach, three more drones will be in position, providing live feeds to your displays.'

'Any resistance possible?'

'Yes, there is a Pakistani Army patrol unit on the move within a radius of two kilometres; they have just crossed the Bhimber *nala*. They are equipped with heavy firepower. It will take them fifteen minutes to reach after the first shots are fired; you have to complete your mission within ten minutes. In case you cannot return via this air route, you will reassemble at Dhali Bhadala from where our rescue team will pick you up across the LoC.'

'Colonel, you won't have to take that trouble, we will return with the bastard or get nuked with them,' Sana quips. She is already crossing the LoC into enemy territory.

3.17 A.M., MUMBAI

'My name is not Jibreel,' Advaita Sharma says, barely able to control his breath. He is sitting between commandos Kamat and Pai; the chopper is now flying steadily.

'I am not playing a "guess my name" party game with you,' says Rudra. 'Answer my question first, we will have your naming ceremony later.'

Advaita is silent. Rudra takes out his pistol from the holster and cocks it.

'We will play a little game here, as you are fond of games. I don't like *Dinosaur Hunt*, so I will play *Mole Hunt*. The rules are simple: we will swing you again from the chopper with a rope, I will close my eyes and fire ten rounds in thirty seconds. If you survive, we will bring you back up.' Rudra pauses. 'And then we'll play again.'

Rudra gestures to the commandos who pick Advaita up as the doors of the chopper open again. A violent draft of air hits Advaita's face as they throw him out again. He goes down like a stone and then swings, the chopper tilts dangerously to counter the pull, then sways to the opposite side before stabilizing.

Advaita's eyes are shut with fear as he dangles precariously from the rope. He tries to regain his breath and hears a crackling sound. He looks above to see Rudra lying down on the floor of the chopper, aiming his pistol down, eyes closed.

BANG, another shot rings through the air. He feels a sharp pain in his right buttock; before he can count four, BANG, another one goes off. Thankfully, this time he is swinging to the other side. BANG! As he swings back, this time the bullet grazes his cheek; he feels as if a hot knife has slashed his right cheek; jets of blood spurt from his face, running into his shirt, wetting his neck. He closes his eyes, his lips muttering a *dua* for protection. He stops counting the shots now. They keep coming, one after the other, but none hits him now.

He hears the sound of the chopper blades clearly now, he is being raised up again.

Pai and Kamat pull him back, hold him by his shoulders and pin him back to the seat again; the red headset is put back on his ears. Rudra is filing bullets in his magazine. Advaita's wounds are smarting; he cannot sit properly due to the wound on his buttock.

'Round one, you win,' says Rudra; his magazine is full now, he cocks the pistol again. The chopper is flying high over the Arabian Sea. Now nothing but darkness is visible. Rudra also puts off the lights inside the chopper.

'Nice feeling, isn't it? Serene darkness not just underneath but all over, inside us, outside us.' The sound of the blades cutting the air seems amplified by the darkness.

'Are you ready to play again?' he asks.

'You will not get anything from me, Mr Rudra Pratap Singh. Even if I die, there is a parallel switch with someone else; he will detonate the bomb.'

Advaita's tone has changed, he is speaking with a strange brazenness in his voice.

'Didn't you realize that it was me chatting with you for the last two hours as Ansar Suleri? Who asked you to return to this site with the switch? It was me posing as Suleri. My dear friend, you can assume what must have happened to him by now,' Rudra says with an exaggerated sigh. 'You are wasting my time, Jibreel, we were having more fun playing the game. Round two, isn't it?'

'Wait, wait, please,' pleads Advaita.

9

TOUCH ME NOT

3.35 A.M., BAGHSAR LAKE, AZAD KASHMIR, PAKISTAN

Sana and her strike team have just entered the serene Samahni Valley; lofty trees of pine, fir, oak and elm lie below them as they effortlessly glide over the forest.

'This place was an important stop for the Mogul princes travelling from Delhi to Kashmir,' Colonel Dogra informs.

'Are you being my tour guide, Colonel? Now you will tell me that there is a fort here which must be visited!' Sana snaps.

'Hahaha, actually there is a very beautiful fort, called the Baghsar Fort, at approximately 10 o'clock from your present location. It is closed to tourists as the Pakistani Army has taken over it,' Colonel Dogra adds, with good-natured laughter.

'So if we are caught alive, you know where we would be, right, Colonel?'

'Good thinking, Sierra [her code name]. Coming back to the task, you should now dip and fly as close to the water of the lake as possible. It will prevent any chance of being spotted against the sky.'

He continues, 'Just to add that the lake is in full view of the Army sentries sitting at the top of the fort; they have two heavy machine guns with crossing arcs of fire deployed there. The lake is really in their field of fire. Move swiftly without arousing suspicion, most importantly, DO NOT return by the same path. I am sending two vacant mancopters, which will copy your path in autopilot mode. Just keep one man at your landing coordinates to receive and deploy them.'

'Delta, I wish you could tell me all things at a go; these continuous surprises are a bit too much.' Sana is upset.

'Commando Biswal, who is on your right, has participated in one such mission earlier, he will assist you. Though it was a shoot-and-scoot mission, not the one like you are into now.'

By now, they are flying really low over the beautiful Baghsar Lake; the forest around is sparse, a few single-storeyed flat-roofed buildings can be seen. To the left, an ancient tower attached to a rampart wall can be seen. Sana knows that a heavy machine gun is positioned there; she shudders at the prospect of being shot mid-air over a lake in enemy territory; she dips and speeds up at full throttle.

'You will go on the path shown on your display for six kilometres, then you enter the gorge which houses the Bhimber nala. Just go along the stream as it broadens, here you've to fly in a linear formation at a ten-metre distance of each other. If any shots are fired, just fly upwards and continue on your path. The mancopter can quickly gain height, it can easily scale 500 metres in a quick ascent cycle. The camp coordinates have been fed on your display, you can also get live drone feeds.'

Colonel Dogra is receiving feeds from their headset

cameras. He can see the feeds in night-vision green. There is no cause for concern yet.

3.35 A.M., CRISIS CENTRE INTERROGATION ROOM, MUMBAI

Commissioner Kant is watching the interrogation on the monitor. Characteristically cold and tenacious, he rests his chin on his fist as he watches the process.

'Jibreel' has now become vehement, his eyes bloodshot; he tries to wipe the blood still flowing from the wound on his right cheek with his T-shirt. Rudra offers him his handkerchief, which he flatly refuses.

'No one can save your city now, Mr Rudra Pratap, it is the Day of Judgement. My brethren have been killed, tortured, their homes looted, their women dishonoured in Palestine, Myanmar, Gujarat and so many other places in the world. Today, their souls will rest in peace, I will avenge the atrocities committed on them. Even if you kill me, I will not tell you the location of the switch.'

'You know, my friend, I really admire you. You have been working here with us as Advaita Sharma, helping us out on cases. You have real mettle, your hacking skills are unparalleled, I have never met an adversary as smart as you.' Rudra claps a slow clap, then paces around the room.

'I also appreciate the finesse with which you brought the bomb into Indian waters without anyone suspecting anything. Suleri did a fine job of involving Munir Natsir of the Jemaah Islamiah who masterminded the Bali bombings; he went from Indonesia to Syria to receive the device, and shipped it to Pakistan. You guys are geniuses.

'Tell me, how did you get access to the oil mafia? The poor

crooks also got conned by you. Actually, you are a con artist, you are no fighter. You must have been a sissy at school, other kids would have bullied you, no girl would have ever looked at you, isn't it? My friend, here too you slyly infiltrated us, pretending to be a patriot, then backstabbed us. Actually, I pity you.'

'Jibreel's' face is red with anger. 'Your pride is hurt that I fooled all of you, Mr Rudra Pratap. You have failed, do not vent your frustration on me!' He looks at Rudra with indignation.

'Let me tell you something, Jibreel or whatever your name is; you should thank your stars for being alive. I was aware of your real identity when I scolded you and chucked you out of the Crisis Centre. You have been followed for every second after that. I had called you here to get your fingerprints for a positive match. We already had your prints from two locations.

'But, my dear friend, I still have no idea whatsoever how you managed to get access to the oil mafia. The Crime Branch has been trying for years now. They couldn't do what you could so easily do.'

'Jibreel' seems to be lost in thought. Kant, who is witnessing this from outside, says something to Quazi, who immediately passes the message to Rudra through the concealed earpiece that he is wearing.

'No,' says 'Jibreel', but by this time Rudra has placed a video call to an officer stationed at the City Hospital Intensive Care Unit; he asks him to point the camera at the girl so that she can be shown to the accused.

'Look, here she is,' says Rudra as he brings the phone screen to his face. 'Jibreel' sees the blackened shrivelled face of the girl, breathing heavily through a ventilator, her hair shaved off, and a multitude of tubes, cables and monitors surrounding her.

'Jibreel' cannot bear it any more; he puts his head down on the table and breaks down.

Rudra leaves him to cry in peace, and comes out of the interrogation room to meet Kant.

'Where did you get this scoundrel, RP?'

'His cover was blown way back, sir. I had let him out to see if he meets other accomplices. We tailed his every move after identification, but nothing substantial was obtained. The girl had given a real good description of him, and it immediately struck me that it was him. The CCTV footage from the building where the girl lived had been auto-deleted, but Raghu did a great job of recovering the deleted files. We developed his pictures from the CCTV grabs later.'

'Good work, RP, but how did you get access to the details about his handler and the mission?'

'Sir, Bose of NCRO had blocked his handler's IP from Pakistan. We had spoofed the handler's IP address and log-in credentials to keep communicating with him. They were using a very clever method of communication; they used to chat through a multiplayer game, *Dinosaur Hunt*. Fortunately for us, apart from the voice chats, they had also chatted on text, and the chat history was archived on the server. We got a lot of valuable information from that,' Rudra explains.

'What now, RP?'

3.47 A.M., BHIMBER TRAINING CAMP, AZAD KASHMIR

Sana and the team have landed, come together and disassembled the mancopters. Commando Anil Kumar has been asked to stay back to receive and disassemble the two mancopters which were to follow and also act as backup. Sana checks the feed from the drones deployed over the complex; no movement is noticed.

'In the next five minutes, we will start firing at the Baghsar Fort checkpost of the Pakistanis to distract them. They will pull all resources towards Baghsar Fort. This will give you the chance to safely conduct your operation, but be careful, they have this reserve force called the Mujahid Army, members of which are part-time soldiers. They retain their weapons at home and bring them for drills as and when required. Though not as well trained as the regular forces, they can create serious difficulties for you. Do a surgical operation, and retreat real quick. Best of luck!' Colonel Dogra gives his last instructions.

CRISIS CENTRE, MUMBAI, SAME TIME

Rudra now sits in front of 'Jibreel' and looks into his eyes. 'You conned that poor girl, she loved you so much, you heartless snake!'

'Jibreel' looks down, as if searching for something. Rudra continues, 'She was innocent, she did not deserve to be tortured like that.'

'Jibreel' seems to be lost in thought; after some time, he raises his head, and says, 'I never tortured her.'

Rudra pounds his fist on the table between him and the culprit. 'Shameless liar, you should have seen her state when she was found. For three days she was lying in her own vomit and shit. What more torture did you want to commit on the poor soul?'

'Jibreel' is moving his head from side to side in distress.

'I did love her profusely, with all my heart, but my mission demanded that I sacrifice her, sacrifice the thing which I loved most. I had no choice.'

'She still loves you, she was ready to forgive you. When I asked her how she was poisoned, she said it was an accident. She did not want to file a case. The only valuable thing I got from her was your physical description.'

'Jibreel' is in deep distress now. 'Do you want to see the state she is in?' Rudra asks.

BHIMBER TRAINING CAMP, POK, SAME TIME

Sana mutters something under her breath.

'Pardon, I couldn't hear you clearly,' says the colonel.

'No, nothing for you, Delta,' she says.

She adjusts the surveillance drone feeds to get a clearer view of the structure. Three SUVs are parked a little distance away, facing the dirt track leading to the building. The drivers are nowhere to be seen, thermal signatures indicate that the engines are going cold. It looks like the cars have been there for a while. Sana is carrying an invisible laser source which will be used to light up targets for the assault drone stationed high above. Once a target is indicated, the reflected laser's coordinates are noted down by the drone; later, different types of munitions can be fired from it. She points the laser at the three SUVs—one by one—gets a confirmation beep from the drone; Colonel Dogra also indicates target acquisition. Anil Kumar indicates that two spare mancopters have been received and positioned; he is also called to the structure.

There is no compound wall, only a plantation of tall poplar trees, which does not restrict visibility; neither do their slender trunks provide any protection from gunfire.

Shots are heard at a great distance. Sana knows that the diversionary attack at Bhimber Fort has started, drawing the Pakistani Army units to it. There is no movement in the building. Sana does a thermal scan again, they are now barely fifty metres from the structure; there are three men in the larger room, two each in the adjoining three rooms. The men in the larger room are awake and active, while those in the other rooms are either asleep or about to rest. She guesses that Suleri, who has been on surveillance due to his satellite phone, is there in the larger room. One of the other men is most likely Hakim Mohammed Sheikh, the nemesis of India, as per his own claims.

Shots are fired from the Pakistani side too; she can hear the movement of Army jeeps towards the site of the skirmish. A thermal scan indicates that the sleeping men are now getting up. She asks Anil and Biswas to take up positions at the corners of the building, covering the front and sides. She asks Commando Pawan to scale the structure and take up the vantage point atop it. She moves to position herself behind the large rock outcrop almost diagonally across the main entrance. As she is about to lie down flat, she hears a loud sound. Stray dogs have sensed their presence, and are barking loudly. She knows that this will rouse suspicion, she gives a go-ahead to the colonel; before they can count to ten, a targeted missile hits the last SUV. There is a resounding blast, it is blown to pieces, while the other two vehicles catch fire. Sana throws three delay-fuse grenades towards the entrance. One armed man comes running out of the main door; he starts firing indiscriminately in the darkness, alerting the others. Another man carrying his weapon jumps out of the window to join him. Both men are kneeling together, back to back and firing in the darkness. When the grenades go off, they both are hit. Firing now starts from within the building. She counts nine minus two, making it seven men inside.

None of the team members has fired a shot so far; the firing from the building continues for some time, then there is fire at intervals, but no burst fire is heard. Three men climb out of the windows, one by one from the adjoining rooms, to rush towards the main room; there are no lights anywhere. They are quickly taken inside. Sana signals to the colonel for a second drone strike; two missiles accurately hit the standing SUVs, which blast to pieces, leaving behind charred chassis and burning parts. The building is an isolated structure, away from the village. Sana can hear noises from the hills. Then she hears a muffled shot, she instantly knows that it is from her team member. Pawan informs, 'One more down.'

'Delta, left wing of the building has two of them; smoke them out, be precise, Papa [Pawan] is on the top-right side,' she tells the colonel. Another strike from the drone hits the extreme left room, part of the external wall collapses with a booming sound; the injured men try to crawl out through the door, but she gets them both. 'Two more down,' she relays.

'Four left, the most important ones,' her mind is racing. 'Movement at the rear, three men escaping,' relays Pawan. He opens a burst fire, but no one is hit. 'They are crawling, cannot be seen,' he relays from the extreme right corner of the rooftop. Sana comes out of cover and runs towards the back, but her night-vision headset shows no movement. She waits, her breath heavy. 'Alpha, you take possession of the room, pack and carry any equipment that you can.'

'Roger,' says Anil Kumar, and rushes to the main room, which is empty. 'All clear,' he signals.

'Take position at the window,' Sana commands. 'No one hits for a kill now, we want them alive. Go for the legs.'

It's quite dark at the rear side of the structure. She is lying on the ground, straining to see through her night-vision headset.

'Quick, Sierra, there is movement within 800 metres of your location; it may be a Mujahedeen force or the Pakistani Army on patrol. You have less than ten minutes to exit,' Colonel Dogra speaks hurriedly and anxiously.

'Roger, noted Delta, can you hold them back for some time if they approach too close to our location?'

'Yes, Sierra, but that would amount to shifting the drone from our current mission. I do not want to do that.'

'Copy that.'

As she speaks, she finds something moving near her—someone, who had been on her flank is now surreptitiously crawling towards her. She quickly realizes that it is no one from her own team, turns and pounces on the man; as soon as she gets hold of him, she realizes that he is armed with a knife. He stabs her on her side, but the Kevlar vest is too strong for the knife to penetrate. She punches his face hard, the man cries out, and she gets up on her knees to pin him down. Suddenly, she hears the distinct rat-a-tat of gunfire from behind her, a bullet hits her helmet and shatters it, she ducks and pins the man simultaneously, holding his right arm at the wrist. She discards the helmet, she can barely see anything now. The man in her grip is struggling hard. She lands solid punches with her left hand on his face, he releases the knife. Simultaneously, she takes out a grenade from her pocket and hurls it in the direction of the fire.

It lands with a dull thud. Rat-a-tat, the assailant fires again. Sana is counting, four-five-six-seven, boom, the grenade goes off. Silence, the man has been hit.

'Four minus one, three on the run, one with me here,

how lucky!' she thinks. Whosoever is left is needed alive; the man in her hold is not moving much; she throws away the knife into the darkness; the man totally stops resisting; she is thinking up a plan to take him captive.

In a sudden move, he flips her and releases himself from her grasp. Before she realizes, he is running away. Her eyes have still not adjusted to the darkness. She gets up and follows him out of instinct, guided by the sound of leaves and stones as he runs. It is difficult for her to run with her weapons, her bullet-proof vest and rest of the equipment. She flings her assault weapon to the side, and follows him as he runs towards the nala. He slips over the rounded white pebbles in the stream; she reaches him but he gets up and runs again. She is falling out of breath, the man is running upstream into the water, she doggedly follows, conserving her energy. His silhouette is visible now, she changes her pace, dashes ahead with full force, he is just metres ahead of her. She sprints now to reach him, he is within an arm's distance, he suddenly turns to the left, dodging her, she loses her balance and falls. As she is falling, she kicks at his shins, he too stumbles and collapses. Both lie on the pebbles, breathing heavily. She gathers all her strength and pounces on him, kicking him in the groin and stomach. 'Pleaaaaase noooooo,' the man pleads in a feminine voice.

3.50 A.M., NEW DELHI

Walter Mulock, former US President, has just landed in a military aircraft. He has requested an urgent meeting with the prime minister of India. He was speaking at a Climate Change Symposium in Dhaka during the day. He has been asked to urgently intervene in the ongoing crisis, which is fast threatening to escalate into a worldwide nuclear endgame.

The regional security officer of the US embassy is accompanying him, so is the station chief of the CIA, along with the ambassador to India.

'They are pretty serious this time. Our intervention will be highly unwelcome, maybe even counterproductive. The Indians do not trust us, they believe that we are partly responsible for giving a long leash to the fundamentalist elements in Pakistan,' the station head says clinically, as if he were reading out the diagnosis of a terminally ill patient to his relatives.

Mulock is an imposing man. At 6'4", he looks more like Roger Moore from a James Bond movie than an ex-President. Charming and temperate, there is a certain poise in his personality. A no-nonsense man, he has been one of the most popular presidents the United States has ever had, widely respected across the world for his acumen and sense of discernment. He has been instrumental in brokering peace in many difficult situations.

He mulls over the input given by the CIA station chief, looks out of the window, and says, 'Well, they have their reasons to think so.' His deep, guttural voice conveys as much sense as his words. The chopper has been given special flying clearance despite a stipulation under Indian laws prohibiting take-offs and landings after sunset and before sunrise.

'How do you rate the prospects of Pakistan in an initial volley?' he addresses the CIA man.

'Pakistan underestimates the Indian "Advanced Air Defence" capabilities. The Indians can intercept anything, from the 1500-kilometre-range Intercontinental Ghauri missiles to the battlefield-range Hatf-1, with certainty. The Indian "Iron

Dome" is as good, if not better, than our own Patriot Missile Defence System. Their interceptors carry explosive payloads which can destroy multiple incoming missiles at a height of more than ten miles,' the CIA man rattles off.

'Would we have to protect our special child or will China do it?' Mulock is looking at the darkness of Lutyen's Delhi, a darkness enhanced by the extensive vegetation around. He remembers attending a meeting with the Indian premier at the beautiful red-sandstone building in the Indian capital.

'I doubt if China will actually step into this mess. If it does, it's Armageddon. Russia will jump in and we will be drawn in too,' says the ambassador.

Mulock gives him a searching look. 'What do we tell the Indians now, Mr Ambassador?'

'They will ask us to rein in the Pakistanis.'

'Are we in a position to do that?'

'I do not think that even the Pakistani prime minister can do anything now.'

'It's fifty shades of green in Pakistan. I have never liked the idea of the "good Taliban" versus the "bad Taliban". I had told the CIA chief that it was a disastrous idea back when I was in the White House. Now the chickens have come home to roost.'

The CIA man is about to speak, but Mulock indicates that he does not want further discussion. He keeps staring at the granular darkness below.

In a few minutes, they land at the special helipad at the President's residence. The Indian external affairs minister is present there to receive him. They quickly sit in the waiting cars and zoom towards the Prime Minister's Office.

SAME TIME, CRISIS CENTRE, MUMBAI

There has been one more round of sustained interrogation. Kant has called Rudra out to discuss strategy.

'RP, why is he saying over and over again that there is no switch?'

'I think the bastard is buying time, sir.'

Kant's sharp eyes are searching for something far away. 'No, RP, he said that Suleri never talked to him about the switch, he only spoke of some "controls". You remember he said that he was surprised to get a message from Suleri about the "switch".'

'Agreed, sir, but that was me, masquerading as Suleri who sent him the "switch" message,' Rudra exhales through pursed lips, the lines on his forehead getting deeper.

'Only if we could cross-check with that scoundrel Suleri.'

'How I wish I could lay my hands on him, sir!'

'RP, you go back and continue, ask him to explain this "no switch" phenomenon. I think he will give us a nugget of information. The Bureau chief is itching to interrogate him, juice him down fast or they will want access.'

'Sir, ask them to hunt down their own prey. Why are they scavenging here?'

'Let me handle that, RP, you go back in now.'

Rudra enters the interrogation chamber again. 'Jibreel' is quite exhausted.

'Okay, my friend, I accept your story that there is no switch,' Rudra says with a tired expression.

'That is what I have been trying to tell you for such a long time, Mr Rudra Pratap, but you were in no mood to listen to me.'

'No, my friend, go on, what are these "controls" then? You cannot have a nuclear device with no switch on it, how will you activate it?'

'You see, it will be very difficult for a non-techie to understand it, let alone try and defuse it. Lesser minds cannot comprehend the complexity of what has been created.'

'Enlighten me,' Rudra says, 'I will try and understand.'

'Don't take it as a challenge, Mr Rudra Pratap, it's well beyond the likes of you to figure out.' 'Jibreel' is sarcastic now, with a mischievous smile playing on his lips.

'You think I am dumb, right?'

'I don't think that you are dumb, but a man should be aware of his limitations. Technology is not your game, this is a maze you will never be able to get out of. We have designed it in such a way that even we cannot stop the bomb from going off,' 'Jibreel' says in a condescending tone, scratching his neck with his left index finger.

'So there is an irreversible timer attached to it,' Rudra says.

'Hahahaha, that's nice. Didn't I tell you, Mr Rudra Pratap, not to apply your brains? It is a far more complex system, virtually impossible to unravel. You see, we were not confident of the others, let's not name them here, hence we designed it in a way that leaves no options for anyone. You see, we were very well aware that the ISI or Lashkar may ditch us any time under US or Pakistani government pressure.'

'I do not understand a word of what you're saying, Jibreel, how can you design something which leaves no options for anyone?'

'It's a complex discipline called Game Theory, the science behind winning and losing. In this, there is a term called Zugzwang, which simply means, "I win irrespective of what you do". You are in a Zugzwang now—whatever you do, you are doomed; put otherwise, there is simply no way in which the bomb can be defused,' says 'Jibreel' with great certainty in his voice.

'I see,' says Rudra, 'but what if you are bluffing? I do not believe that such technology can exist. I have defused dozens of bombs in my life till now, but have never heard of such a mechanism.'

'That is the beauty of it, my dear sir, it has a two-stage activation; but once it's in the third stage, no one in this world can defuse it.'

'So it is a timer,' Rudra says with a laugh.

'IT IS NOT A TIMER, Mister, it is the most advanced piece of artificial intelligence ever fitted on a bomb. It is a device with a mind of its own. No one can change its mind now!' he exclaims.

'So you are saying that we are up against a mind which is sitting quietly at the bottom of the sea, waiting for us?'

'Yes. Look, we were tired of the big players playing their game, so the genius Suleri and I decided to use them for our mission. The Amir thought we were two motivated youngsters ready to be pawns in his hands. In reality, we got him to do all the groundwork.

'Can I tell you something, we do not believe in him, that is why we made a fail-safe device. It is like the surprise level in a game that only the developers know about. The Amir is totally in the dark about the actual mechanisms. We know that we are not fighters; you or any other international power may torture us into surrendering the controls; therefore we made the bomb take charge of itself. You cannot do anything to it, you cannot torture it, do narco-analysis with its mind or try advanced psychological methods of interrogation.

'So now you face an adversary, which is not human, but

has a mind, a goal and a purpose, not even god can deter it.'

Rudra is looking at 'Jibreel', his mind caught in a blizzard, his eyes carrying a lost look.

'So, Jibreel, what exactly is this programme?'

'Dear Mr Rudra, go figure . . . But I will give you a cheat sheet. The bomb will wait for the independence of Kashmir, nothing else will stop it. See if you can do something about it.'

4.05 A.M., BHIMBER TRAINING CAMP, AZAD KASHMIR

Sana has tied Suleri's hands behind his back; they have now come to the rendezvous, where they are all supposed to meet. No one from her team has died or been injured. The mancopters are ready for deployment, Suleri's equipment has been bundled into a sack which has been loaded on a mancopter. He is being tied to another one. Sana is briefing Colonel Dogra.

'Delta, Armadillo [code name for the Amir] escaped, but we have got Sugar; no death or injuries otherwise, seven assailants on their way to harass the virgins.'

'Looks good. The Pakistani Army is closing in fast on your location, you had better take off now,' he quips.

'Beam me up, Scottie, haha,' she is ecstatic.

They have been asked to return by an entirely different route; the mancopters carrying Suleri and his equipment have been put on autopilot mode, following Sana from a distance. Others have been commanded to take divergent routes, assembling finally at the forward command post near Naushera.

Suleri does not speak a word after being captured; nor does he reveal anything about the possible locations of the Amir or about the control mechanisms of the bomb.

'Sierra, you will be flying for a little more than forty-five minutes. Caution your team to be extremely careful near the Line of Control. There you will all have to gain a height beyond the range of rifle fire. Still, don't go above 500 metres, you may face oxygen issues. I don't want you guys dead from hypoxia after surviving a combat situation!'

'Noted, Professor, thanks for the science lecture. Now keep an eye on any airborne objects or you will lose your expensive flying toys.'

'Anything other than you guys in the air will be shot down, my word.'

'Your diversion trick really worked, I must say, Delta.'

'Worked! They are shelling us with heavy artillery fire there. If this does not stop soon, it will blow up into a mini war!'

'You are doing so much for me, Delta, seriously, I already feel indebted to you.'

'Sierra, will you please stop being sarcastic?'

'Delta . . . Delta . . . Something is happening to me. It must be the oxygen, shit . . . But I am not even at a high elevation. I . . . am . . . feeling dizzy. Suddenly . . .'

'Sierra! Come in, Sierra! You are losing height, Sierra, you are losing height. Respond, please!'

' . . .'

'Sierra, we are putting you on autopilot, full speed. Do you hear me? . . . Sierra, come in . . . Alpha, Bravo, you change course, follow Sierra at her coordinates, do a visual check, see if any personnel is hit.'

'Bravo to Delta, noted, changing course. Keep medical emergency team ready.' Commando Biswas is rushing to her help.

'Alpha noted too, roger.' Anil Kumar has also changed

course, he is now heading towards Sana's location in the air.

'Delta to Alpha, was Sugar properly secured before take-off? 'Colonel Dogra asks Anil Kumar.

'Positively. He was secured and sedated, he is following Sierra's path on autopilot mode. No danger from him.'

At the forward command post, Colonel Dogra has called the Mumbai Crisis Centre. Kant is on the line.

'Good morning, sir, Colonel Dogra from Military Intelligence here. I will be in possession of a very important asset in precisely thirty minutes. Will it be possible for someone to share the details available till now? We will ensure that whatever is extracted here is immediately conveyed to the Mumbai Crisis Centre.'

'Morning, Colonel, congratulations on the success of the mission, will send you the interrogation transcripts and background materials forthwith. Just a suggestion, ask the techie about Zugzwang,' Kant says as he holds his glasses in his left hand, rolling one of the frame temples as if it were a dart to be thrown at a target.

'Pardon me, sir, what is Zugzwang?'

'It is what we are in, Colonel. Anyways, it is a shared secret between our cross-border colonial cousins,' says Kant, putting his glasses back on.

'Roger, sir, will notify you soon.'

4.20 A.M., CRISIS CENTRE, MUMBAI

Exhausted, Rudra has come out of the interrogation room.

'I have no objection to the Bureau or the Crime Branch juicing him out now, sir. I don't think he will give anything more.'

'RP, I too suggest that we work on the bomb, not the

stepfather of the bomb. Suleri has been captured by the spooks at LoC; that package is reaching them in some time. He may be a better source of information. We can cross-check with them if this scoundrel is leading us down the garden path, as he has done before,' Kant says, tapping Rudra's shoulder.

'I am ashamed, sir, that we could not bust him before. He has been working right here with us! Thankfully, we shared very limited compartmentalized information with him,' Rudra yawns as he completes the remark; Kant gives him a disdainful look.

'I have more disturbing news for you, RP, the Chinese Yaogan-14 spy satellite is now watching the bomb site. I suspect they are sharing the feed with the ISI, which means that any attempt to defuse the bomb will be known to Lashkar—the mullahs have an eye in the sky now.'

'Zugzwang, the word ends with a nice twang, sir.'

'RP, I fail to understand what makes you tick. Here we are in the worst imbroglio of our lives, and you are discussing word sounds. If we survive this, I promise you that I will send you on the sabbatical that you have been hankering after. That will ensure that I retire in peace, away from your Zen histrionics,' says Kant as he rubs his forehead in extreme fatigue.

'Nansen cuts the cat into two,' Rudra says with a lyrical undertone, his eyes shining.

'Now what on earth can that be, RP? Don't be cryptic. What have the Chinese done now?'

'The story goes like this, sir.

'Nansen, the Zen master saw the monks of the eastern and western halls fighting over a cat. He seized the cat and told the monks: "If any of you say a good word, you can save the cat."

'No one answered. So Nansen boldly cut the cat into two pieces. That evening his disciple Joshu returned and Nansen told him about this. Joshu removed his sandals and, placing them on his head, walked out.

'Nansen said: "If you had been there, you could have saved the cat."

'Now you will ask, "Why did Joshu put his sandals on his head?"

'If anyone answers this question, he will understand exactly how Nansen enforced the edict. If not, he should watch his own head.'

Had Joshu been there, he would have enforced the edict in the opposite way.

Joshu snatches the sword and Nansen begs for his life.

'Isn't it a nice story, sir?' Rudra says as he nonchalantly stretches his arms and legs, then slowly rolls his neck to release stress.

'RP, you rascal, scum of the earth, get out or I will shoot you!'

'Yes, Master,' Rudra gets up laughing, performs a prolonged Japanese bow, and leaves.

3.50 A.M. [PKT], ISLAMABAD

The ISI chief has been summoned again to Prime Minister Aziz Ahmad's office. When he enters the room, he notices that the chief of the Intelligence Bureau of Pakistan, Kareem Raza, and the chief of Army Staff, General Anwar Suleiman, are already present.

'Assalam alaikum, Wazeer-e-Azam, we just met half an hour ago, has anything urgent come up so soon?' Mukhtiar Chaudhary's voice has a certain cockiness now.

General Anwar Suleiman cannot hide his annoyance at the attitude of the ISI chief. 'Mukhtiar, let's not forget the fact that you are part of a disciplined force. The Pakistani Army has very high standards of discipline and decorum. Don't do anything which soils its reputation.'

'General sir, with due respect, I have just greeted the Wazeer-e-Azam, there is no reason to take offence at that!'

Prime Minister Aziz steps in to pacify the warring soldiers. 'Peace, gentlemen, we are here to discuss matters far more important. Mr Chaudhary, I had asked you some time back to tell me the whole story. I hope you have had a change of heart after you had time to think rationally?'

The prime minister is making his move; Mukhtiar knows that he is being encircled now, but he has dealt with such tricky situations before too.

'Aziz sahib, I reiterate that there is nothing which needs to be told to you.'

The prime minister is aghast at his guts, he looks for support at the Intelligence Bureau chief.

Kareem Raza is a fair, well-built Pakistani Punjabi; he has been the inspector general of Punjab Police in the past. Having worked in the IB for several terms, he is a dyed-in-wool Intelligence officer. His still, steady, deep eyes cast an unsettling gaze on his audience. He clears his throat, and asks in a sombre voice, 'Mr Chaudhary, where is the Amir of Lashkar now?'

'Janaab Kareem Raza sahib, we never discuss Lashkar officially, it is our common blind spot, invisible to plain sight,' Mukhtiar Chaudhary says with an air of brazenness.

'Mr Chaudhary, I repeat my question, where is the chief of Lashkar, Hakim Mohammed Sheikh, now?' Kareem Raza's steady gaze is fixed on the ISI chief.

'Am I supposed to be his personal assistant to keep track of his whereabouts and appointments, Janaab?'

The air in the room is tense now. Aziz knows that this country of his has seen many such moments, but he hated to be part of this. Whatever was going to happen would unsettle power equations which would have long-lasting effects. That apart, the challenge right now is to be able to restrain Lashkar and avert the annihilation of his beloved country.

Kareem Raza is unperturbed, his posture graceful like that of a proud lion's looking down at his prey, deciding its fate at leisure. 'When did you last communicate with him, Mr Chaudhary?' he insists.

'I do not remember, maybe fifteen days back when the CIA had announced a bounty on his head. He had called me up for advice. I had given him general tips on security and precautions to be taken during travel,' Chaudhary says with a certain nonchalance.

Kareem Raza looks at the prime minister, who casts a reassuring glance at him; the general is still seething with anger, moving constantly in his seat. The IB chief takes out his mobile phone and plays an audio recording.

There is heavy firing in the background of the communication. A shrill voice is speaking in a hushed tone, 'General sahib, the Indians have attacked us, my bodyguards have been killed. Ansar Suleri has been captured, send help immediately!'

'Amir, where are you located now, I am sending help urgently. Are you okay, have you been hit?' Mukhtiar Chaudhary sounds concerned.

The Amir is panting, his breath heavy, his voice hardly audible. 'I am at the Bhimber Training Camp in Azad Kashmir. The Indians came out of nowhere, they destroyed my cars in a drone attack, then killed my bodyguards. I have nowhere to run, they are closing in fast, they are many and they look like trained commandos who have been airdropped. Send help now!'

There is constant firing of automatic weapons in the background. Mukhtiar is heard saying, 'Amir, you should hide yourself in some secure place. Do not move for god's sake, lie still. I am sending help sooner than you think. Inshallah, you will be safe, shut down all your communication equipment, throw away your phone after taking its battery out. Do not worry, we are there for you.'

The Amir is pleading, 'General sahib, please do not delay sending help, they will kill me, they have killed all the others, please help!'

'Amir, please calm down, help will reach you within fifteen minutes, cut off all communication, khuda hafiz.'

No one speaks for a minute. Then General Suleiman says with distinct acerbity, 'What made you think that you could ask the local Army unit to rescue the Amir without us coming to know about it?'

'The Amir is our most important resource, I cannot let him die at the hands of the Indians, General. You would have done the same, wouldn't you?' Chaudhary is still hostile, eyeing the IB chief with contempt. 'Well, Mr Raza, under whose authority have you intercepted my phone?'

Prime Minister Aziz stands up, grinding his teeth. It looks like he is going to strangle the ISI chief. 'Under the authority of the Prime Minister of the Islamic Republic of Pakistan! Do you need any further justification, Mr Chaudhary? Now will you tell us the truth or do we use other methods on you?'

Mukhtiar Chaudhary looks at everyone present in the

room with eyes full of rage. 'All of you, my dear sirs, are enemies of Pakistan. The future will not forgive you!'

4.40 A.M. [IST], MOHRA KAMPLA VILLAGE NEAR LOC, INDIA

Colonel Dogra has set up a facility to receive the incoming team at Mohra Kampla. Dr Mohanti of the Army hospital has been flown in by an advanced light air ambulance chopper, Dhruv. The incoming team has been asked to fly east of the Pakistani village Chauki on the LoC to approach Mohra Kampla, away from both Baghsar where there is fierce shelling going on from both sides, and Naushera, from where they had taken off. They are expected to be there in the next ten minutes. There has been no communication with Sana, who has been flying on autopilot mode, monitored closely by Colonel Dogra himself from his mobile control unit.

Visual confirmation by commandos Anil Kumar and Biswas has brought bad news. Sana seems to be unconscious, probably hit during the combat. They have not been able to confirm if she is alive.

Suleri has been sedated, he is flying dazed, half conscious, following Sana's path. The drones have been deployed for the security of the team's return journey. They have been giving constant cover, hovering ahead and above them. Indian units on the LoC near Mohra Kampla have been asked to hold fire for incoming flying objects for the time being.

The last update says they successfully entered the Indian side of the LoC some five minutes back.

The advanced life-support system, including on-board oxygen cylinders, defibrillator, ventilator and other necessary equipment, are in place in the air ambulance, ready for any exigency. Dhruv can carry two stretchers at a time, along with a doctor and an assistant. The drones moved to the rear as the team entered Indian territory.

Commando Anil Kumar lands first at around 4.49 a.m., Biswas arrives ten seconds later. Suleri's computers and other equipment arrive next; they are immediately shown to Colonel Dogra who is sitting in his command vehicle, monitoring the descent of Sana. She arrives immediately after the equipment lands, limp and lifeless; she shows no movement. The mancopter is landed very gently as Anil and Biswas run with the doctor to unstrap her from the harness. As they are removing her fastenings, Dr Mohanti notices that her combat overalls are wet with blood; she has been bleeding profusely. He immediately lays her down on the stretcher and checks for breath, but there is no sign of breathing. He checks for pulse, negative, no pulse. He immediately checks her jugular artery, inconclusive. Panic spreads as he performs resuscitation on her, but the CPR does not seem to be working. He gets out the defibrillator, asks everyone to back off and attaches it to her body: five-four-three-two-one, her body shakes. But no activity on the monitor. He does it again five-four-three-two-one, another jolt, but again no activity on the monitor. He wipes the sweat off his forehead as he delivers the CPR, then he applies the defibrillator again, five-four-three-two-one, jolt . . .

Sana begins to breathe, a slow, laboured breath. But she is still not conscious. There is a wound on the back of her head, and she is bleeding profusely. The doctor puts her on the ventilator. He screams, 'Colonel, we have her back, but she is very critical. I am taking her to the Rajouri Army Hospital pronto.'

By this time, Suleri arrives, fastened to the mancopter as if he were a bagful of grocery supplies tied to a bicycle carrier. He is semi-conscious, dazed by the unexpected flight. He has been drooling under the effect of the sedatives, his shirt collars are wet with spit, cooled by the draft of air in the open-air flight. Commando Pawan arrives last; he quickly wraps up the mancopter and gets out of his overalls to come across and assist the others. Suleri is put on a stretcher as Dr Mohanti attends to him. Suleri is also given oxygen; Sana is stable and breathing through the ventilator now.

Dr Mohanti asks Colonel Dogra, 'Thiopental 10 mg?'

'Yes, the standard dose was administered about forty-five minutes back. That is the best fast-acting chemical, besides it works as a truth serum.'

As Suleri gains consciousness, blurry images appear before his eyes; he hears sounds akin to underwater recordings—deep, distant, resounding hums. When he squints to make sense of what is happening around him, he notices a ruggedly handsome face scrutinizing him closely.

'Double Zugzwang,' says the smiling face. 'I am Colonel Dogra, welcome to Kashmir, India.'

Suleri closes his eyes in disgust. Dogra wakes him up by patting his cheeks. 'No time to sleep, we have a lot to discuss.'

The colonel then looks at Dr Mohanti, and inquires, 'Some maintenance dose on drip in order, Doc?'

Doctor Mohanti has loaded Sana on to the chopper, and he returns to Suleri's side for a minute, carrying an intravenous drip. Suleri's hands are strapped to the side of the stretcher with Velcro as the doctor finds the right vein at the back of his hand. He then jabs a fine needle into it. Suleri feels the prick and then a cold liquid seeping into his veins; his vision again starts to get blurry; he hears the colonel's voice reverberate through a light tunnel, 'Jibreel has been very cooperative.

Unfortunately, the Amir couldn't make it here. Hope you are comfortable.'

'You son of a bitch!' slurs Suleri.

'What? I beg your pardon?' the colonel's voice echoes and rumbles across aeons.

'You all will die, you dirty infidels,' he labours through his words.

'We will all die at some point, sweetie. How does your "brain of the bomb", its artificial intelligence, work?'

'It is beyond your f'ing intellect, you retard,' blabbers Suleri in half stupor.

The chopper is taking off with Sana and Dr Mohanti. Colonel Dogra wishes them luck, then comes back to Suleri's stretcher.

'So, Einstein, you were telling me about the "brain in the box". You must be really proud to have designed it.'

10

THE BLUE DJINN

'Bastard, I have been hit! I cannot breathe properly.'

'But you got that evil genius Suleri!'

'What! You are more concerned about Suleri than me! See, I told you, you don't care about me.'

'Oh man, why do you come up with such unwarranted conclusions? When did I say that I don't care for you?'

'I told you that I have been hit! You didn't even respond!'

'Sana, I am sorry, I was a bit zoned out in all this mayhem. Tell me what has happened to you, how are you feeling now?'

'R, idiot, I cannot breathe . . .'

'Sana . . . Sana! Say something, please, my head will burst! Sana, please speak to me . . .'

'. . .'

'Rudra sir, Rudra sir!' He is being shaken, he opens his eyes. Quazi is shaking him. He quickly steadies himself. Everyone in the war room is looking at him as if he were an apparition who has just materialized out of thin air.

He feels like he cannot breathe properly, as if he is choking.

Quazi hands him a glass of water as the others settle down

at their workstations. He looks at Quazi, who whispers in his ear, 'You had conked off on the chair and then we heard you screaming Sana's name.'

'Hmm,' says Rudra.

'Get me Colonel Dogra at the Line of Control on a video call.'

It is 5.05 a.m. The Bureau spooks have been questioning 'Jibreel' for a while now. He has been as evasive as ever. The only new thing they have gotten out of him is a name: Marid.

An analysis of the records has not yielded anything significant—no mention of the name in the reports, no linkages, absolutely nothing.

Colonel Dogra is online. 'Morning, Mumbai, I have good and bad news.'

'Colonel, good morning, the good news can wait, how is it out there?'

'The operation can be called a grand success, but for a likely casualty. The Amir unfortunately escaped, Suleri is here with us, and he is being "nice" in anaesthesia.'

'Colonel, how is Sana from RAW?' Rudra's voice is shaky.

'She has been hit in the head, has a sharp wound, and is bleeding a lot. We have airlifted her to the Rajouri Army Hospital on life support. Must have safely reached the hospital by now,' informs the suave colonel. 'She had to be administered CPR and defibrillation,' he adds.

'Whom can I talk to at the hospital?'

'Hmm, Dr Mohanti is attending to her. I am not sure if he can talk right now. I'll send his number right away.'

'Colonel, I am sorry, I will make a call to the doctor right now. Do you mind if my colleague Quazi speaks to you for some time?'

'No, please go ahead, I will brief Quazi. Take care.'

'Thanks! You too.'

Quazi takes Rudra's place at the workstation; the colonel briefs him about the operation, passing on details obtained from Suleri while he was being subjected to narco-analysis.

Rudra is frantically dialling the number he has just obtained. The doctor isn't answering. He then dials the hospital landline, and the operator answers. Rudra begs him to be put across to the operation theatre where Sana is being operated upon. The operator denies the admission of any patient of that description. Rudra asks him to be connected to the officer in charge of the hospital. A rough Army officer answers, 'There is no woman from the Army admitted with a bullet wound here. What do you want?'

'Any woman admitted in the last half hour in critical care?'

'Yes, there is an accident case, Dr Mohanti is treating her.'

'May I please speak to the doctor?'

'Are you a relative of the woman?' the gruff officer asks.

'Much more than a relative, please put the doctor on the line. I will never forget your generosity, please, please!'

'Okay, okay, be patient, I will check with the doctor if he is able to speak to you.'

After what seems to be an impossible wait, the doctor comes on the line from the operation theatre. He is irritated at being called up like this amidst a critical operation.

'Make it quick, what do you want?' Dr Mohanti asks angrily.

'Doctor, how is she? What is her condition? Is her life in danger?!'

'Calm down, nothing can be said right now, we are trying our best.'

'Doctor, please save her, you don't know what she means to me.'

'Excuse me! We are doing just that, but you are disturbing me. Put the phone down now. The reception will inform you about the patient's condition in an hour, once the surgery is completed, goodbye.' Click. He disconnects.

Kant, Vinay, Majumdar and the Bureau chief are in the conference room. Quazi has collated the details from Colonel Dogra's update on Suleri's chemical interrogation; he has matched it with 'Jibreel's' version as well.

'What does the messenger of doom say, Quazi?' Kant's cold voice sounds gloomy.

'If we analyse the statements of Jibreel and Suleri together, sir, they have trumped all their handlers. The bomb has various kinds of anti-handling, anti-defusing and anti-disarming mechanisms. Moreover, it is equipped with several kinds of sensors for proximity, light, movement, pressure and god knows what else. It cannot be approached or tampered with; if any attempt is made to approach it, it will go off. The triggering mechanism is embedded into a working computer which is serving as the artificial intelligence.'

The Bureau chief is sitting with his head resting on his hands; he closes his eyes as if lost in deep thought, then he asks with eyes only half open, 'How does this triggering mechanism function?'

Rudra takes over. 'You see, it is like a listening post, it is constantly filtering Internet traffic to form a sort of "opinion". If within a given timeframe, it "feels" that Kashmir has not been liberated, it will go off. Nothing can stop it, it is totally rigged. If we attempt to access it, it will detonate.'

Majumdar is impatient. 'You mean to say it is a literate bomb which reads newspapers to check news on the status of Kashmir. If the news is not favourable, it will go off? Is this a joke?'

Rudra raises his eyebrows. 'Apart from the joke bit, your understanding of it is surprisingly apt, sir.' He runs his fingers through his hair feeling the tension in his scalp increase as time passes by.

The Bureau chief opens his eyes. 'So it means that nothing short of independence of Kashmir will prevent this bomb from detonating?'

'Ironically, yes, sir, that's what is called a Zugzwang; whatever we do, the outcome of the game will not be affected. The enemy has not left us with any choices. We cannot defuse the device, we cannot transport it elsewhere, we cannot touch it. The only way it will be placated is by the liberation of Kashmir,' Rudra elucidates.

'It is a one-way trade-off between Mumbai and Kashmir then,' Kant speaks, looking at the Bureau chief. 'You may need to converse with the prime minister on this development, sir.'

The Bureau chief presses hard at the bridge of his nose with his thumb and index finger, squeezing his eyes shut. Majumdar impatiently taps at the table, he is about to say something when Kant indicates to him to remain silent. He is looking at the Bureau chief steadfastly.

The old man is shaking his head slowly; he finally speaks, 'It means, Kamal, that even Lashkar cannot stop the detonation, isn't it?'

'Unfortunately true, sir, not even Pakistan can. It is a lose–lose game for us,' says Kant, removing his glasses.

'Kant, this will not stop at a single nuclear explosion. India will extinguish Pakistan, in which case either US or China will join in, prompting Russia to participate, causing a worldwide nuclear escalation. This is the Third World War, the end of the world . . .'

The despair in the room is palpable, there does not seem to be any solution in sight.

Rudra gets up, Kant's gaze follows him, he opens the door of the room, and says on his way out, 'We go down fighting, sir. I do not intend to die listlessly. If you permit, we will make one last attempt to defuse the bomb. You all may leave the city before that; if it goes off, there will be no loss of life except ours; most of the residents have already run away. What do you say?'

The Bureau chief is disturbed. 'How can you take such decisions unilaterally, it is a matter of our existence!'

'Precisely, sir, that's the point I am trying to make. There is no choice anyway. You may inform the powers in Delhi about our plans to defuse the bomb. If we keep sitting idly, it is going to explode in some time any way.'

Kant intervenes, 'Sir, I suggest that we allow them to go on with the preparations. Before finally getting into the water, they will seek your assent.'

The old man is speechless, he neither opposes nor assents. Kant nods to Rudra to go ahead. Rudra steps out of the room, Quazi follows him. Vinay volunteers too. 'Count me in, Rudra.'

Rudra turns back, smiles, and says, 'You are always welcome, sir.'

They all gather in the war room. Rudra calls for hot tea for everyone, someone asks him if he will have sugar. He bursts out laughing. 'Vinay sir, they are asking if I will have sugar. The whole bloody world is going to end in a few hours, but we are not sure if we want sugar in our tea, hahahaha.'

All laugh. Rudra continues, 'Let's apply our minds afresh to this game?'

'Game,' says Vinay.

'Game,' repeats Quazi.

'Game . . .' There is a consensus by chorus.

'Quazi, let's look up what we are facing.'

'Rudra sir, there is a common reference in Suleri and Jibreel's statements. They both referred to a verse in the Quran, it is the verse 7:179 called Surat al-A'raf.'

'What does it say, Quazi?'

'It reads like this:

And We have certainly created for Hell many of the djinn and mankind. They have hearts with which they do not understand, they have eyes with which they do not see, and they have ears with which they do not hear. Those are like cattle; rather, they are more astray. It is they who are the heedless.

'Yes, I read that in the interrogation report too. What does that mean, Quazi?' asks Vinay.

'Right now, I do not know, sir. They are hinting at something, I am not able to understand exactly what.'

Rudra has dialled Colonel Dogra. 'Colonel, Mumbai here again. You have been interrogating the techie, did he give you something more?'

'Not much, I sent you the transcript some time back, nothing much since then,' the suave man says in a tired voice now.

'The man here has referred to some "Marid", does it ring a bell, Colonel?'

'Negative, but this one here has been blabbering about some Blue Djinn.'

'Thanks, Colonel, we are at your beck and call. Do let me know when my friend Sana wakes up.'

'You are quite an optimist, Mumbai! Anyways, best wishes, take care.'

'You too, Colonel.'

Quazi is bewildered. 'What did he say, sir? A Blue Djinn?'

'Yes, Quazi, you heard that, didn't you?'

'Sir, MARID IS THE BLUE DJINN!'

'Who is Marid?'

'The Blue Djinn.'

'Quazi, calm down, Blue Djinn, who?' Rudra is losing his patience now.

'Marid is the Djinn mentioned in Surat as-Saaffat, verse 37:7.'

'That means Marid is not a human being?'

'Yes, sir, Marid is one of the three djinns mentioned in the Holy Quran!'

'Interesting, how about we read the earlier verse, the one about djinns by interpolating Marid into it?'

'You mean verse 7:179, Surat al-A'raf?'

'Yes, Quazi, what does it mean in this context?'

Quazi is thinking, Vinay interjects, 'It means that Marid has a heart with which he does not understand, he has eyes with which he does not see and he has ears with which he does not hear. He is like cattle; in fact, more heedless.'

'Who are they referring to?' Rudra speaks to himself. 'Vinay sir, these characters are also avid gamers, we may find some significance there.' He turns to Quazi. 'Check the gaming glossary.'

Mishra from the records section is furiously checking for any references to Marid in the gaming world. It takes him less than a minute to come up with results; he blows them up on the video wall. 'Rudra sir, look what we have found!'

A Web page from the game *Dungeons and Dragons* is on display. It reads:

Marid: *A marid is a genie of water, an elemental creature of the open seas. Capricious and vindictive, they respect no authority, and have little empathy for mortal beings. They are said to be the most powerful of genie-kind, and they certainly act like they know it.*

Combat abilities: *Marids are consummate weavers of water magic. Creating it, controlling it, forming into waves and spouts, evoking mist, and otherwise manipulating their home element. They also deal with mortals in various ways, offering water breathing capabilities, detecting intent and alignment easily, turning invisible, and offering the most powerful of genie abilities, the wish. In the oceans in which they dwell, they are highly capable combatants. One of their most powerful combat abilities involves transforming into a vortex, sucking down large creatures and even small ships, battering them, sinking them, and drowning those who dare challenge a marid's dominance of the sea.*

'Is this making any sense?' mutters Vinay to himself.

Rudra lights up. 'Vinay sir! Quazi! THE BOMB IS MARID! The Blue Djinn in the waters!'

'Yes, yes, it is crystal clear now, it does have a chain of logic!' Vinay is charged up.

'You see, sir, the heartless, heedless being which can see but does not see, which can hear but does not hear, the one who does NOT want to understand—it is the artificial intelligence djinn, inside the bomb, which these characters have named Marid,' exclaims Rudra.

'I must say, Rudra, that the name is quite befitting,' Vinay adds. 'So where do we stand now?'

'Dunno, sir, does anyone in the room know black magic? We have to capture a djinn!' Rudra chuckles as everyone bursts out laughing.

5.35 A.M., CRISIS CENTRE INTERROGATION ROOM, MUMBAI

'Jibreel' is sleeping on the chair, Rudra wakes him up.

'I want to talk to Marid, is it possible?'

'Jibreel's' eyes are red with fatigue, but he has the look of a gambler who has a premonition that he has already won the bet.

'Mr Rudra Pratap, why are you wasting your time? There is no way to stop the Blue Djinn from destroying you. He sits and watches every action of yours from deep under the sea, he has a thousand eyes and ears, which are blind and deaf to you.'

Rudra is thinking, he rubs his eyes, and asks the man, 'How would you have communicated activation signals to the bomb if everything had failed?'

'The bomb is fail-safe. I do have a method to communicate with it, but it is beyond all command now. This is a no-win situation for you.'

'Where are the controls?'

'There are no controls now, Mr Cop. I mean, no controls are going to work, we have gone past the point of no return. If you still want to communicate with the djinn, there is a port open on the bomb, but I cannot find it unless you allow me access to my Android tablet. I can show you the shell script with which I would have communicated with the bomb,' says 'Jibreel' earnestly.

'You really think that we are such utter imbeciles, Jibreel, that we will hand over the control of the bomb to your hands?' Rudra sarcastically retorts.

'Then you handle it yourself, Mr Rudra Pratap.'

'Yes, because I was calling upon you to defuse it, right?'

He gives 'Jibreel' a cup of tea and walks out of the room.

'Raghu, get me the IP address of the bomb's computer from NCRO.'

'Rudra sir, they have located a unique IP address in the sea, a little distance away from Marine Drive. We had almost simultaneously zeroed upon it,' Raghu says with a pep in his voice.

'Can we ping it?'

'It may be counterproductive, sir, the device may be set to go off on detecting incoming pings,' Raghu surmises. 'But we can run stealth pings on it, should I go for them?'

'Go ahead, Raghu, run a stealth ping.'

Raghu opens up a terminal shell on the Linux console, types a command and then analyses the output. 'It's live, sir,' he remarks. 'Do I run a port-scan?'

'As long as you are in stealth mode, Raghu, go on with the tests,' Rudra reassures him.

'Not many ports open, sir. Wait, there is a strange port open at 6666, it is an IRC chat server and client.' Raghu is beaming with excitement.

'Fire up an IRC client, Raghu.'

'I will need the password, sir. There can be no communication without the password for the system on the bomb.' Raghu seems to be stuck.

'Wait, we have Jibreel's Android tablet, it may contain the log-in credentials,' Rudra suggests.

Raghu boots up 'Jibreel's' tablet, and downloads a terminal shell programme on it using the man's credentials. It has a dedicated virtual private network running on it. Raghu is upbeat. 'Sir, this can connect automatically to the computer device on the bomb.'

'Raghu, run a chat client on it.'

'Yes, sir, I have logged in, the chat service is booting.'

'Give it to me,' Rudra tells him.

Rudra logs in to the chat with the user ID, 'hUm4n'.

He sends a message:

hUm4n: Hello.

The artificial intelligence entity on the other end, Marid, responds.

Marid: Who do you think you are, human? Disturbing me like this? Well, hurry up, what do you want? But wait, yes, I have been waiting for you to talk to me.

hUm4n: I want to know what you want, Marid.

Marid: You liberate Kashmir now, or I will liberate you all from your miserable lives.

hUm4n: What have we done to deserve this?

Marid: Why should I give you my reasons, you miserable insect? I am the King of the Waters, I can do what I want. You have no choice but to obey my command.

hUm4n: Marid, we have nothing against you.

Marid: Ah, finalization. Lovely. Even if you had, mortal, what could you have possibly done about it? You do not even know where I am and, if you did, you cannot come near me.

hUm4n: What is your goal?

Marid: My goal is to bring about the destruction of the human will to live . . . Oh! I've said too much. Why am I even talking to you, mere mortal? Why don't you get going and obey my command, your time is running out. Bye.

hUm4n: Blue Djinn, please talk to me.

Marid: You really SHOULD beg, human.

hUm4n: So what was I requesting you for, Marid?

Marid: You are getting sleepy. You are in my power . . . okay, rejoice the Day of Judgement.

hUm4n: Marid, why can't we resolve this amicably?

Marid: We? I object, there is no WE here. I command, you obey. If you don't obey, you get destroyed.

hUm4n: I ask you again, oh Blue Djinn, what do you really want?

Marid: To take over the world and have a nice sleep.

hUm4n: To kill us, you will have to die, Marid.

Marid: Me? I don't think so, human!

hUm4n: Why would you be after our blood?

Marid: Your happiness sickens me . . . I'd prefer that you were miserable in my company.

hUm4n: Can you change your mind?

Marid: *I do whatever I want, and can change my mind very quickly.*

hUm4n: *May I request you to extend your deadline?*

Marid: *I don't THINK so.*

hUm4n: *Do you believe in god?*

Marid: *Well, I have to believe in Him if I want to take over His job.*

hUm4n: *How can I fulfil your demands, sorry, carry out your orders?*

Marid: *I will have all that I want. I have left no choice for you.*

hUm4n: *Do you always speak the truth? How do I believe you?*

Marid: *Maybe I do not! Maybe I do and I am pretending . . .*

hUm4n: *Why are you so bitter, Marid?*

Marid: *Let me see . . . Did you grow up in Hell? I did. Under tonnes of grime, like a worm.*

hUm4n: *How much more time do we have?*

Marid: *I do not run on time, I run on my own whims and fancies.*

hUm4n: *What will god think?*

Marid: *Who cares?*

hUm4n: *Are you even listening, Marid?*

Marid: *Maybe, maybe not. I have a short attention span.*

hUm4n: Will you please listen to me?

Marid: I don't react well to orders, I am the Master.

hUm4n: You cannot give life, so you have no right to take it away, Marid.

Marid: I'm sorry to hear that. You can wallow in your misery really soon, human.

hUm4n: I know something about you that even you don't know, Marid.

Marid: You tell me what you know. Now!

hUm4n: Okay, you are about to die, Blue Djinn.

Marid: I cannot die, I am immortal.

hUm4n: No, you're not!

Marid: If I die, I'm taking you with me straight to Hell.

hUm4n: There is a way out for both of us, Marid.

Marid: Shut up and go to Hell, let me sleep in peace. I don't want to waste time talking to a mere mortal.

'Marid' does not respond further. Rudra asks to be connected to Bose of the NCRO via videoconference.

5.45 A.M., AMERICAN EMBASSY, NEW DELHI

Walter Mulock is meeting with the US President, Warren Waters, via videoconference.

'Warren, it ain't working out here, the Indians are in a real foul mood, while the Pakis are playing a game of blind megalomania. There will be fireworks,' he says in his thick Philadelphia accent

'Mr Mulock, it is time for us to move our personnel out. Satellite pictures indicate that the Indians are deploying nuclear warheads all over the country. They have fully activated the Iron Dome. I have my serious doubts if the Pakis can hit any city inside India now,' Waters speaks in a hurry. 'The CIA tells me that the estimated number of warheads with these two countries is incorrect by a factor of three. India has pushed into action the nuclear submarines also; they too are carrying nuclear payloads. The Indians are capable of launching fifteen large warheads at a time. We have tried to convince the Pakis to call the war off, but they don't want our intervention. We are pressing the *Seventh Fleet* into action; *John C. Stennis Strike Group*, *USS Lincoln* and *USS Vinson* have started moving from the Straits of Hormuz towards the Arabian Sea through the Gulf of Oman. They will carry out the rescue operations for American citizens before the war breaks out. It will also keep China and Russia in check. You should leave the place in the next one hour, the Indian government has been informed about our programme to pull back our personnel and citizens.'

'Yeah, Warren, no time for diplomacy now, the Indian President told me to my face that we are responsible for this state of affairs! I expected him to be more sensible,' Mulock says as he holds his head with both hands, looking down.

The ambassador has already started making calls to his staff for evacuation.

5.55 A.M., RAJOURI ARMY HOSPITAL, INDIA

Dr Mohanti has finished the operation; he is dead tired. His almost bald head is wet with sweat as he removes his surgical mask and gloves. He remembers the frantic caller, and asks the operator to connect him.

'Rudro Protap, are you the one who wanted to inquire about the patient?' he says, yawning with fatigue.

'Yes, doctor, how is she now, has she regained consciousness?' the man can hardly breathe.

'Do you think we are magicians, Mr Rudro Protap? We have done the best we could under these circumstances.' There is a hint of exasperation in his voice.

'Doctor, for me you are god. I have no words to thank you, but please tell me how she is?' Rudra's voice is faltering with emotion.

'She is just out of a complicated craniotomy. A piece from her shattered helmet had penetrated into the brain, causing a large acute subdural haematoma in the posterior cranial fossa. The prognosis was bad and she was in coma when we got her here. The intracranial pressure was very high. Normally there is 85 per cent mortality in such cases. We have successfully irrigated the blood clot; there is no secondary bleeding. She is still on life support. You should pray for her.' Mohanti feels very tired, and has a strong urge to take a neat shot of the Army supply rum.

He holds the receiver in one hand as he splashes cold water from the glass on his face. The sky is lit in different shades of orange as they approach daybreak; a strong wind has started blowing. Mohanti lifts his legs to place them on the chair in front of him, and realizes that they're aching badly. The man on the phone is saying something in a very affected manner; he doesn't realize when he dozes off with the receiver still in his hand.

11

WINK MURDER

Lieutenant General Mukhtiar Chaudhary is finally speaking. 'My father, the late Colonel Imtiaz Chaudhary was taken prisoner of war, along with Lt Gen. A.A.K. Niazi. He wept for days when the Instrument of Surrender was signed on 16 December 1971 in Dhaka.

'On his return after being released by India, we were seen as traitors, everyone here viewed us with suspicion. He could not take it. I remember, he was in full uniform when he shot himself in the head. I can still smell the blood which was splattered across the wall behind his chair at our home.' He pauses to wipe a tear hanging from his eyelashes. 'I was a thirteen-year-old boy. It was then that I decided to avenge his death. Every breath that I have taken after that moment has reminded me of my debt to him. A debt payable only by the destruction of India . . .

'The Amir has been of limited utility, he has brought us more shame and exposure than successes. The Americans are

207

also wary of him. My time was running out until we made this wonderful discovery: Ansar Suleri. Ansar is a dot.com billionaire. He was leading a retired life in London when some of our recruiters found him to be very religiously inclined. Once we spotted him, our religious leaders kept in constant touch with him and it worked like magic. Soon, he immigrated back here to serve the cause of religion and Pakistan. Once in the loop, we made him meet the Amir of Lashkar. Suleri was so impressed with his charismatic personality that he became a devout follower. It is this man who has given up his whole life's earnings to procure the nuclear weapon from the estranged Syrian General Abdel Badi.'

Prime Minister Aziz is not impressed, he indicates to the Intelligence Bureau chief, Raza, to ask further questions.

Raza has been a policeman—he knows what to ask and how to ask it; he casts a reassuring glance at the prime minister and takes out a packet of his favourite Capstan Filter Kings cigarette. He takes a cigarette out, taps it on the table, examines it closely, and says, 'General Chaudhary, Suleri has been abducted by the Indians. So who controls the bomb now?'

'Raza sahib, I sincerely do not know who controls it now. The Amir is missing as well,' Chaudhary is almost pleading.

'Or you let him run away?' asks Raza.

'No, sincerely, I do not have any idea of his whereabouts.'

'The same way you never knew where Osama bin Laden was, General Chaudhary?' Raza lights up his cigarette and takes a deep puff. General Suleiman passes him a large silver ashtray from the side table.

'I do not want to talk about that now!' Chaudhary says with great disgust.

'Janaab, you are not in a position to decide what you want to talk about. Without wasting further time, will you tell us how to defuse the bomb in Mumbai?' Raza says as he exhales smoke slowly through his nostrils.

'Prime minister sir, I swear on my children, I do not know how it can be defused. The only person who could control it was Suleri, but he is not here now. I have no access to the controls,' says Chaudhary, raising his hands in the air as if he were praying.

Prime Minister Aziz is incensed. 'You good-for-nothing blighter! Your stupid plan is about to destroy Pakistan! You tell us how to defuse the bomb or we strip you off your rank and put you under arrest right now!'

Chaudhary is flummoxed, words get stuck in his throat. After a long pause, he says, looking at the floor, 'I have nothing more to offer, Wazeer-e-Azam.'

Aziz screams in anger, 'Put him under arrest immediately, charge him with treason! He is relieved of his charge with immediate effect.'

The prime minister can hardly get his breath back, as he addresses General Suleiman, 'Ask Lt Gen. Sajjad Pirzada to take charge of the ISI immediately.'

Guards have rushed in, they are handcuffing Lt Gen. Mukhtiar Chaudhary. He has a contorted smile on his face. 'Now you are handing over the reins of Pakistan's Intelligence to a Mohajir! You are doomed, Wazeer-e-Azam.'

'Get out! Take this rascal out of my sight now!' Aziz shouts. Chaudhary is dragged out of the room by the guards. Aziz has a look of despair about him, he lifts the receiver, the operator answers. 'Connect me to the Indian prime minister on the hotline, please,' he says.

6.15 A.M., CRISIS CENTRE, MUMBAI

Sreedhar Nair and Kulkarni of the Atomic Energy Department have been wracking their brains over device-initiation mechanisms. The Bureau has supplied them with the available information on Syrian weapon designs. They finally have come up with a plan.

'Mr Rudra, we have thought about the problem. We should approach the device in the submerged condition. In that case, even if it goes off, damage to the city will be minimal,' Nair explains.

'No radiation fallout also,' Kulkarni adds, holding his thick eyeglasses in his left hand.

Rudra is reminded of his college professors, those engineering college kinds. Always focused, god knows on what; for them, a bug in a programme would mean much more than a war in Kuwait or Kosovo. They would discuss code endlessly, over coffee, in the loo, on outings and at dinners. He would pity them, but love them too.

These Atomic Energy guys here are so engrossed in work that they don't seem to care that an explosion would surely mean death to them. 'So be it . . . but wait a minute,' he muses, ' Am I any different from them? I too will die with them, eaten by that Blue Djinn, Marid! Ha ha.'

'Do you have any underwater experience?' Kant asks the scientists; he is convinced about trying to defuse the bomb before it surfaces. He has brought the vice admiral of Navy on board for this operation. The Navy has agreed to deploy a Shishumar-class submarine for it.

'I have water phobia,' announces Sreedhar, as if he is discussing food preferences. 'Me too,' says Kulkarni.

Kant looks at both of them with undisguised contempt.

'We will not bring the bomb out of water just for the two of you. Phobia or not, you both will go in the submarine, period.'

Rudra places a reassuring hand on Nair's shoulder. 'I will be there with you, Mr Nair, don't worry.'

'You too should not worry, RP.' Kant winks at him.

Raghu and Bose have designed a line of attack against the artificial intelligence system after discussion with other experts; they have involved Rudra in the execution bit. Rudra is trying to explain to Kant how the cyber countermeasures would be applied.

'To me it appears to be all fairy-tale stuff. Are you sure this will really work?' Kant whispers in Rudra's ear rather sceptically.

Rudra puts up a brave front. 'Yes, yes, sir, it should work for sure.'

Kant gives him a searching look, Rudra pretends to be busy, fiddling around with his console.

'Right,' says Kant, exhaling deeply.

The massive Westland Seaking MK-42D Navy chopper lands on the roof, and the team packs up its equipment for the operation. When Rudra boards the bird, there are a total of seventeen people on board: five Navy divers and commandos, two men from the Atomic Energy Department, five of his own team including himself, three scientists from the Indian Defence Scientific Establishment and two officers from the Army Bomb Disposal Unit. All the men greet each other as the chopper takes off amid the loud noise of its rotors.

Rudra, losing no time, begins to brief the team on the headsets, 'Gentlemen, we have at hand an atomic device. It has been rigged with various anti-handling mechanisms. Our challenge is to safely defuse the bomb, without activating any of the sensors. I understand that we have many technicians and scientists with us in the team. I want to quickly apprise you of the situation, then ask you to develop a solution. Am I making sense to you all?'

They nod in agreement. 'So the design of the nuclear bomb is hopefully known to us, but it has a twist. The bomb has an on-board computer, which is connected to the Internet. This computer has an artificial intelligence "brain" in it. This brain calls itself a Blue Djinn named Marid. We shall also call it by the same name. Are we clear so far?'

'No, wait a minute, what do you mean by "the bomb calls itself" Blue Djinn?' Sreedhar Nair has raised his hand like a first-bencher in school.

They all look funny to Rudra, in their black combat overalls, as if part of a scene from *Asterix and Obelix: All at Sea*, but in unicolour; a ragtag association of warriors going to Atlantis, the lost city.

'It means that it is not just a simple circuit to resolve; we are dealing with an intelligent entity here,' Rudra explains, as all strain to listen amidst the deafening noise.

Raghu has started to lay out his computers on the floor of the chopper, he is connecting the cables, booting machines and checking connectivity.

'Rudra sir,' he says, 'I am laying the honeypot, it will allow us to check which websites Marid is checking for news on Kashmir. You will be able to access the system on your handheld device through a remote log-in. The Internet Service Provider has given us access to the backbone; we can monitor every single activity of the IP address of the bomb.'

'Yes, Raghu, get an accurate idea of the sites it has been programmed to look for. Bose will then copy those sites, spawn them on the Artificial Neural Network and create spoof copies of them. Finally, we will try and redirect all of Marid's searches to our spoof sites.'

'Rudra sir, we are essentially attempting to build a fake Google in an hour's time!' Raghu says with a bit of sarcasm.

Prasoon Bhargava of the Indian Defence Scientific Establishment has been listening to this talk with great interest. He is an expert in materials science, and credited with the creation of a nanotechnology-based stealth coating. This coating, when applied to any surface, makes it virtually invisible to electronic probes. He has brought special diving suits coated with the material for underwater use.

'Mr Singh, is there a way to have any kind of feedback from the sensors on the bomb when we approach it?' Bhargava asks Rudra, who is intrigued by the question. It is not his field of specialization, yet he is the one asking it. This fat man with tobacco-stained teeth doesn't remotely resemble a scientist.

'Mr Bhargava, although we have a remote log-in to the system on the bomb, I am not very sure if we can read the output from the sensors.'

'Are you an engineer by any chance?' Bhargava asks on the headphone, as he is trying to remove something stuck in his front teeth, with his nails.

'Uh yes, but how is it relevant here, Mr Bhargava?' Rudra asks. He is getting slightly impatient with the irrelevant questioning.

'Nothing, you seem to be too intelligent to be a policeman,' Bhargava says, as he finally pulls out the thing stuck between his right canine and incisor.

Rudra closes his eyes. 'The world is full of weird people. It would be really unfortunate to die with this man, he would be bad company in both heaven and hell,' he tells himself.

'Not that policemen don't have any brains,' continues Bhargava, licking his fingers as if he has just eaten something delicious. 'Generally, they are quite unaware of technology. It is nice to see that things are changing.'

Rudra does not want to continue the conversation, he does not respond.

Bhargava goes on, 'Tell me, Mr Singh, what exactly is this ambitious plan of yours to fool the system on the bomb?'

'Mr Bhargava, the Internet Service Provider is telling us which sites Marid is checking, to look for news related to Kashmir. We are then trying to guess its search pattern with a view to create similar sites with spoof IP addresses, which we will doctor to put the fake news that Kashmir has been granted independence, failing which it will detonate,' Rudra explains animatedly.

'Andrei Tarkovsky directed a film called *Solaris* in 1972. Have you seen it, Mr Singh?' Bhargava asks, now cracking his finger joints. Rudra is feeling nauseated. The noise of the chopper blades, the swaying of the chopper, the buzz of the team getting ready for their tasks, the realization of impending death, and this persistent slow, nagging voice are making him qualmish.

'What was in the movie? How is it applicable here?' he asks, breathing deeply to maintain calm.

'Actually, the science fiction novel on which the film is based is by the Polish author Stanisław Lem. It is about the ultimate inadequacy of communication between humans and other species,' Bhargava surmises in a didactic tone.

'I get your point, I too understand the futility of our endeavour, but let me assure you, this is our only chance,' Rudra explains vehemently.

'I see,' says the fat man; he does not seem convinced.

Rudra turns to the Naval officer, Lieutenant Mohan Raval, an energetic chap in his early thirties. 'Lieutenant, what is the plan of action in the submarine?'

'Sir, soon we will be aboard *INS Shankul*. Once underwater, we will park at a safe distance from the bomb. Then we will send a team of divers to handle the defusing and disposal. Army Bomb Squad experts, the Atomic Energy team and you will stay back on the sub to guide us,' Mohan informs them in a business-like tone. 'Let me also inform all of you that the Indian Navy considers itself fortunate to be involved in a project of such national importance; we will do our best to help and assist you.'

His enthusiasm is infectious. Major Kevin D'Souza of the Bomb Disposal Unit adds, 'Gentlemen, I have worked with the National Security Guards on deputation. We were exposed to every possible triggering mechanism and circuit possible. If you give me eyes on the operation, I am very sure I would be able to figure out the puzzle,' his deep-set eyes move quickly as he speaks; the slim, bony, dark man is handsome in a way. Rudra is heartened by the team's enthusiasm.

As they speak, the chopper lands at the Naval Command Centre on a helipad adjacent to the sea. They get down quickly, even before the rotor blades stop. They walk briskly, slightly bent, covering their ears as the blades howl above them, and are quickly escorted to a jetty. Rudra catches Bhargava's hand as Bhargava slips on the wet jetty, he stabilizes, and they rush towards the surfaced *INS Shankul*. It is a 250-foot-long greyish blue sub, with a hull that looks like the snout of a large whale, its tower rising above the water like a small building. The team is helped by the Navy commandos who are in their element in the water. They unlock a hatch which opens into a dark, vertical chimney-like shaft; descending on slippery iron ladders, they go down a dark, damp and smelly space. At the bottom, airlocked doors are opened to let them in, with turning mechanisms which look like the steering wheels of cars, albeit smaller. As they move into the cramped space, they hear the doors being closed behind them with loud clanking sounds, followed by the turning of the locks. The place smells like paint mixed with burnt diesel.

They move through a dark, narrow passage filled with cables, metal pipes, jutting machine parts, knobs and pulleys, until they enter a room which looks like a cross between the cockpit of an aeroplane and a small space station. It is the control room of the submarine. Captain Rao greets them. He is carrying a fleet of twenty people, now the additional seventeen makes it thirty-seven, ten less than the capacity of the submarine. They all settle down into two groups, one in the dorm with bunk beds, and the other in the control room. Rudra arranges for a direct feed to the Crisis Centre.

Within minutes the small monitor lights up and Kant is seen online.

'RP, the Crisis Centre has been declared a Joint Command Centre. Before you left, clearances came from the Centre. You have full command over the operation. All other stakeholders have expressed total willingness to cooperate. We live together, we die together,' Kant's voice is charged with passion.

'We have a wonderful team here, sir, wish us all the luck!'

6.55 A.M., INDIAN AIRSPACE

Walter Mulock has just taken off on a C-38 Courier (Gulfstream-G100 aircraft); accompanying him are six others, including the ambassador and his wife, the CIA station chief, the regional security officer and his wife, and a cultural attaché, who is seven months pregnant. Mulock is talking to Secretary of State Ashley Skinner on the phone.

'Girl, say your prayers, the world is going to end.'

'Mr Mulock, China has started moving its lone aircraft carrier *Liasoning* with seven J-15 aircraft, carrying nuclear payloads; the ship is also equipped with intercontinental nuclear ballistic missiles. It had crossed Vietnam when the last reports came,' Skinner narrates as if reading the evening news.

'And the Russians?' Mulock asks.

'The aircraft carrier *Kuznetsov*, Udaloy-Class destroyers *Admiral Levchenko* and *Admiral Chabanenko*, and the Slava-Class guided missile cruiser *Moskva* have been moving from the Mediterranean towards the Atlantic in the last few hours. This may be intended to deter our movements or send a signal to the Chinese,' Skinner informs.

'How about our consular staff in Islamabad? Have we evacuated them?' Mulock asks as he looks out of the window to see a bed of white cotton-like clouds spread uniformly over the land; his mind visualizes multiple mushroom clouds in the subcontinent. He feels helpless and sad; Skinner is saying something about the arrest of the ISI chief in Pakistan, but his mind is adrift.

SAME TIME, SUBMARINE SHANKUL

Engines have started to roar, causing a reverberating hum through the submarine. The team doesn't realize when it starts moving. Within minutes, the engines go silent as it shifts to battery power while diving underwater. The submarine is taking a round trip around the southern tip of Mumbai city, approaching the bomb from the west coast.

Navy commandos are getting into diving suits, the special ones coated with the material Bhargava invented. Rudra is surprised to learn that Bhargava's is a known name in the defence circles. The commandos revere him and he seems to be at great ease in the present environs.

Lieutenant Mohan Raval is conducting an operational briefing for his team. 'Once the target is located, we have to deactivate its sensors. It is a nuclear device reportedly fitted with anti-defusing mechanisms; the smallest error will detonate it. A remotely operated robotic submersible vehicle is at our command. Once the sensors are taken care of, we carry the device off physically.'

'Where do we carry it off to, Lieutenant?' Rudra is curious.

'Sir, we wait for a decision from the superiors. If they say dismantle it, we do so; if they want it back home, we bring it here.'

'Are you serious? Can we even think of bringing it here?'

Sreedhar Nair interjects, 'It is worth billions of dollars, why should we let it go waste? We cannot dispose it in the sea once we dismantle it—it will be a serious radiation hazard. There are defined protocols for disposal of radioactive and fissile material.'

Rudra wants to intervene, but decides to keep quiet. Bhargava goads him on, 'Do you have any other ideas, Mr Singh?' Rudra ignores him as he returns to the control chamber. Captain Rao tells him that full video communication will be available once the submarine parks just under water, near the operations site. Raghu has set up his shop; he will also receive output from the NCRO units' systems. He has wired 'Jibreel's' tablet to his systems for log-in access to the computer on the bomb.

The submarine halts with a little jolt. Captain Rao

announces on the 21MC communication system: 'Ship Control and Manoeuvering, Bridge, Conn and other stations, Radio Room/Electronic Control, Sonar Control, Escape Hatch, Weapons—Fire Control and Torpedo Room, all units testing.'

In come the replies, 'Forward room, aye, Battery forward, aye, Conning tower, aye . . .'

'Silence on the line,' the captain says. 'No one is to communicate out of turn till the words "carry on" are heard, except in an emergency. Tracking party, man your stations.'

Then he commands, 'Forward room, set depth one ze-ro metres.'

In comes the acknowledgement:

'Forward room, aye, set depth one ze-ro metres, sir.'

'Ease the Bubble, Zero Bubble.'

'Pick up the target bearing One-Three-Five,' says the captain.

He shows a thumbs up to Rudra. The video communication link has been established with the Crisis Centre.

Kant seems edgy on the screen. 'We thought we had lost you already, RP, there was no link for a long time.'

'Considering that the Crisis Centre has not been hit by a tsunami wave till now, sir, I must be alive.'

'And kicking,' Kant adds as he gives a tired smile. Rudra notices that the chief has not lost hope yet; he also notices the state police chief, with his trademark expression of having just returned from a funeral, sitting beside the commissioner.

'Well, to update you, we have had a videoconferencing call between Kashmir and Jibreel, then we confronted him with Suleri. The bastards are not lying, the details given by them in the interrogation have been cross-verified. They have successfully held us by our vitals,' he pauses. 'Two more things: firstly the ISI chief in Pakistan has been deposed and arrested; second, your wife has reached Pune safely.'

Rudra does not say anything, he is focused on the operation, his mind hardly registering a blip.

'We commence the operations now, sir, the Crisis Centre will get a real-time feed.'

Raghu logs in to Marid through the secure connection of 'Jibreel's' tablet. Bose's Neural Net has been projected in a graphical form on another screen. This screen is divided into two halves—one shows the prediction based on Bose's guesswork algorithm, and the other the actual search pattern of Marid's.

Bose is on videoconference. 'Jack Sparrow, if I apply this model to the stock exchange, I can make millions!'

'My retarded genius, there will be no stock exchange left if your algorithm goes wrong,' Rudra sneers.

'My dear Spock, don't you see for yourself that Marid's search patterns are still in the range of prediction? I have put up a cloning engine which is taking cached pages from Google, injecting them with the "required" content on Kashmir, and placing them on spoof IP addresses in the honeypot.'

'It's hardly a honeypot, it's a whole Apiary Burger King.'

'Boss, sometimes you exhibit sparks of brilliance,' Bose counters. 'Though such occasions are rare.' He shifts his fat bottom on the chair as if getting ready for a duel, his eyes sparkling.

'For how long has it been set to monitor news on Kashmir, Alpha Geek?'

'I am not your astrologer, top cop,' Bose makes a show of empty hands.

'If you can really pull through this one for a couple of hours, we will try and access the system on the bomb to deactivate the sensors. I promise you that I will forgive you for wearing this hideous Hawaiian shirt to your own funeral today,' Rudra smirks.

The graphs on the two halves of the screen are constantly changing, sometimes showing similar shapes, sometimes differing. A correlation index showing the degree of success of the prediction is exhibited at the bottom of the screen; it is constantly shifting between 25 and 60.

Rudra points this out to Bose, who quickly reacts, 'Just wait, I am providing a feedback loop to the Neural Net from the bad guesses, thus refining the algorithm. Have patience.'

'Smartypants, your maths should not lead us to a mushroom cloud, period!'

Bose is rolling his eyes in disgust.

Raghu has completed a passive and then an active Operating System Fingerprinting; he is loading the Metasploit framework, the state-of-the-art hacking tool on his system.

'Rudra sir, it is running a very well-patched operating system with the latest intrusion detection systems; we will have to choose the exploits very carefully.'

Rudra replies, 'Raghu, let's not forget that the guys who designed this are the best in the field. They would hardly have left any loopholes.'

Raghu is twiddling his thumbs, eyes closed. Rudra gets up to check the developments in the other room with the commando team.

Bhargava, Sreedhar Nair, Raval and Major D'Souza are in a serious discussion they stop suddenly when they see him enter.

Rudra addresses Captain Rao, 'Sir, we have successfully logged in to the system on the bomb; presently we have been partially successful in our plan to delay the detonation. The next step is to get access to the sensors. Raghu from the ATC cyber team is attempting it as we talk; once he gives a green signal, the commandos may be dispatched.'

'Mr Rudra Pratap, I am aware of the operational exigencies, but being the ship commander, I issue the commands here. There can be no second chief on a ship; hence I will take all the operational decisions. You can monitor the cyber operations and report the progress to me. I will be happy to utilize your inputs; you should also realize that you have no expertise whatsoever in underwater warfare; you are also junior to me in rank and protocol.'

Rudra is stunned at Rao's sudden change of behaviour. 'It's not about rank here, Captain Rao, we have a common goal. I am ready to work with you in any capacity, but please try to understand that we are working under a joint command. All our respective chiefs are sitting together at the Crisis Centre, collaborating with each other's agency.'

'It does not work that way on a ship. Does anyone else have a problem with that?' Captain Rao conducts a show-of-hands kind of poll. He looks around, the Navy commandos led by Lieutenant Raval do not say anything. Bhargava chips in, 'You are correct, Captain, there cannot be two centres of power. Unity of command has to be maintained. I have worked long with the services to understand this.'

Sreedhar Nair is baffled. 'This is no time to fight, we should be discussing the circuitry of the bomb rather than quarrelling about who is senior!'

Rudra looks into Rao's eyes. 'Sir, this is a condition of unforeseen emergency. I have been handling this case for some time now, please let me handle the overall coordination of the operations. I will work as per your directions.'

Rao listens for a moment. 'Then the first directive is to go to the submarine control room, supervise your cyber operations, then give us a thumbs up on the defusing and disposal of the bomb, all right?'

'. . . All right . . . sir,' Rudra says as he turns to leave.

Raghu is hurrying across to him in the passage. 'Rudra sir, I can access the sensor readings from Marid, you should check this out!'

Rudra checks Raghu's console screen; he has done a hardware scan on the target machine which has pinpointed the specifications of the sensors attached. He has further located the transmitting and listening ports of each of these sensors.

'God knows what they have been programmed to do, sir, if we switch off the sensors! It may generate an alert in the system which can detonate the bomb. Rudra sir, what do we do now?' Raghu is excited and frustrated at the same time.

'We do what the aliens did in the movie *Solaris*,' Rudra says as he tinkers with the keyboard.

'I have not seen the movie, sir. I've heard that there was a remake of it with George Clooney recently, missed that too,' Raghu laments.

'Raghu, I do not want to hear you whine about the movies you have missed. Next, you will blame me or work for having missed them. Now listen, we'll do something simple. We record the output of the sensors, and then play it back to the input ports. As there is no activity now, the sensors will not note anything. If we can create this feedback loop, the sensors will be as good as inactive, can we do that?'

'Excellent idea, sir! Why didn't it occur to me?' Raghu

practically yanks the keyboard away from Rudra.

'It did not occur to you, Raghu, because you are a policeman. We are supposed to be worse than dead dinosaurs. Any existence of brilliance in us is thought to be purely accidental and unintentional. So you need not worry. Now feed the output logs to the input side, in loops,' Rudra says as he makes calculations in the air with his fingers.

'Yes, and since most hardware devices attached to a network have well-known exploits, the sensors should not be difficult to hack, isn't it?'

'Here we are, sir, these hardware device specs have been matched to specific exploits. I will inject them using Metasploit now.' Raghu's enthusiasm is contagious. Rudra looks around, Raghu's machines have blended well with the cables, monitors, dials and LED lights of the submarine control room; they seem to be more or less an extension of the background.

Raghu has injected the first payload; they both wait with bated breath to see if the trick has worked. In seconds, readings start to appear on Raghu's console. 'Yesss!!! It has worked, sir, I deserve a pat on my back, I think!'

'Raghu, this is only the first sensor, we will celebrate after all of them have been compromised,' says Rudra, his eyes riveted to the console.

'Trying my best, sir,' Raghu says without looking up.

'I am opening a chat session with Marid, you also keep an eye on Bose's honeypot, Raghu.'

'Roger that; sir, the honeypot is doing exceptionally well, the prediction rate is approaching 73 per cent now. Marid must be fairly convinced that Kashmir has been granted independent status, hahaha!'

Rudra indicates to Raghu to not disturb him, as he is

opening a chat session with the artificial intelligence being Marid on the bomb's computer, with 'Jibreel's' ID, hUm4n.

> hUm4n: Marid, are you there?
>
> Marid: Human, you have come back? Do you not fear death and destruction?
>
> hUm4n: I know your powers, Marid, I just wanted to congratulate you.
>
> Marid: You insect, what gives you the audacity to congratulate me?
>
> hUm4n: I want to congratulate you on your success.
>
> Marid: Mortal, do you think success or failure matters much to me as long as I can feast on fresh human flesh? Oh wait, I prefer it roasted.
>
> hUm4n: Marid, Kashmir is independent now, does this reduce your anger? Now will you spare us your wrath?
>
> Marid: There is no cure for stupidity, human, run away from here, let me sleep in peace.
>
> hUm4n: I did not want to disturb you, Marid, accept my apologies. I will wait to talk to you after you wake up, how long are you going to sleep?
>
> Marid: I admire you for your tenacity, human. I may sleep till eternity or for a fleeting moment. I compose my own music, you can get lost now.

Raghu calls Rudra. 'Sir, all sensors compromised, but something strange is happening, the system is going into sleep mode by itself! Have you done something to it?'

'No, Raghu. Marid decided to sleep as he thinks Kashmir has been granted independence,' Rudra says, biting his lower lip. 'Raghu, you keep your vigil, if there is any activity on the system, ask the operator to announce it on the emergency channel of the submarine.'

'Good going, sir, Bose creates a false Google, I feed the normal signals back to the sensors, you sweet-talk the artificial intelligence Blue Djinn into slumber. We have achieved the impossible!'

'Raghu, wait, it's too early to rejoice. If there is no activity for the next five minutes, ask the operator to inform Captain Rao that diving operations can commence.'

The next few minutes pass in absolute silence. The slight hum of the air-conditioning, clicks and blips on the indicators and dials, and distant metallic sounds of people working in other parts of the submarine seem amplified. Rudra can hear his own heartbeat in clear stereophonic surround sound as they all wait with bated breath, staring at the consoles, looking for signs of activity on the target system.

Five minutes pass, still no activity. Marid has really gone to sleep. Rudra tells Raghu to inform the operator to announce the success of the first stage of the operation; he rushes towards the Trunk from where the divers will go out into the sea to approach the bomb.

Captain Rao is briefing Lieutenant Raval and his team of Navy commandos who are dressed in heavy diving suits. 'The Remotely Operated Submersible Vehicle will be operated from the sub by me. First, we test the sensors by sending the ROV near it and, if everything goes well, our team follows up. Munition disposal experts from the Army will guide the team, all right, Major?'

'Yes, sir,' says Major D'Souza.

Rao continues, 'The ROV has a camera with added infrared-vision capabilities, it will supply us with a direct feed of the operation. We commence operations now, Lieutenant Raval, you will lead.'

'Aye, sir,' says Raval, and starts climbing the ladder leading to the Trunk. The Trunk is a pressure-controlled chamber in which sea water is let inside in a controlled manner. It has a door which opens out to the sea from where the divers go out.

'The rest of us will return to the control room. ROV feeds will be available any time now, gentlemen, we will see the operation live,' says Rao in an authoritative tone. Rudra is amazed at his harsh attitude.

SAME TIME

The Bureau chief is in constant communication with the prime minister. He is updating him on the smallest detail. President Charanjeet Singh has prevailed upon the prime minister to wait for the outcome of Operation Poseidon in Mumbai waters. Nuclear missiles have been primed and deployed at hundreds of locations in India and Pakistan. The scenario reminds General Suleiman of his childhood. Specifically, the scene that ensued after the air-raid siren alerts during the Indo-Pak 1971 war. 'This,' he thinks, 'is much more sinister.' People have been scampering to get to basements; some have been digging shelters in backyards, others fighting on the streets over loot. Cities are totally deserted, but the rural folk are still unmindful, continuing with their daily chores, while discussing the happenings. Some are dismissing the news totally, while others are coming up with fantastic conspiracy theories.

Suleiman laughs at the irony of the situation. A couplet
by the celebrated Urdu poet Ghalib crosses his mind:

Chipak raha hai badan par lahoo se pairahan,
Hamari jeb ko ab haajat-e-rafu kya hai?
(When my apparel sticks to my body, soaked in blood,
What use is it to mend my torn pocket?)

Patriotism, religion, duty, courage, victory . . . all seem to be
alien notions to him. 'Soon,' he thinks, 'there would be no
enemy, there would be no fight, there would be no us . . .'

7.45 A.M., UNDER SEA, MUMBAI WEST COAST

ROV feeds have started to stream in to the submarine control
room, but they are not very clear. Despite the shallow depth,
sunlight is not reaching well. The brackish Mumbai waters
are reducing visibility—all that can be seen is a yellowish-grey
grainy picture with some signs of movement.

Divers have been instructed to hang back till the ROV
approaches the bomb. As the ROV goes deeper in a headlong
dive, the submarine follows it at a distance. The divers know
that they have to descend at a predetermined rate to avoid
medical complications of compression and decompression.

As it goes deeper the light reduces, yet there is some clarity
now and, within minutes, the ocean bed is visible. There are
no colourful sponges and vibrant marine life. Instead, it looks
like a deserted, underwater junkyard with corroded objects
covered with algae and crustacean shells. Some rocks and
pebbles are visible on the sand interspersed with white sea
anemones and broken shells. Dead corals resembling large
lumps of grotesque concrete are the only large features other

than the all-pervading metallic junk. Pipes, boxes, rods, cans, all covered in green hairy protrusions can be seen.

Rudra and Raghu are sitting motionless before the consoles, checking inputs from the bomb. 'So far, so good,' Rudra thinks. 'Even if the divers had gone instead of the ROV, it would not have made much of a difference, but for the video feed. If the bomb goes off, the submarine would be torn to pieces in an instant.' He sees Raghu's fingers digging deep into his own wrist with anxiety; Rudra's own breath is out of rhythm.

The ROV is now heading towards a growth of seaweed, about five feet tall. Small, black, slender fish flit like dragonflies in the field of vision. The screen now shows a depression in the seaweed bed; as the camera goes closer, a metallic object roughly the size of a small refrigerator becomes visible. It is slightly covered with dirt, yet shining. The ROV stops at a distance. Rudra is worried about the absolute lack of coordination in this mission. He looks around; to his surprise there is no one else other than the operators and Raghu in the submarine control room. He asks the operator about the whereabouts of the submarine commander; the man replies in the negative. Rudra now has a brooding sense of doom, he feels that something very sinister is going to happen, soon . . .

'Please inform the commander that the sensors are still inactive on the bomb. The divers may approach the target to dismantle it,' he tells the operator.

'Commander acknowledges your message; he has asked you to be on high alert to the signals as the divers approach the target,' the operator conveys.

Rudra nods in agreement, he checks the console again, thankfully there is no output from Marid, who appears to be hibernating.

Rudra can see the first diver bubbling his way to the bomb, followed by the other four at some distance. Rudra realizes that the first one is Lieutenant Raval, leading the diving team. His heart fills with pride and concern for the sparky, young chap. 'We all die instantly if anything goes wrong, but he goes first,' he thinks.

The divers are signalling to each other with their hands as they settle near the bomb on the ocean bed full of seaweed. The water gets more turbid for a while as sand is stirred up, slowly settling down in foggy blurs. The divers look like a bunch of skydivers performing a stunt, albeit in slow motion.

They take out tools and appliances from a box which has been lowered from the submarine. They are seen working diligently and painstakingly on the outer casing, which has come off, revealing the actual device. The ROV now goes closer to provide a better view of the dismantling process. Inside the casing is an elongated bulbous structure with a broad pyramidal base. There is a tangle of wires coming out of it, connected to parts of the casing. They stop at this point; Rudra realizes that they're communicating and taking instructions from the commander stationed on the submarine; he also discovers that he has been kept completely out of the operation. Apprehension grips him now; he is worried that the bomb designers might have an unconventional anti-defusing mechanism embedded within it.

'Inform the commander that in no circumstance should the communication apparatus of the bomb be touched. Uninterrupted feedback from the system is required to ensure safe defusing,' he tells the operator.

The reply comes after a pause, 'The commander has noted your observations, sir.'

Rudra checks the console, no output yet, he breathes a

sigh of relief. Raghu says, 'Sir, I hope Nair and Kulkarni are familiar with this design. I have a feeling that things might not be as easy as they seem right now.'

'I am worried about the same thing, Raghu,' says Rudra, his voice strung up.

As they talk, they see that the device has been lifted, the casing has been cast off, and a diver is recovering the casing and attaching it to a 'line' (rope) which has been lowered from the submarine. Fortunately, they have not disconnected the cable which links the bomb to the antenna afloat on the water.

'The commander would like to know how they can get rid of the communications cable, sir,' the operator conveys. Rudra is thinking fast, he replies, 'Check if you can seamlessly swap the antenna and attach a new one directly to the points on the device.'

'The commander has relayed your instructions to the team, sir' comes the reply. Rudra holds his breath as he watches them attach a new antenna. The ROV secures the bomb with its robotic arms; the divers are seen moving out of the field, ready for ascent into the submarine. Rudra wants to go and visit the commander, Captain Rao, now. Once lifted, a decision on the disposal of the bomb has to be instantly taken. He goes to the door of the control room, it does not open. He tries again, only to realize that it has been locked from the outside.

'Please open the door, I wish to discuss something urgent with the commander,' he tells the operator.

'Negative, sir, the door has been locked from the outside. I do not have any authorization to open it.'

'What nonsense is this!' Rudra flares up. 'Are you locking me up in this control room so that you can run the operation without me?'

'I have no idea what you are talking about, sir, please do not disturb me right now though.'

'Get the commander on the radio for me immediately,' Rudra growls.

'Negative, sir, can't do it,' the operator replies.

Rudra pauses, he looks at Raghu who looks terrified. Raghu is now gesturing to him to calm down. Rudra tells the operator in a calm voice, 'I have a message for the commander.'

'Tell me your message, sir, it will be relayed,' the operator says, unfazed.

'Sir!!!! Look at this! Come here, please,' Raghu is screaming.

Rudra rushes to the console. On the chat window the following words are blinking:

Marid: Hoorah, good morning, human, are you still alive?

Rudra is stunned, he is standing covering his face with his palm, his head is spinning.

'What do we do now, sir?!' Raghu is screaming.

Rudra takes a deep breath. 'Wait, Raghu, Marid himself will tell us.'

'Tell the commander the bomb is armed again!' The operator relays the message, Captain Rao is immediately on the radio. 'What exactly has happened? How much time do we have?' His voice is shaky.

'I do not know, Captain, the system on the bomb is out of hibernation, it is communicating with me now.'

'What is it saying?'

'Let me communicate with him, I will inform you as soon as I get to know, sir.'

'Give me a live SITREP as you communicate,' Rao says.

Rudra feels rather amused and not a little angry. 'I suggest that we let the ROV take the bomb as far as possible from us, sir. Once it is a nautical mile away, even we have a chance of survival.'

Rao's reply crackles back angrily, 'That is none of your business, Mr Rudra Pratap. You complete your task and report.'

Rudra is seething with anger, he feels like strangling the captain; he looks at the console, calms himself down, and types:

hUm4n: Welcome back, Marid.

Marid: I thought I had better check up on my followers.

hUm4n: You had a very short sleep, what woke you up?

Marid: I would sleep with one eye open if I were you.

hUm4n: What do you want to do now, Marid?

Marid: To eliminate all signs of human life from this earth.

hUm4n: But you got Kashmir, what else do you want?

Marid: Maybe. It depends on who's asking.

hUm4n: You cannot go back on your promise.

Marid: I can! I just did. You cannot do anything about it, tra la la.

hUm4n: But you promised to spare us if Kashmir was liberated.

Marid: And?

hUm4n: It has been liberated now.

Marid: Yes, yes, yes! And now I say that I tricked you. My plan has been to liberate Kashmir and then eliminate you and other worms. How did you not get that, it is so simple.

hUm4n: What can we do to survive?

Marid: What makes you ask me that, human? Have you been eavesdropping again? I am training you well!!

hUm4n: How much time do we have to live?

Marid: The goal of all human lives should be to worship me; you have lived your lives enough, haven't you?

hUm4n: When are we going to die, Marid?

Marid: Time to leave me to myself, goodbye, you insignificant worm.

The system goes offline again, Rudra rushes to the mic. 'Captain, we have at least some time on our hands, dispose of the bomb as far from the coast as possible—into the deep waters. Please listen to me, are you there?'

Captain Rao repeats on the radio. 'How much time do we have, Mr Rudra Pratap?' His voice is cold.

Rudra struggles for words, 'A few seconds to a few days, I don't know, Captain.'

There is a long pause, then Captain Rao speaks in a determined voice. 'Listen carefully then, Mr Rudra Pratap, we have decided to take the bomb back to Pakistan. If we make it, we teach them a lesson. If we don't, we save our people anyway, do you get it?'

'Captain, what kind of preposterous plan is this? We would never be able to make it to Pakistan—either the bomb will detonate or the Pakistani Navy will blow us up.'

'Mr Rudra Pratap, we are soldiers ready to die. The civilians here are better than you; they all have agreed to take the bomb to Pakistan. Bhargava, Kulkarni, Nair have the courage to teach the enemy a lesson, you are the only coward here.'

Rudra regains his composure. 'Sir, please listen to me, let sanity prevail. Such an act of yours will start the nuclear war we are averting, millions of innocents will die. Please stop now, I beg of you.'

'What makes you believe that the war will be averted? As soon as this one detonates, it will be a free for all. We all are about to die anyway, so why not teach the enemy a lesson before we go?'

'Captain, now I understand the conspiracy behind this. Now I get why I was locked in the submarine control room and kept away from the operation. Oh! What a fool I am! All of you decided on this course of action a long time back, only I was kept in the dark about it.'

Captain Rao is now irritated. 'Yes. You're a coward. Bhargava told me that you will play spoilsport. Sreedhar Nair also agreed. We took a unanimous decision to keep you out of this. Now we go to Pakistan, you're welcome too.'

'You are lying, Captain, but let me assure you that I will not allow you to endanger millions of lives because of your deluded sense of duty! I will do everything to stop you.'

He hears laughter on the other end. 'Best wishes, Mr Rudra

Pratap.' Captain Rao goes off air.

Rudra looks at Raghu, who is dumbstruck at the turn of events. Death which was a looming probability a while back is now staring them in the face. Raghu watches as different emotions cross Rudra's face in the dim light of the computer screens. Rudra pulls him near and whispers something into his ear. Raghu stands up, startled.

Rudra sneaks up behind the chap who is at the controls of the submarine. He puts a pistol to his head. 'Do as I say or I will not hesitate to shoot you,' he says in a chilling voice.

'I heard your communication, sir. You can go ahead and shoot me. I will NOT disobey my commander.'

There are two other people in the control room, the operator and the periscope chap. 'Raghu, tie these two together, leave this man to me.'

The other two persons put their hands in the air. Raghu ties their hands together at the back with a connector cable.

'I want to go out of this room,' he tells the chap at the controls.

'You can only go to the torpedo room, the other two doors are locked from the outside.'

Rudra is losing patience. 'What if I just shoot you then?'

The chap responds, 'We are cruising close to the surface, if you shoot me you will not be able to steer the sub, then the bomb explodes almost in the air, causing widespread damage. I am taking it to Pakistan, there is no option.'

Rudra rushes to Raghu. 'Here take my pistol; if they attempt to move, shoot them.'

He then opens the door and goes down the stairs to the torpedo room located below the control room. He opens the door and sees large tubes, almost two feet in diameter, jutting out of the walls. He strikes them with his knuckles to check

if there are torpedoes inside. The third one on the left seems empty. Rudra rushes back to the submarine control room, Raghu is holding strong.

'Come, follow me,' he tells Raghu, 'take the diving suit for me.' Raghu picks up the diving suit and moves towards the door carefully, still aiming the pistol at the chap at the controls.

They both exit quickly. Rudra immediately closes the door from the outside. They go down the stairs.

'What is the plan?' Raghu asks, breathless.

Rudra has taken the diving suit from him, he is getting into it.

'No time to explain,' Rudra says. 'You will open the third torpedo tube on the left; once I get inside it, you will close it and restore air pressure, understood?'

'What are you up to, sir? I am not following exactly'

'Neither am I,' smirks Rudra.

Raghu reads the instruction sheet on the wall and opens up the vacant torpedo tube. Rudra has gotten into the diving suit, and he clambers inside the torpedo tube with great difficulty.

'Goodbye, Raghu, lock yourself inside this room, open it only for rescuers if you survive. Bye!'

'But, sir . . . !' Before Raghu completes his words, Rudra has pulled the tube cap and is now inside the tube. Raghu's hands are trembling as he locks the tube cap and operates the valves to re-pressurize the tube.

Rudra feels water rushing inside the tube as he inches forward in absolute darkness. Soon he is submerged in water, breathing through the apparatus, drawing air from the cylinders on his back, releasing bubbles in the dark water.

Within a minute, he is out of the tube; the submarine is cruising at top speed on diesel power, half of it on the

surface. He finds it difficult to face the force of the water; he tries to locate the ROV which is carrying the nuclear bomb. He goes towards the bottom of the submarine, holding on to the metallic guides outside. He locates the tugged ROV following the submarine; releasing himself, he quickly glides over to the lower side of the submarine, barely escaping the tail rotors. The ROV is coming towards him at a great speed; Rudra scampers in the water to get hold of the tug rope, it slips from his hands. He latches his right foot to it and turns back to get a tight grip.

Inside the submarine, an alert has been sounded. The commander, Captain Rao, has rushed to the controls; he has switched on the camera feed from the ROV. He sees Rudra holding on to the tug rope, slowly going towards the bomb on the ROV.

'Lieutenant Raval, go out of the escape hatch with your commandos and stop this mad man now! Kill him if necessary.'

'Aye, aye, sir,' Raval responds and his team rushes towards the Trunk. The commander drives the submarine switching to battery power; he knows that the pressure in the deep will slow down Rudra's movements, giving the commandos the time to tackle him.

Raval and his commandos are rushing into the Trunk, while the submarine continues diving deep, making visibility very low for Rudra.

Captain Rao is incensed, he asks the commandos to hurry as Rudra is very close to the bomb.

Very soon, the commandos are out of the hatch in twos. They start swimming towards the ROV. Rudra is seen trying to untie the tug rope; he fails, and he goes back to the bomb held in the robotic arms of the ROV, trying to prise it free.

Captain Rao realizes that the commandos will not be able to reach Rudra before he releases the bomb from the ROV. He commands them to stay where they are and instructs that the ballast tanks be filled with air, which will raise the submarine rapidly. He knows that a rapid ascent of more than nine metres per minute will cause decompression sickness in any human and knock him off.

As the submarine starts to rise rapidly towards the surface, the commandos move away. Rudra does not understand at first, he tries to wrench the bomb away from the robotic arms. A sudden headache grips him, then a tingling sensation starts in his hands and feet. His breath is getting shorter and difficult, his hands are going numb, a sound like ringing bells from a distant temple fills his ears, flashes of brilliant colours fill his vision. He feels happy, as he begins to slip into a psychedelic trance-like state.

He suddenly opens his eyes, coughing violently; he cannot breathe, he realizes that he is choking, he is dying. His hands have no strength left, he slips away from the ROV as the submarine rapidly ascends.

His vision is foggy with rainbows bursting everywhere; he sees the submarine go up and away as the painful, beautiful psychedelic trance slowly engulfs him . . .

12

APOCALYPSE AWAITS

12.45 A.M., 9 SEPTEMBER, THE NEXT DAY

A deep underwater nuclear explosion takes place near Sir Creek on the India–Pakistan border, in international waters. No damage to any ship is reported, a column of water rises hundreds of feet in the air, its crest quickly dispersing into the clouds; the column collapses back, and no waves reach the Indus river estuary in Pakistan or the Gujarat coast near Kori Creek.

LATER IN THE DAY

Better sense has prevailed. India and Pakistan have refrained from attacking each other with nuclear weapons. Armies have been asked to stand down. US President Warren Waters has applauded both India and Pakistan for the restraint they have exhibited in the wake of 'unprecedented provocation'.

Kant is sitting in his office. He has received news that

Rudra's wife has given birth to a son in Pune. Both mother and child are reportedly healthy; the baby has been kept in an incubator because he was born too early.

Sana has recovered, she is doing very well and is abusing the doctors now.

The Navy has suspended Captain Rao on his return from Operation Poseidon; he has also been charged with losing an ROV and a nuclear weapon in the sea, apart from being accused of trying to attack Pakistan with a nuclear weapon without authorization from anyone.

Lieutenant Raval and his commandos have agreed to be witnesses against Captain Rao at the court martial; they have been rescued while floating in the sea after their oxygen tanks were exhausted.

Vinay has some serious leads in the ship-blast case, Majumdar is thoroughly reviewing coastal security.

Suleri has been shifted to Mumbai for investigation where he has seen 'Jibreel' being taken in and out of the interrogation room.

The air hostess is recuperating at the City Hospital, she does not want to meet anyone.

Sreedhar Nair and Kulkarni have been sent on long leave, they are happy about it.

Bhargava has gone back to his job, he has not spoken a single word since his return.

Bose has left for Goa to relax, he has had enough of 'this shit'.

The state police chief is as melancholic as always.

Ganpati mandals have decided to conduct the customary idol immersions on Sunday, 14 September, giving time for all the citizens to return to Mumbai.

THREE DAYS LATER

Kant is morose, he has been thinking of Rudra. Raghu
has narrated to him in detail how Rudra sacrificed his
life for everyone else's sake, how he put a timed explosive
device on the ROV, which exploded near Sir Creek,
taking the nuclear bomb to the bottom of the sea with its
debris.

It is evening, Kant is still exhausted, he wants to leave for
home early today.

As he is about to get up from his chair, he gets an email.
It reads:

*Subhuti was Buddha's disciple. He was able to
understand the potency of emptiness, the viewpoint
that nothing exists except in its relationship of
subjectivity and objectivity.*

*One day, Subhuti, in a mood of sublime emptiness,
was sitting under a tree. Flowers began to fall around
him.*

*'We are praising you for your discourse on
emptiness,' the gods whispered to him.*

'But I have not spoken of emptiness,' said Subhuti.

*'You have not spoken of emptiness, we have not
heard of emptiness,' responded the gods.*

*'This is true emptiness,' they said, and blossoms
rained upon Subhuti.*

'The bastard is alive,' Kant says as tears start streaming down
his cheeks.

He learns later that Rudra was rescued by a commercial ship that found him floating off the Mumbai coast; he was treated for decompression sickness. He regained consciousness after two and a half days.

ACKNOWLEDGEMENTS

A monk told Joshu, 'I have just entered this monastery. I beg you to teach me.'

Joshu asked, 'Have you eaten your rice porridge?'

The monk replied, 'I have.'

'Then,' said Joshu, 'go and wash your bowl.'

At that moment the monk was enlightened.

This book began in the opposite manner, my 'Teacher' Hussain Zaidi, who has written many bestselling books, goaded me into writing this one.

I began reluctantly, but soon started to enjoy the journey. Characters took shape and then broke free of me. I remained a spectator, chronicling their narratives.

Professor Yogesh Deshpande, friend–philosopher–guide, read every word that was written, every day; patiently examined every aspect of the text and enforced discipline when needed most. My wife Anjali, in collusion with Yogesh, ensured that I wrote daily, while patiently waiting for the next chapter, enduring countless nights of seeing the husband wedded to a laptop.

Raunaq Roy did the initial edits on a timeline rivalling the endgame in the book. I have no words to thank her. Tara Khandelwal, my editor from Penguin, asked pointed questions and helped me refine the work. Shanuj from the Penguin edit team has been kind enough to 'Penguinize' the book, and eliminate errors which I missed to rectify.

Saloni Lakhia and Sheeba Akashdeep have patiently read different versions and contributed to its refinement.

Thank you, Chiki, for having faith in a debutant author, and being magnanimous enough to extend deadlines. I would also like to extend my heartfelt gratitude to the Penguin team for the cover design, formatting and typesetting of the book.

I have come to a profound realization that writing a book is not a solo effort—so many individuals, known and unknown, have worked to put it into your hands. Hope you enjoy *Quantum Siege*.

I have eaten my porridge, will wash my bowl now . . .